ECHO
AFTER
ECHO

ECHO AFTER ECHO

Amy Rose Capetta

CANDLEWICK PRESS

Copyright © 2017 by Amy Rose Capetta

First edition 2017

Library of Congress Catalog Card Number pending
ISBN 978-0-7636-9164-6

17 18 19 20 21 22 BVG 10 9 8 7 6 5 4 3 2 1

Printed in Berryville, VA, U.S.A.

This book was typeset in Minion Pro.

Candlewick Press
99 Dover Street
Somerville, Massachusetts 02144

visit us at www.candlewick.com

For Cori,
who lights me up

ACT I

i

This is the Aurelia Theater.

Zara's body curls around the open stage door. Her feet are a rushed whisper. She would die before she would disturb the auditions that are, according to a sign, already IN PROGRESS.

Backstage is black and empty. Not so much a world as the darkness before the world begins. Ten stories of fly space yawn above Zara's head, ready to swallow scenery — a tangle of woods, the twisted spine of a mountain range.

The greenroom throws light through an open door. Zara stops outside. Breathes. There's always a moment like this, a quiet one before the nervous, giddy plunge into auditions. Zara wants to make these seconds last — forever, if possible. She has no interest in going back to her assigned life. The one where she is a senior in high school, pulls decent grades, does a scattering of school plays, has a string of minor crushes.

This is already better. This is already *more.*

She stands in the theater's dark body and pictures its face, pale marble with a gilded blush. Any actress with half a dream to her name knows the Aurelia Theater. Still, it doesn't seem possible that Zara is actually here. The casting notice she found in *Backstage* must have been a mistake.

Open call.

For *Echo and Ariston.*

They wanted a video audition, so she signed up for an hour of studio time at the arts annex where she takes acting workshop. She could have made the video at home, just cleared her throat and dived into Echo's lines headfirst. But Zara needed to feel like more than a teenage girl pretending in her bedroom, and that meant a real rehearsal space. She set up her phone on a borrowed tripod and turned strips of recessed lights on and off until she found the magical combination that gave her face a slight glow. She still felt a jab of nerves as she hit RECORD. She sounded ridiculous, saying her name and age for the phone's little black eye. She had to restart her monologue twenty times before she had a decent version to send.

By the time she was done, Zara felt sure she would never hear back.

She auditioned on something stronger than a whim — but what's the name for that? Zara tests words to find one that fits. It's a game she plays, inspecting and weighing things in her mind, seeking matches. Being an actor is all about finding keys from the real world that open imaginary locks.

What's stronger than a whim, but with the same push to it, like a knuckle of wind?

Urge? Desire?

No. Too many bad novels have coated those words, turned them slick.

Inclination?

Weak.

Impulse.

Yes. Something gentle and sure clicks inside her.

Yesterday, Zara got the call from the casting director. Today, she skipped school for the first time in recorded history.

A woman in the obligatory black of a crew member comes out of the wings and catches Zara standing in the doorway. "Auditions?" she asks.

Zara nods, her neck still tight from the train ride.

The woman leads Zara into the greenroom. The space is choked with girls. And every single one wants the same role as Zara, which is a problem, because now that she is here, she can't imagine leaving.

This is the Aurelia Theater. It feels like coming home.

ii

The greenroom is delightfully shabby. Ancient couches have been pushed aside to make room for the actresses. A cornered snack machine hums resentfully. No one's buying. These girls, in their stylish dresses, with their stylish bodies, do not look like they have ever snacked.

Zara makes the error of comparing herself to them. She is soft, a collection of circles. She wears a skirt that is too old and a sweater she used to think was perfect but now feels unforgivably tight. A forgotten gland at the back of her knees comes to life, pushing sweat down her legs.

The assistant stage manager takes one girl and then another, leading them away like this is some dark fairy tale. The rest of the girls do what actors do when they're penned in a small space, waiting: they warm up. Some sing scales. Others stretch themselves into improbable shapes. Most show off their knowledge of the famous Greek tragedy.

The room bears only a slight resemblance to other auditions Zara has attended, where people find their friends or make new ones as quickly as possible. Where everyone talks in warm, brash voices, wishing one another broken legs as they run their monologues and grab their sides.

These girls are focused on themselves. On their work.

On the need to win over Leopold Henneman.

Just thinking about the famous director makes Zara's nerves double over. She grabs for her purse and the aggressively loved copy of *Echo and Ariston* she found at a library book sale when she was twelve. The year that she got her first kiss. She walked around for months afterward feeling blank, and then she found this tiny book with the flaking cover. By the time she had finished the first page, she was different.

She was in love.

The darkly printed words and the wide margins in Zara's script calm her. She knows the play by heart — three different translations. Looking at it right now isn't strictly necessary. But it keeps her safe from the greenroom's whirlpool of pride and politics and low-carb tendencies.

The assistant stage manager is a black fly, hovering.

"Evelina Robbins," she calls.

A girl tilts her chin and marches a few steps toward the door. Then she seems to remember her purse. It's especially large and bulky, and with no other visible options, she leaves it in the care of the nearest girl, who perches on the arm of a couch drinking from an unmarked white cup.

As soon as Evelina is out of sight, the other girl peels the lid off her latte and pours steaming milk into the purse.

Everyone goes back to her own business.

iii

Eli has no business sitting at the table between the mezzanine and the wide fan of the orchestra seats. This table is meant for designers, like Roscoe.

Most of all: it's meant for the director.

Leopold insisted they fling the auditions wide open, so the Aurelia is overrun with what feels like every actress in New York who either *is* a teenager or thinks she might be able to pass for one. Eli knows that this is only a tiny fraction of the girls who sent in video auditions. She can't imagine what it was like to weed through those, to tell so many girls that their talent and their prettiness and their dreams weren't enough. Which is why she's the light-board op, not the casting director.

The current redhead wraps up her monologue. There's a lull between girls, which gives Eli a minute to dig out the food she brought from home. Eli keeps one Tupperware for herself and hands the other to her boss. Roscoe takes it with a wide-lipped smile. He gets so busy thinking about the lights that he forgets to eat. Almost forgets to breathe. That's why Eli is here today: to help Roscoe. To take care of him, a little. He is lighting god and first-grader and nothing in between.

Leopold Henneman rattles out of his seat. He paces down the aisle and then right back. He hunches over the table with a pen, working his way through a pile of headshots. He draws a slow, deliberate X over each girl's face.

His assistant, Meg, gathers the papers quietly and walks them over to the trash. As usual, she's brisk and blond and mostly silent, and does whatever needs to be done.

Leopold uses two fingers to wave the casting director to his side. "I was under the impression you knew what I wanted for Echo," he says in a low voice. "Was I unclear in some way?"

Eli tenses every muscle. In her family, if someone has a feeling, they all hear about it. None of this pinched whispering. Theater people are usually loud, which is part of why Eli loves them.

The assistant stage manager leads another actress out from the wings. There is a snicker of paper as her résumé is passed. Eli doesn't even look down. She's painfully aware of how skimpy her *own* résumé looks. Eliza Vasquez, nineteen years old, with a string of off-off-off-Broadway hits under her belt. Follow-spot operator. Light-board operator. Lighting designer, but only once. At some point Leopold is going to decide she's not good enough to be here.

And then what?

Eli can't let herself think about that. Thank God, or whoever is up there in the flies, the girl onstage is a very good distraction. Eli has watched every one of these actors and thought about how to clothe them in light and shadow.

This new actress Eli has to adjust to. She is already better. She is already *more.*

It's about how she inspects the curtains. She sticks to them, lingering in their heavy shade, running a finger over their infinite redness. It pushes the Aurelia's beauty to the front of Eli's brain.

The girl's smile is crooked in the best ways. Her hair hangs to her waist, a warm shake of cinnamon, eyebrows a few shades darker. About thirty white girls in a row have read for Echo: it's not exactly *Hamilton* up there. But this actress becomes the first one in hours that Eli can *see*, instead of skimming over with tired eyes. And the way she looks at those curtains — Eli thinks, for a second, she might climb them.

Eli steals a glance at Leopold, to see if he notices the difference. He's still pouring quiet words into the casting director's ear. Eli can't help thinking about *Hamlet*— wasn't somebody poisoned through the ear? Not a good way to go.

11

Leopold puts a hand on the casting director's shoulder. She nods and sinks back into her seat. Eli gets the feeling that she won't be doing much casting today.

The girl onstage leaves the curtains behind, squares her feet, and says her name.

Zara Evans.

Then she launches into the act 1, scene 2 speech. The one that Echo spits at her parents before leaving the kingdom.

Echo and Ariston.

God, Eli hates this play.

Or maybe she just spent too much time with it, the way she did with Hannah.

They met during Eli's first show in the city, and Hannah pulled Eli in with all that eyeliner and lava-soft kissing. She was the one who convinced Eli to move to the city and chase a full-time career as a lighting designer. Being with Hannah was being on the verge of every good thing. And then one morning over diner pancakes, it was done, before Eli even had time to pour the syrup.

Zara Evans is halfway through the monologue, and Eli should be falling asleep, but she's not. Actor voices are usually sanded, smooth, powerful. Zara's is garden-variety sweet. A little on the breathy side. Sometimes she takes a step forward, then back, a spiky dance that no partner would be able to follow. What she lacks in perfection she makes up for in honesty.

"I would live in this home and then the home of a man
Of your choosing. This Ariston. Your *Ariston.*

I would touch without feeling,
Kiss without taste."

The girl is digging these words up, dredged in fear, glowing with possibility. It makes Eli want that feeling back, the one she had with Hannah. But now she's older. Wiser. She knows what's waiting on the other side of that feeling. She's permanently, painfully aware of how it ended with Hannah. Not in death, like it did for Echo.

But it still wasn't pretty.

She looks down the table and finds the whole crew staring. Even Roscoe is staring. Are they having the same sort of flashbacks? Eli can't imagine Roscoe in love. She can barely imagine him tying his shoes.

Zara Evans ends on a trembling note.

No one claps.

Eli knows the monologue was good, but she also knows how little that matters when it comes to casting. Who's beautiful? Who's connected? Who does the public want to see smeared across the Arts section for months? There are parts of this that aren't magic at all, cruel parts that balance out the pretty.

Eli takes out her Leatherman, not because she needs a multipurpose tool, but because she's developed a habit of flipping the knife blades when she's nervous. *Let this girl stay,* she thinks. A callback, at least. Because Eli has fallen a tiny bit in love. Not the whole feeling: she's not a lunatic. But the first piece is there, a sliver of brightness that makes the rest of the moon inevitable.

iv

Zara's audition piece ends, and she's still onstage. All she can see is the bright, cutting circle of the spotlight. Zara doesn't want to leave, but the longer she stands here and hopes, the worse it will be when Leopold Henneman sends her back to Pennsylvania.

And then —

A voice in the dark.

"Indulge me," it says.

Zara knew the director must be out there, watching her, but it's one thing to imagine it and another thing to have evidence. Leopold Henneman is talking to her — that has to be a good sign, right? His voice is low but not smooth. It crackles and curls. When it says *Indulge me*, everything in Zara's body leaps to say *Of course*.

"Miss Evans? Are you still with us?" he asks.

Leopold Henneman is the world's most-famous living theater director, a fact that Zara finds as distracting as an itch between her shoulder blades. There's also the matter of the visions. When most directors use that word, they mean some vague and dreamy idea of what a play should be.

Leopold Henneman claims to have *actual* visions.

Zara has to focus, to fight her way back into the story. *Echo and Ariston.* Love and death.

"What would you like me to do?" Zara asks. "The casting director said to bring one monologue —"

"I would prefer something else," the director says. "A game." His voice has grown hard, the tight bounce of a rubber ball. She wonders how many of the other girls have been invited to play.

"Who do you love most?" Leopold Henneman asks.

Zara has no idea what he wants her to say. The question takes on a new life inside her head. It seeks out memories, possible answers. The words ring and rattle. She can't stop hearing them.

Who do you love most?

Her boyfriend? He has soft brown eyes and soft brown

15

freckles. They spent most of the summer at the movies, sharing oversalted popcorn. They kissed in the sun at the lake, wrapped in towels, beaded with water. Zara likes him. But the distance between *like* and *love* suddenly seems like the distance between Earth and the sun.

Who do you love most?

The first person she kissed? That was a girl from summer stage. She was playing Wendy in *Peter Pan,* and Zara was one of the Lost Boys. It happened at one of those theater parties where everyone kisses everyone. The kiss itself was nice. But then the blankness set in. Besides, that couldn't have been love because they've barely talked since.

Who do you love most?

Her parents? She loves them, of course. But it's the *of course* that rules them out.

Who do you love most?

The Ariston to her Echo. How can she describe a person she's never met? Her thoughts grow frantic and fast and hot to the touch. "I . . . I guess . . ."

"Don't *guess,*" Leopold says. The weight of his voice tells Zara that she's running out of time. "Show me."

She stares out into the blank brightness of the theater. The director's words thrash around inside her. *Who do you love most?* It's a trick question. There's no love wide enough to measure against Echo and Ariston. They're legendary — Romeo and Juliet, but better. Less hormonal, more epic and defiant. Zara craves that kind of love, but she hasn't found it. The closest she's ever gotten is standing onstage.

Then — Zara looks down. She's standing on a skin of black paint, a thousand layers of story beneath her.

"Who do I love most right now?" Zara asks.

Leopold Henneman's voice takes on a hard crust of boredom. "Are you so fickle that the answer will change by tomorrow?"

Zara shakes her head, trying to chase off embarrassment and get back to a clearheaded feeling. *Neutral,* her drama teacher calls it. But that word always sounded too calm to Zara. She feels it like the moment on a diving board, right before jumping. She lines up her toes. Takes a deep breath.

And then she starts to change.

It happens to her body first — shoulders pinning back, chin exploring a higher tilt. Her palms float upward. Before she opens her mouth, she imagines what her voice should be: plush as a red velvet chair, tall and reaching as the fly space above. "You should know that I'm very pale," Zara says. "Pale, and dressed in gold."

There is no answer from the audience. But Leopold Henneman hasn't told her to leave. Not yet.

It's a stay of execution.

Zara twirls her fingers with a stolen grace. "I've given people so many reasons to love me. *Death of a Salesman. The Misanthrope. Mourning Becomes Electra.*" Zara is listing the plays that have been performed on this stage. She feels the need to touch every bit of the theater like it belongs to her — no, like it's *part* of her. She rushes from the thick pelt of the curtains to the lip of the stage, where it tumbles into the orchestra pit. She stretches her arms up, toward the streaming lights. "*Twelfth Night. The Trojan Women.*" She works backward in time, excavating story after story.

Who do you love most?

Leopold Henneman gave Zara a trick question, so she gave him a trick answer.

"Interesting," he says, a new lightness at his edges. "Very interesting."

Satisfaction floods Zara, brighter than the lights. The director is playing along. And for one sharply outlined moment, Zara sees that she would do anything to keep this place. This feeling.

"And who is this charming creature?" Leopold asks.

Zara curtsies so deeply that one knee kisses the stage. "Aurelia."

There is no callback.

Zara settles into the fact that she has lost the part. That she never could have won it in the first place.

"Open casting was a stunt," says one of the girls in the senior class play. Zara is sitting in an orange plastic seat in the high-school auditorium, trying not to remember the Aurelia. It feels like holding back a tidal wave with one hand. "Leopold does stuff like that," the girl continues, as if she and the director are old friends. "It drums up attention for his shows."

Zara nods. She doesn't offer up her story. Zara doesn't want anyone to be nice to her and give her a series of consoling nods while secretly thinking that she wasn't good enough.

She learns her lines for *Hello, Dolly!*

She makes a date with her boyfriend. Watches him eat all the breadsticks in the basket at Olive Garden, order more, eat those, and then break up with her. He tells her she's been acting weird.

Zara can't deny it.

She settles into the fact that she has lost the part. She does not settle as well into her old life.

There's college to think about. Applications. She shoves those thoughts down, but they keep coming back like the *tap, tap, tap* of a headache at her temple.

The first week of October, her name surfaces in a headline in the *New York Times*. Her parents get the paper every weekend, although they hardly ever read it. Zara is the one who inhales the Arts section every Sunday. So she's the one who sees: NEWCOMER EVANS PAIRED WITH WARD IN FAMOUS TRAGEDY. Zara reads the first paragraph, about how she beat out two thousand girls for the chance to act opposite Adrian Ward, one of Hollywood's prettiest young leading men. Her mind drifts over the rest of the article in a detached way that makes her think she must be dreaming. Or dead.

A second shock follows. As she's running around the kitchen getting ready for school—late because she spent too long staring at the newspaper—her phone rings in her pocket. A soft, troubling pulse. When she looks at the screen, there's an unknown 212 number. Zara picks up, expecting the casting director, maybe the assistant stage manager or the AD.

Leopold Henneman is on the line.

"Is this Miss Evans?" he asks. Zara noticed his slight accent during auditions. She tries to trace it to the country of origin but dead-ends somewhere in Europe. "This call is the most delightful part of my job," he says. "Of course, I should have been the one to tell you the news. Our cast list must have been leaked to the press."

"Oh," Zara says. "Right."

His voice pushes through the phone, making him feel much closer than New York. "Strange, I know, not to hold callbacks. The Aurelia producers wanted to fight over it." He laughs. Gently. "Don't worry. I convinced them that you're perfect for this role. For this production. I'm sure you'll prove me right. And this is a nice little moment, don't you think? Your dream has come true." Zara doesn't know what to say. Her words have flown away, like birds before a storm. A few seconds later, when she still hasn't answered, he says, "You must be overwhelmed."

Zara sits on the kitchen floor. "A little." The tile looked like a good idea when she was standing up, but now that she's down here it's cold and gritty.

"That's natural," Leopold says. "Your life is about to change in so many ways. But I'm going to be with you, from the moment you arrive at the theater. If you need anything, you come directly to me."

Zara nods. Then she remembers that Leopold can't see

her. "I will. Thank you." She says it again, knowing the words will never be big enough. "Thank you."

Zara asks her mom to drop her off at school, because it's still possible she's dead, and dead people shouldn't drive cars.

Her weekly acting workshop takes place that afternoon. The teacher is waiting in the lobby of the arts annex, and when he sees Zara, he gives her an endless hug and congratulates her on being his first student to "really make something of herself."

So the article was real. The phone call actually happened.

She's going to play Echo.

Zara rushes to the bathroom where the girls warm up because the tile has such good acoustics.

"What if it doesn't work out?" one of the girls says, right after hugging her. From the tone of her voice, it sounds like she wants to prepare Zara for the worst. "The Aurelia's a really big deal."

"I know," Zara says.

The girls — all five of them — lean toward the mirrors to retouch their makeup. Zara has thought of them as her friends, but they don't study together or talk about their lives. They don't spend time together outside of class. They work on their scenes and talk about their dream roles.

Your dream has come true.

The girl standing closest bumps Zara playfully with her hip. "Are you going to be okay standing this close to Adrian Ward? I think he might blow your sweet little mind. He's really famous. And hot. I can't tell if he's more hot or more famous."

"Hot," says the first girl. "Definitely."

They all laugh. The sound turns hard when it hits the tile.

"There's a curse on the Aurelia," another girl says. She tries to sound like she's just teasing, but an edge breaks through. "You're not worried about that, are you?"

Zara knows they are saying these things to bother her, but the last one stays with her longer than it should. Which is silly. Theater superstitions are like Ouija boards — everybody loves them, but nobody really believes in them. The Aurelia's curse is just a string of accidents made to sound ominous.

It's nothing.

The play is everything.

Late that night, Leopold calls. He lights up her cell phone, rips her out of sleep. "Apologies," he says. "I didn't realize it was so late." He calls the next night, and the next, and just when Zara is getting used to it, he doesn't call for six days.

When he finally does, Zara grabs her phone and stares into the painful glow of the screen. It's 2:37 in the morning.

"Hello, my dear. I'm sorry if it's late where you are." Leopold fans out his excuses. He's in Brussels. He forgot she has school in the morning. He's so excited about a detail of act 2, scene 3 that he didn't even think about the time.

"What is Echo feeling here?" he asks.

Zara has thought about this before. She stares up at the ceiling and says words that she never thought anyone would want to hear. She is telling a famous director what she feels. "Echo wants to run away, she's ready. But it hurts."

"Because she's leaving so much behind?" Leopold asks.

23

"No." Zara shakes her head. "Because she's taking so much with her."

"Mmmmm." Every time Zara tells Leopold something about Echo, he makes an appreciative sound, as if she's laying out a feast for him. Leopold acts like everything she thinks about Echo is delicious.

The next night, he tells her about a vision.

"I saw you onstage in white," he says. "Organza, I think. It clung to you in a very becoming way."

Zara wants this to be true. She *needs* it. In just twelve weeks she's going to be in front of hundreds of people, and they will expect her to be beautiful. "How do they work?" she asks. "The visions?"

"They're simple, really. The visions show me how to create a perfect story. And then, if need be, I help things along."

"Have they ever been wrong?" she asks, thinking of the white dress.

He is quiet for so long — not even breathing — that she thinks the call must have been cut off. "No."

Zara wakes up in a haze. She doesn't tell anyone about the phone calls that keep her up until dawn — who would she tell? Her theater friends are so jealous their faces curdle when they see her coming. Her parents wouldn't like it if they knew she was up so late, especially because of the play. It's already disrupted her life so much. So Zara keeps Leopold a secret. She waits for the soft, dark center of the night, and the call that might be coming. She thinks about Echo, who is completely fictional, but feels more solid than anyone she's seen in weeks.

Zara's last day of school is here and then gone. She won't graduate with the rest of her class in the spring. She won't go to prom. She'll miss the spring play, which used to matter so much, and now has been eclipsed to the point that she can't even see the bright edges of what she used to care about. Her parents are the ones who worry about her missing out on all the normal teenage milestones. They support her decision, but in the next breath they make her promise to finish her coursework, promise to take the GED, promise to apply to colleges for next fall, even if she has to defer. They wince as she picks out school after school in New York City. She adds Carnegie Mellon in Pittsburgh, to make them happy, and then promises herself she won't go.

"We know how much this means to you," her mom says, which only proves it doesn't mean as much to them. Still, they cluster her with hugs, douse her in support. They even throw a small party a few days before she leaves. There's ice-cream cake and a fistful of balloons, because they don't know how to celebrate in a way that is not identical to her eighth birthday.

October flares like a match, then dies. Wind strips the trees. The world that Zara called real for so long is falling away.

vi

When Roscoe looks down, the theater hovers far beneath his feet. The walkway he's standing on is a series of open spaces and thin metal slats.

He won't be hanging lights for another few weeks, but he needs to be up here. Other places don't have the power to make him this happy. In the subway, he yells at the pigeons that ruffle the rails. "Feathered assholes!" In Grand Central Station, he is buffeted and kicked while he tries to watch the light move across the floor, while he says the prayers he learned as a boy, a few of the words gone, like fallen-out teeth. In winter, he sits on park benches and stares at the people hurrying past, their cheeks scratched with cold.

Red and red and red.

He picks up his stack of gels and an X-Acto knife and gets to work on gobos. Sliced plastic films, thin as breath, that he will spend hours and days teasing into the perfect shapes. Slim trees for act 2, scene 3. Dappled cave light. And water for the ending.

So much water. Enough to drown a girl.

But will it be good enough for Leopold? That's the other reason he needs to be up here — to figure out what went wrong. To fix it. His design was due this morning, and Leopold hated the light plot, hated the whole thing, wanted to throw the graph paper out and start over. Wanted to throw Roscoe out and start over.

But it's no real trouble. Roscoe will get it right, and Leopold will love him again.

He has Eli, too. She was a find, a girl who doesn't run from his mutterings and the smell that makes other people step back and back. She is a kind person, true kind, underneath the bluster and the boots. Sometimes she brings him food from home. Sometimes she picks up sandwiches from the deli two blocks down, with extra turkey for Roscoe. He likes the way that she makes coffee, swimming with hot milk, a little scalded, a little sweet. He likes how she talks to the lights just like he does, although she usually switches to Spanish. But that's all right. He doesn't need to understand what she's saying. He knows that it's a private conversation.

He wishes Eli were here right now. He gave her the day off.

He shuffles his gels and gets to work on another gobo. Pure white, this one, as sweet as Christmas lights.

That is one time Roscoe likes the city, and it's coming on fast. Winter. Cold and cold and white and red. They're already a few days into November, which means millions of lights will go up soon. If he made a god, that god would hang Christmas lights everywhere, including a few in Roscoe's brain, just to brighten things up.

He's not allowed to hang *Echo and Ariston* lights yet because *Death of a Salesman* is still running. Roscoe is just here to think. To plan. The series of catwalks above the stage connects to a hidden strip of a balcony above the orchestra pit. From there, he can reach the booth. He will get a sandwich soon, because tomorrow Eli will ask if he ate, and Roscoe doesn't want to disappoint Eli. But right now he will visit his light board. A few hours hunched over the slides and buttons will make him feel better.

He will work and work and never stop until he gets this right.

Then Roscoe hears a sound — the door from the lighting booth. A person can climb from the booth, up a ladder, to a secret walkway that connects to this one, a walkway hidden by a false plaster ceiling covered in painted angels. Not many people come through that way.

It could be Eli. Maybe she didn't want her day off. Maybe

she's figured out that this is the best place and never, ever wants to leave.

Roscoe stands on the lip of the balcony, because that is where he pictures what the lights will look like when they hit the stage. He reaches out, pretending that each finger is a beam of light, but he reaches too far, everything wobbles, and in that wild second he sees the wooden edge of the railing. Below that, air. Then the deep red carpet of the orchestra pit.

It would be a long fall from here to the ground.

vii

Zara is back in New York — finally.

Her parents made her promise to get off at Penn Station and immediately take the subway uptown, but after a few hours of that flattened train feeling, Zara follows a new impulse through the doors of the subway car, into the tight press of bodies in Forty-Second Street Station.

Zara climbs the stairs toward the gray sky, her suitcase announcing each step with a clunk.

If you need anything, come directly to me.

Broadway is awash in tourists. There are probably people from twenty different countries and as many states on this block alone. Each square of sidewalk holds something new — mismatched buildings, forty posters for the same album on a construction wall, roasted-nut vendors, obsessively brisk women in heels.

The sky simmers with bad weather.

Zara's new roommate is expecting her. Zara knows she will turn up at the apartment late, probably wet. She fiddles her phone out of her purse and sends a quick text. *Wanted to see the theater.*

Then she's off, wheeling as quickly as she can, bumping the suitcase over tiny breaks in the sidewalk. She can't help running through the important dates in her head. It's November 5, the day before the first read-through. *Echo and Ariston* opens on December 29.

The Aurelia is there, waiting for her. The white marble gives her the same feeling as good poetry.

I'm going to be with you, from the moment you arrive.

Leopold might not be in the building right now. Zara knows that. If she can't find him, she'll call, but it would be better to see him in person. They've had a dozen late-night talks and it hasn't been enough to banish the worst of Zara's nerves.

She isn't ready for this read-through. She still feels like she should be sitting in the theater instead of up on the stage.

Zara presses her forehead against the glass doors. She jolts the bars. Locked.

When she goes around back, she assumes that the stage door will be locked, too — but it pushes right in. The audition signs have been cleared. The emptiness of the hallway pulls her toward the wings.

Zara steps onto the stage. It's all hers. No one waiting in line, pushing to take her place. She tells herself: *If the door was unlocked, it must be all right for me to be here.*

She tells herself: *I belong here.*

Heel-toe, one step at a time, she starts to walk the boards. One of her directors taught her to do this, and it stuck. *It's about learning the space,* that director said. It seemed important to Zara, like learning the body of a person you love. She spent time on every boy she dated, finding out their details. She savored that part: the freckles, the skin, the secrets. Zara spent time on girls, too. Certain ones. Maybe it was just theater — how it's supposed to make you notice everything — but Zara found herself painstakingly aware of the way one girl would tilt her head when she sang her scales, how another would smile to herself as she waited for her entrances.

Zara discovers the Aurelia, one step at a time. Heel-toe, heel-toe. The stage is giving her a grounded feeling that nothing else could. This is better than going straight to Leopold. Now when she sees him, she won't be frantic and afraid. He'll know that he made the right choice when he cast her. If she comes up with some new insight into Echo, he might even be impressed.

As she walks, she tells herself the story of *Echo and Ariston.*

I was born to inhabit a kingdom, but that's not a blessing.

Zara pinches off bits of the stage with each step.

We've been at war since before I was born.

More steps. More stage.

My father promised me to the heir of the neighboring king-dom, a boy I've never met. Ariston. So I ran away. I ran through the woods, and I made it to the sea. I met a boy, and I didn't know he was Ariston — of course — so I fell in love with him, of course. A series of famous love scenes follows. Zara's blood rises and swells. This play taught her everything she knows about being in love.

But the story doesn't end there. Echo and Ariston share everything, except their true identities. That's what makes it a tragedy. Ariston doesn't figure out who Echo is until it's too late to save her.

So Echo dies.

Of course.

The ending shouldn't have the power to hurt Zara after reading the play so many times, but it does. Zara has to stop. Breathe. The darkness of it wraps around her, so when she takes the last step, to the edge of the orchestra pit, she almost doesn't notice.

There is darkness down there, too.

And the outline of a body.

"Hello?" Zara asks. She thinks she must be seeing some-thing wrong — that it's a trick of the shadows. They're different in theaters. Heavy, like the curtains that sway at the edges of the stage.

"Hello?"

There is no answer, and Zara has almost convinced herself she was wrong. But then she hears a thin groan. She sits down and pushes herself off the edge of the stage into the orchestra pit. It's dark down there — she uses the firefly glow of her phone to light a vague area. A man on the ground. Blood spreads from his body, a shade darker than the carpet and the seats.

Red and red and red.

viii

Kestrel opens the door to the hallway, revealing her new roommate, who is chubby, bedraggled, and plain as unflavored yogurt.

Then Kestrel remembers that she should give Zara a significant break. She did just find Roscoe in the orchestra pit.

Kestrel leans in and hugs her. "Poor thing. You must want to turn around and go right home." That would fix all of Kestrel's problems. It's a perfect solution, really. She's proud she thought it up.

Zara pulls away. "I just got here."

Kestrel doesn't know this girl any better than a stranger in Times Square, but she can see in the set of Zara's wide, stubborn lips that she isn't going anywhere. The Aurelia didn't want to pay for housing for a nonfamous out-of-town actor, so Leopold asked Kestrel to take the girl in like a stray puppy. And she certainly couldn't say no to Leopold.

Kestrel is too nice. That's her problem.

She shakes her head and feels the end of her bob skimming her shoulders. Her fresh red dye can't possibly look good in the bright hallway. They should go inside — but that's so *final*. "This isn't right at all," she says, and she can hear the whine souring her tone. She tries to brighten things up. "I always script my meetings, don't you? We only have one day to get to know each other before the read-through. One. Day. I thought we would go out for tapas." As long as this girl is here, they might as well get to know each other. It's not like Kestrel has had a friend her age in a long time. She likes that her friends are older — sophisticated — but the idea of having another teenage girl to talk to about teenage girl things has been vaguely exciting.

"I'm not hungry," Zara says, stomping all over Kestrel's plans. "I'm sort of tired, actually." Zara peeks around her, through the door. Behind them is the apartment — stainless steel and tasteful curtains and cream furniture. "This building is nice," Zara says. "Really, really nice."

Kestrel wants to snap at her, because that's really, really

obvious. Doesn't this girl have anything better to say? Kestrel doesn't snap, however. She shifts her weight onto one foot, hitches a sole up to the other knee. Yoga is one of the things that keep her calm when she is on edge. "This is just the New York apartment. Mama and Alec will be in Florence for at least six months. They haven't lived in the city full-time since I was a baby, but I won't budge."

She waits patiently until Zara asks, "Why?"

"Because of the food and the people and the *Aurelia*, of course." No way was she spending a season with the Italians and their stunning lack of deodorant while Leopold Henneman directed *Echo and Ariston*. Kestrel prepared every day for months, and went in for five different auditions. She remembers having to break the news to Mama and Alec over the phone, hiding the tears behind her well-trained voice.

Her phone starts up a dull buzz in the living room. She snatches it off the side table and comes right back. "Stage manager," Kestrel announces. She reads the short message, feeling her brain tighten around the news. "Roscoe died in the hospital." Kestrel isn't surprised. Not really. Zara looks surprised enough for both of them. Her eyes are full of harsh, reflected light. She's not breathing. And then she's trying to breathe too much.

Kestrel runs into the apartment. She's seen this sort of thing before. She goes straight for the medicine cabinet and hunts down her Xanax. There are only a dozen pills at the bottom of the prescription bottle, and they make a skittering noise as she runs back to the door. She twists the cap, thrusts a pill at Zara. "You're having a panic attack," she says. "Take this."

Zara shakes her head like an idiot, and Kestrel almost throws the entire bottle at her. "I shouldn't . . ."

"Fine," Kestrel says. "Your choice."

She downs the pill instead.

The girl looks like a disaster, so Kestrel tries to make her feel better. "It's not really a surprise that Roscoe would fall from the balcony. You wouldn't know because you never met him, but he was just so odd." Kestrel repunctuates. "Just. So. Odd."

"I didn't know he was the lighting designer," Zara says, her breath starting to smooth itself out. "I thought he came in from the alley. It was cold out. The stage door was unlocked."

"Right," Kestrel says, and before she can stop herself, she adds, "*anyone* could wander in." But being terrible to Zara Evans doesn't actually make her feel better. She finds tree pose with her other foot and lets out a breath. "It was probably the curse."

Zara's eyebrows go up. Besides being cliché, they're dangerously unplucked. "You believe in the Aurelia's curse?"

"Short answer? Yes." Zara stares at her, looking confused and needy. "Fine. Long answer. Theaters are strange places, and you have to walk into one with an open mind. If we wanted to be unimaginative and live flat, boring lives, we would have done people's taxes."

Zara smiles a tiny bit, and Kestrel gets the summery feeling that comes from giving a good performance.

But it blows past and they're left standing in the hallway. This unwanted Echo is right on her doorstep, and what does Kestrel do? Bring her inside, along with her hideous suitcase, and offer her tea.

Too nice. Every time.

ix

Meg made place cards for the read-through: curled hand-writing on plain white card stock. It's not necessary, but it's a nice touch, she thinks.

The table is the same one they used at auditions, favored in the theater even though there are much grander ones lying about. Supposedly its swirled grain and scuff marks originate from the 1956 production of *Waiting for Lefty*. It bleeds history, like everything else at the Aurelia.

Meg squares the corners of each card. The little rectangles give her a pleasant feeling. Meg likes to plan, to arrange things.

This business with Roscoe has been regrettable, and Leopold surprised her by taking it personally. Maybe he doesn't want anyone to believe that he is the reason Roscoe pitched himself to the ground.

It's no secret that he was unhappy with the lighting design.

And then there are the other things, the ones that Leopold whispers to Meg when he should be sleeping.

Meg wants Leopold to forget that for today. She has changed the location of the table read from the stage to the studios. There will be a small furor from the older actors — it's not *tradition*— but the police aren't finished in the theater.

Besides, a death lingers over the orchestra pit. Meg doesn't want anyone too close to the truth of that moment. Theater patrons who sit in the front row always live to regret it. They're too near the bodies of the actors, able to feel their strain, to count their tears. Distance is what turns life into a story. Distance will turn Roscoe's death into a small, simple tragedy.

They can mourn quickly and then get back to work. Leopold will like that. And that's what Meg needs, more than anything. A happy director.

More cards, more squaring, and then Meg stops. She brushes her thumb over the imprinted letters of a name.

Zara Evans.

Leopold's pet nobody. Meg knows what Leopold will do to her. Not the details, but it's the same story, every time. And this girl will go along with it, like they always do — swept up and not even noticing, at first, how strong the current is.

As Meg sets a script in front of each seat, a song scratches at the inside of her head, begging to be let out. A song she used to love. She releases the sound in a small, tight hum. "Tonight." *West Side Story.*

The table is ready, but when Meg looks back, she sees it through Leopold's eyes. She knows his thought process as well as she knows her own. The cream cards would look perfect in the vast, gilded theater. In the studio, they seem out of place.

Meg changes directions, counterclockwise, undoing all the work she has done. She spent hours on these cards, but no matter. The rectangles of paper accumulate in a little pile, then melt away into the trash.

Yes — a clean table. A blank studio. A fresh start.

This will make Leopold happy.

For today.

X

Kestrel and Zara arrive at the read-through late, but they come bearing gifts — small gold boxes of chocolate. Kestrel insisted on stopping at a specialty shop in the Village, forty minutes out of the way. "People need comfort right now," she said. "They need to be reminded about life. How it's here — a moment, melted on the tongue — then gone! A bite of perfect chocolate does that."

Zara tugged away from the ridiculous plan at first, but then she was charmed by the odd taste of pear caramels, taken in by the rustle of fancy paper, even half-convinced by

Kestrel's words. She could almost forget the body crumpled in the orchestra pit.

As soon as Zara enters the studio, she remembers everything. Roscoe's ragged breathing. How she never finished walking the boards.

The actors are already gathered around a long table. Everyone turns to look at her. Kestrel breezes away from her side, setting down the chocolates on the table. Zara is left standing alone, empty-handed.

And then she sees Leopold Henneman at the head of the table. Leopold Henneman, smiling gently at her.

Zara has seen pictures; she recognizes his uniquely light brown eyes, the steep angle of his features. What can't be shoved into a frame is the amount of heady, unfocused energy he gives off. "My dear," he says, and his voice wraps around her like a coat on a cold day. "Come." He nods to the empty chair next to him.

On his other side is a woman with pink-white skin and short blond hair tucked behind her ears. "This is Meg," Leopold says. "My personal assistant. Meg, you remember Zara Evans."

Zara's lips stretch into a thin, nervous string of a smile.

Meg gives a nod. Her pale-blue eyes have a dark stone of pity at the centers. Why? Because Roscoe died? Because Zara had to sit there, waiting for the ambulance, and watch?

She doesn't have long to wonder, because Leopold stands. He takes in the room with a single, sweeping glance. "Welcome," he says. "Or, as is the case with so many of you, welcome back."

Zara knows those words aren't for her. She's not really one

of the company yet. But she has to start somewhere — right? This is what Zara has been waiting for. Sitting in a plain studio on a spittle-gray afternoon. This is when she becomes one of the initiated, the people behind the curtain, making the stories. Someone who can be welcomed *back*.

"This is not what I would have wished for, but as always in the theater, we work with what we are given. Thank you, all of you, for cooperating with the police." Zara had her moment with them, after the ambulance and hospital and before Kestrel's apartment. She was so tired and their faces were so blank. They asked over and over again how she knew the theater would be open. *I didn't.* Then how did she open the door? *I didn't.* Then why was it open? *I don't know.* Why did she go in that way? *I just wanted to see the stage.*

I'm an actor.

"They must follow their procedure," Leopold adds. "The more help we give, the sooner they can leave our space. And while I cannot say anything officially, the police have informed us that Roscoe's death was most likely an accident, caused by an unsafe lighting session." These words are the air that Zara has been waiting for. *Accident. Unsafe.* She takes a full, round breath for the first time since yesterday.

"This is what we do," Leopold says, "We push on. At the Aurelia, we stop for nothing, not even death. Perhaps it is most important to be making art when death is all around. This is when we need the perfect story."

Leopold lets the room fall back into silence. His words make Zara feel bold and terrified all at once.

The stage manager invites them all to go around and introduce themselves. Zara shifts in her seat. Maybe things will settle in now. This could still be everything she dreamed, with no more dark edges.

The crew goes first. Sound design, set design, dramaturg. Leopold nods with each addition.

His energy changes, tightens, as the turn falls to a young man who fits the description of tall, dark, and handsome a little too snugly. "Barrett," the young man says. "But you can call me the God of Props."

"I make costumes," says a woman whose deep voice is touched with an Italian accent. A white braid runs down her back, sleek against wrinkled skin. She's unspeakably elegant. "My name is Cosima." She must be the oldest person at the table by at least twenty years.

Next, they come to a girl with blue-green tattoos twining up her arms. A girl almost as young as Zara. She has curly black hair, glowing amber-brown skin. Her hands are filled with nervous energy. She's so pretty that Zara assumes she's an actress, then immediately changes her mind.

"Eli," she says. "Assistant lighting designer."

The silence shimmers with tension.

"As you know," Leopold says, "the Aurelia has seen few designers with Roscoe's level of dedication. We are sure that his assistant will be able to carry out his wishes for *Echo and Ariston.*"

"All right." The stage manager sounds a too-sudden clap. "On to the actors."

First up is a wisp of a woman with vaulted cheekbones. She might be in her early forties, but she looks a decade older. Her light-brown hair is brittle, her voice as pretty and sharp as a smashed mirror. "My name is Enna, and I'll be playing the role of Echo's mother, Amalthea."

Then comes Echo's father, a heavyset man with a blunt red face and stunning blue eyes. "I'm Carl."

As soon as Zara sees the man playing Ariston's father, she wishes she could swap. Toby is short, bald, and gay in every sense of the word. "I'm so glad to be back here with all my favorite chickadees," he says. "Minus one, minus one. But Roscoe is going to the great big show in the sky."

Toby's words and his warm voice are almost enough to convince Zara that Roscoe is in a better place. But then her Jewish atheism kicks in, reminding her what she believes — when you die, you die. Besides, Zara doesn't need a heaven. She has the Aurelia.

"I'm Kestrel," her roommate says, standing up in a way that demands attention. "I'll be playing the chorus leader." Her fake smile lasts long enough for her to sit down, and then it vanishes.

Zara is the only actor left.

"Aren't we waiting on one more?" she asks.

"She's excited about Adrian Ward," Leopold says with a dry chuckle. Zara shifts in her chair. That wasn't what she meant. Still — how can she be Echo without Ariston? "We have a week before actors are called again, and Adrian, our Adrian, is still filming scenes for his upcoming release. Something about a warlike species of bugs that intend to take over the planet. He has to slay a few more before he can join us." Leopold folds his hands and turns back to Zara. "Now. Shall we?"

"I'm Zara Evans," she says as she stands up, even though her knees don't seem to think it's such a great idea. Her chair clatters, making twice as much noise as anyone else's. "I'll be playing Echo." The words came out tilted, like a question. *I'll be playing Echo?*

Into the silence, she blurts out, "I've loved this play since I was a little girl."

Enna studies her with a series of rapid, dramatic blinks. "You mean since last Tuesday?" Laughter rises around the table.

Zara looks down and closes her eyes. Sees Roscoe on the floor.

Leopold rushes up from his seat. He puts a hand on her back, five points of pressure holding her up. "Our Echo has had quite the arrival," he says. Then, like velvet in her ear, he adds, "Sit down, my dear." She does. He tells the company how perfect she is, while Zara keeps her eyes on the scuffed table.

The stage manager calls a ten-minute break. Zara thinks it might finally be safe to look up.

The girl with the blue-green tattoos is watching her.

Eli spends five minutes of the break wanting to talk to Zara Evans and the other five trying *not* to talk to her.

The girl she thought would climb the curtains is right here, slipping out of the studio, disappearing into the bathroom. She comes back with paper-towel scratches like claw marks on her cheek.

Zara Evans has been crying.

It punches Eli in the gut: she hasn't cried yet. She's been too busy. Her entire family has been on the phone, talking to her, leaving messages. Her mom: *We'll send flowers to the church.* Her dad: *Is that theater safe? ¿Estás segura?* Both of her brothers called, although they clearly had no idea what to say.

The visit from the police this morning didn't help. They had a list of questions for Eli that seemed to go on for hours. They were mostly interested in whether Roscoe and Eli had been sleeping together.

"He was my boss," she told them as they did an inspection of the lighting booth, grabbing random pieces of equipment and calling them evidence. "Also, he was thirty-four years older than me."

They looked at her like those statements made it more likely, not less. So she added, "I'm a lesbian, officers. Actually, a lesbian and a half." The policemen scowled at her. Eli enjoys outing herself sometimes. This was not one of those times. "Do you have any idea what actually happened? Because I *know* he didn't fall."

"You don't believe what happened to Roscoe was an accident?" one of them asked.

"No," Eli stated.

The policemen exchanged tight-assed looks. They didn't want to figure out what happened to Roscoe. They wanted to give her a hard time, fill out their paperwork, call it an accident, and go home.

The stage manager claps her hands, bringing Eli back to the studio.

Read-through time.

Eli does everything she can to focus on *Echo and Ariston*

instead of Roscoe and more Roscoe. She follows along with every word in the script. When they hit Echo's first scene, Eli thinks about Zara and her paper-towel-scratched cheeks, and Eli can't stop herself from sending a spark of encouragement across the table.

Zara looks up at her.

Again.

Zara's eyes are warm and brown and Eli is in trouble. She reminds herself not to do this. Things play out badly for Eli: siempre, siempre. She crushes too hard and then falls on her ass. That's how it went with her not-quite-a-girlfriend in high school. That's how it went with the assistant stage manager who eyed Eli all summer, took her down to the techie love nest under the stage, then stopped the makeout just long enough to let Eli know she had a girlfriend in Maine. That's how it went with Hannah. When Eli met *her*, she was playing Juliet. That should have been a hint. Juliets want to run around the city acting rebellious and turning every feeling they have into poetry, but they don't stay with a girl after the curtain goes down. Hannah liked having Eli around — blissful, stupid, in love — until she didn't. Even then, she swore that her feelings for Eli were real, but they weren't *enough*.

Zara's voice fills the studio.

"I have done your bidding these many years,
But this I will not do."

Eli shovels Roscoe's old notebooks on top of her script. The police looked through them, but when they saw the thicket of math — nothing that looked like a suicide note — they gave

51

the notebooks back to Eli. What she needs to do now is use them as a template to come up with a better lighting design. It's like spitting on Roscoe's grave to even think about changing his plan, but she doesn't have a choice. Leopold hates it. He gave her a week to revise it *and* submit a light plot.

Which is impossible.

Eli stares at page after page. Her brain is a mess of grief and equations. When her eyes are almost dead from strain, Eli closes them and lets the rest of the play wash over her. Here comes the famous love scene, which sounds weird with the stage manager reading Ariston's part. Like half a love scene, which is really nothing at all.

And then —

Echo, caught by the soldiers. Echo, pitching herself into the sea. Echo, wreathed in saltwater and drowning.

And then —

The read-through is over.

Eli is left sitting at the table, holding back the tears that wouldn't come all day. Roscoe should be here next to her, muttering and making those enormous gestures, his hands flying around the room like two drunk birds.

Zara did a good job with the read-through. That's all Eli is feeling. She's just responding to what Zara can do with her voice, with her body. Ay, maybe don't think about her body.

The cast and the crew break up. Zara stays at the table and lingers over her script, setting down a few notes in the margins. Eli wants to offer herself — she'd make a good margin. Zara could write on her in that careful, slanting script.

52

Shit.

Did she really just think that?

Eli makes for the door. She's halfway down the hall before she realizes Zara Evans is following her. Eli's entire body celebrates and panics at the same time.

The girl is clearly rushing to catch up. It would be rude not to slow down. So that's what Eli does. Zara catches up and slows down and then just — stares. Warm brown eyes, all over Eli. "I wanted to say that I'm sorry."

"For what?" Eli asks. She can't think of any way that Zara Evans has wronged her. And she'd like to keep it that way.

Zara blinks hard, like maybe those blinks are powerful enough to keep her upright. "Roscoe."

Eli shrugs. "Why? You didn't know him." Her voice is ice. She doesn't like the sound, but it's a necessary precaution. Otherwise she'll warm up way too fast.

"I was there," Zara says. "Not . . . when he fell, but . . . I found him."

"God," Eli says. The first thing she feels is sorry for Zara. Then another feeling hits, so strong it almost cancels out the first. She's glad Zara was there. Glad that Roscoe wasn't alone. "So when Leopold said that thing about your arrival . . ."

Zara nods.

Kestrel's voice wafts out of the rehearsal studio. "Zara Evans! Paging Zara Evans! Do people even page people anymore? Oh well! Zara Evans!"

Zara shrinks toward the wall.

"What does she want?" Eli asks.

"I'm staying with her," Zara says. It doesn't take much digging to hear the stress in Zara's voice. "You know how we have a week before rehearsals really start?" Eli nods. "Well, I convinced my parents that I needed to stay here. But now I have to spend the whole time in Kestrel's apartment."

Eli feels a path opening up in front of them. She needs to learn what happened when Roscoe died. Zara needs an escape. "We should hang out tomorrow."

Kestrel catches sight of Zara and waves madly at her from down the hall. "I'll grab your bag!"

Zara says quickly, "As long as it's a real tomorrow."

"What else could it be?" Eli asks.

"In plays, they're always saying, 'We'll meet tomorrow. We'll see each other soon. We'll run away in the morning.'" Zara's eyes widen, like that last part hit her ears sounding different than she thought it would. "They never actually do."

Eli drags one of her curls into a long, slinky spiral, which means she's flirting. Wait. Who authorized this flirting? She flicks the curl away. "Yeah," she says. "Let's make it a real tomorrow."

xii

Zara's second night at Kestrel's is harder than the first because sleep is replaced by red, red dreams. She commits to being awake around dawn, and does everything she can to distract herself. Runs her lines, unpacks her clothes, kills a week's worth of homework. A few hours after waking up, she leaves the room to snatch breakfast — nothing that requires the stove or the shiny appliances. They look like they could be dusted for fingerprints and come up clean. Zara grabs a yogurt from the fridge. Kestrel is on the couch, flipping back and forth from reality TV to a French film without subtitles.

"Are you going to the funeral tomorrow?" Kestrel asks, her face sad in a way that looks measured — like she had to think about just how much sadness would be appropriate before she pursed her lips and wrinkled her forehead.

"No." Zara thinks back to what Eli said. "I didn't really know him."

And going to the funeral would mean facing the company again, without Leopold. At the read-through, he was the only thing standing between Zara and complete humiliation. He's gone for the entire week, in Toronto.

"I'm going to stay here and work on my lines," Zara says.

"Right," Kestrel says, suddenly interested in her toenail polish. "You have *so many* lines."

Zara hurries back to the guest room. She can't help that she's been cast as Echo at Kestrel's theater, but living in her space makes everything sharper. Zara's afraid to be caught touching Kestrel's things. Breathing her air.

She settles onto the bed, her script in one hand. She has a whole week to sit here, trying not to think about Roscoe. She won't be able to do it, though. He'll slip into thoughts of the Aurelia. He'll visit her dreams every night. A week of this, before she goes back to the theater. It's like sitting shiva for someone she never knew.

Zara's phone comes to life. Maybe it's Leopold. They can talk about the play and forget all this for a while. Zara sets her yogurt on the bedside table and checks the screen.

It's her mom.

She's left seven messages since Zara got to the city two days ago. Zara knows that she can't put this off forever. "Hi." Her voice is fluttery, weak.

"Zara, love," her mom says in a way that she usually pairs with a hug or a kiss on the cheek. Zara misses that. She could have gone home this week, but she was afraid that when she came back to New York, she would have to start all over again, from scratch.

Besides, she's going home for the holidays. Some of them, at least. Thanksgiving is only a few weeks away. And Christmas isn't their holiday, anyway.

"How is the city?" her mom asks. "How is the theater? Did you leave anything at home?"

"Good, and beautiful, and no, I did not."

Her parents pile on the questions like this. It's one of their rituals. Now she's supposed to ask her mom at least three questions back.

"Something happened," Zara says, breaking the pattern. She can feel her mom waiting for an explanation on the other end of the line. She can picture her in the kitchen — black coffee in one hand, a to-do list on the table in front of her. She probably just crossed out *Call Zara*.

Zara smiles, knowing that it will infuse the way she speaks. "First of all, everything is fine." This is the right way for them to hear about Roscoe. Newspapers would make it sound cold, sensational, or terrifying, and it was none of those things. It was an old man who fell, and a trip to the hospital. Zara can make her parents see it that way if she tries hard enough.

Isn't that what acting is for?

"When I came in on the train . . ." she starts. It takes ten minutes to tell the story and another forty to convince her mom not to drop everything and immediately come see her. Zara promises to call her dad and tell him, too, although her mom will get to it first, so the hard part is done.

At the last second, after a round of good-byes, her mom's voice goes flat. "You shouldn't be there. You never should have gone." This is exactly what Zara needed her not to say. "It's just a play." Zara winces like she's been thrown into cold water. "If you were good enough for them to pick you once, someone will pick you again."

Not at the Aurelia.

Not by Leopold Henneman.

Not as Echo.

A new text comes in, from a New York number, with no name attached.

Is today tomorrow?

"Mom, I have to go," Zara says.

And she hangs up. Without a good-bye. She's never done that before. Zara reads Eli's text again.

Is today tomorrow?

Plays are usually filled with people who become close for weeks and months, who spend every minute together and learn each other in ways that normal friends never do. They confide, reveal, peel back fears and secrets to see what's

58

underneath. They dream together. They wrestle and fight and laugh too loud and kiss for no reason. Zara has her mom's words trapped in her head, like a line that she memorized and will never be able to unlearn. *It's just a play*. She needs a friend who knows better.

Eli looked at Zara like she belonged at that table, like she was meant to be there.

Zara takes a quick breath and types.

Tomorrow and tomorrow and tomorrow.

As soon as it's sent, she falls backward on the bed and hits the pillows with a hard thump. Zara can't seem to get anything right. Who quotes the most morbid monologue from *Macbeth* when someone just died?

Eli worked with Roscoe. Zara watched him die. Maybe that's why Zara needs Eli to like her.

Her phone lights up.

All our yesterdays have been shit. Let's get new yesterdays.

Zara smiles, lying on her back and holding the phone up with both hands as she types.

Where do you want to meet?

Eli picks the Aurelia, which is perfect. Maybe Zara should want to avoid it, to get some distance, to forget what happened to Roscoe. But the truth is, she would have been intimidated if Eli picked any other place. The rest of New York City overwhelms Zara: the subways and the choked sidewalks, the people who would happily murder her for not walking fast enough.

The Aurelia feels like hers.

xiii

The greenroom is dim. Zara doesn't turn on the lights, just in case she's not supposed to be in here.

She finds the most comfortable spot on the well-loved couches and looks over the printed and bound pages that the stage manager handed out at the read-through. This is the fourteenth version of *Echo and Ariston* that Zara will add to her collection. But it isn't just another copy of the play. This is Zara's *script*. It has Echo's lines highlighted. Soon it will hold her stage directions scribbled in light, hasty pencil. There is a promise in these pages that was never there before.

For the first time, Zara feels the threat that comes with it.

What if she can't fall in love like she's supposed to? That's what she's here to do. That's what Echo's story is about.

Zara's secret ripples inside her like dark water. She thinks back to the auditions, Leopold needling: *Who do you love most?* Zara's never been in love. Now she has to hope that her director doesn't notice.

Eli shows up and flicks on the lights. "Have you been lurking here in the dark?" She's wearing the same sort of outfit she wore at the read-through: gray T-shirt, ripped jeans, stomping boots.

"I wouldn't call it lurking," Zara says.

"Skulking?" Eli asks. "Lying in wait?" The words fly out at a pace worthy of David Mamet. Eli is pretty enough to be an actress, smart enough to be a playwright, talented enough to be a lighting designer. Zara feels an inner flutter — *intimidation, envy?* It can be hard to tell flutters apart.

Eli sets one hand to each side of the doorframe, looking at Zara with an intensity that locks her into place. "I need to ask you something that will make your day much worse." Zara lets out a small laugh. Eli cocks her head. "I did say *worse*, right?"

"Yeah. But the way you just . . . said it. I like that." Zara holds up her script, butterflied open at the spine. "It's what a character in a Greek play would do. They always say what they feel."

The small smile that Eli gives Zara goes straight to her

head. Eli finally leaves the doorway, but doesn't make it all the way to the couch. Instead, she hovers halfway across the room and takes the Leatherman out of her belt holster, flipping out several blades in one swift, shiny motion.

"What did you want to ask?" Zara says.

Eli speaks while shifting a long knife back and forth, "What you saw. That day. With Roscoe."

Zara blinks, and he's there. His body on the ground. His blood everywhere. She can hear broken breathing, and her own starts to shatter. Zara needs to be done with this story. She recited it to the police, slowly, carefully, and then did her best to forget.

"I'm sorry," Eli says, curls flying as she shakes her head. "It's just . . . Roscoe's death is the wrong color."

"What does that mean?" Zara asks.

Eli puts away the Leatherman. She paces, stubbing the reinforced rubber toe of her boot against the wall. "So when I'm deciding how to light a scene, there's a lot of practical stuff I'm thinking about, a lot of little choices that have to do with the equipment and the setup. When it comes down to it, though, whether a moment has the right color is — a *feeling*. This feels wrong." She turns directly to Zara. There's a sadness in her eyes that can't be faked, even by the world's best actor. "They're making it sound like he was some old man whose brain came unwired. Like he couldn't keep his balance. I've seen Roscoe walk a tightrope with two forty-pound lights in each hand."

What happened to Roscoe was an accident. Zara doesn't

doubt that. But how can she refuse to even *talk* to Eli about it? That's how her parents deal with hard things.

They just stop.

"Okay," Zara says.

Eli leads her out of the greenroom in a disorienting rush, down halls and through an unmarked door. Up a thin metal ladder that never seems to end. Zara looks up and finds herself staring at the bottom of Eli's boots, the dark valleys of the treads. She wonders what she's gotten herself into.

When she arrives at the top, there's nowhere to go except a thin strip of a balcony. "I'm not afraid of heights," Zara says.

"Good," Eli says, already halfway across.

Zara raises her voice, to hide the quiver. "I'm not *not* afraid of heights. I respect heights."

Eli doesn't give Zara the pep talk she hoped for, or the rolled eyes that probably deserves. Instead, Eli just stares at Zara, eyes dark and unblinking. That look could pull someone across a room, across an ocean.

Zara takes the balcony one careful step at a time.

When she makes it to Eli's side, she assumes the worst is over. Then Eli leaps onto the railing. Zara's heart slides in her chest. Eli settles into a crow's nest posture, perfectly casual. "Roscoe was here. He comes up here when he wants to think about the design. It's the best view in the theater."

Zara tips her face over the edge of the railing, and the world falls away. She's looking at the Aurelia the way a bird would look down on the earth. White scrollwork like sand. Rows and rows of red seats, waves on a bloodstained sea.

"It wouldn't be hard to fall," Zara says.

"It would if you know what you're doing," Eli counters. "Would you die making a cross from upstage left to downstage right?"

"No," Zara admits.

"Of course you wouldn't," Eli says with satisfaction. "That's your job. That's what you do."

Zara spent her first rehearsal at the Aurelia as an outsider, the answer to *one of these things is not like the other.* In one offhand comment, Eli made her feel like a real actress.

"So . . ." Eli says. And Zara can tell that it's time to revisit what happened to Roscoe, to crawl back inside that moment. She doesn't want to tell it numbly, the way she did to the police. She takes her time, looking for words that have the shine of truth. The keys to the story. "I was walking the boards. When I got to the edge of the stage, I saw Roscoe in the orchestra pit. I didn't know who he was then. I rushed down the rehearsal stairs. And I . . . I knelt down. And I called 911. And I talked to him, although he never talked back."

Zara wants to rush ahead—past the part where worry and fear hit her in a fresh wave—but she holds herself in the moment by force. "No. I'm sorry. I'm wrong. I asked all these questions and he never answered them, but he mumbled something. I don't know if he even knew I was there. He was staring up and he said . . ." Zara can't quite grab the word. It's there, like a character waiting offstage, impossible to see behind the curtains.

Eli waits while Zara presses her fingers to her forehead. "He said . . . *angels.*"

Eli cants one dark eyebrow. "Angels?"

Zara asks weakly, "Was Roscoe religious?"

Eli puts a thumb to the soft hollow of her neck. "I wore a rosary one day and he went out of his mind with happiness."

"You're Catholic?"

The question almost asks itself.

Eli shrugs. "It's how I grew up. I converted to theater. They have a lot in common: rituals, costumes, a voice that fills this big echoey space and makes you believe in something." She smiles, and there's teasing in there. "What about you?" She bounces on the balls of her feet, still crouched on the railing, and Zara feels it in her nerves. "Let me guess. Episcopalian. No. *Lutheran.*"

Zara knows her last name throws people off. Her dad's father converted when he married Zara's grandmother, the one with the theater heritage and the perfect sufganiyot recipe.

"I'm Jewish." And since there are a hundred different ways to be Jewish and Zara is only one of them, she adds, "Culturally Jewish."

Eli nods. She drums her fingers on the wooden railing. Zara's eyes are drawn to her wrists, where the tattoos start. She follows the path all the way up Eli's arm, to her slim shoulders. There are stars and moons, islands and seas. Flowers that bloom in unexpected places. Zara wants to tell her it's beautiful.

But that's not why they're up here.

"So what do you think it means?" Zara asks. "Angels?"

"Roscoe saw some, I guess. White beams and whatever. He was probably trying to figure out how to do a light plot for it." Eli's smile dies a quick death. "What else?" She's been patient so far, but now there's an urgent boil underneath her words.

"That's it," Zara says with a useless shrug. "Angels."

She feels it again, how high up they are. Zara looks down at the floor of the balcony, littered with cables and cardboard boxes that hold extra bulbs. But looking down just reminds her that Roscoe fell a very long way.

So she looks up instead.

On the plaster ceiling right above her head, there are paintings of gods and men. And angels. Not the kind with gentle smiles and softly feathered wings. These angels have faces that storm with righteous anger.

Zara taps at Eli's wrist. She points to the fake sky.

Eli jumps down from the railing to the balcony. She works a cluster of keys from her belt and puts one into the wall right below the angels. Zara doesn't even notice the door until it's opening.

On the other side is a sort of dark cave. Its floor is the plaster ceiling of the theater, and a few feet over that, a walkway spans the empty space. It's even less safe-looking than the balcony. A skeleton of metal and air.

"Where does this go?" Zara whispers. The theater has

secrets everywhere, and it feels like speaking too loudly might shake the wrong one loose.

"This leads to the lighting booth," Eli says. "Only people who know the Aurelia would come this way."

Eli strides onto the walkway like it's nothing.

Zara takes a step, looking straight ahead. Eli doesn't look back, expecting Zara to be brave. But Zara's nerves tell her that she's falling. She reaches out and grabs one of Eli's hands.

And everything stops.

Eli turns around to face her, long, delicate fingers twisting to lock with Zara's.

Eli holds on tight.

Eli asks herself: What if someone used this walkway to come up behind Roscoe? What if someone planned it? What if someone *pushed*?

She lets go of Zara's hand. Ay, carajo. She crushed the girl's fingertips. Of course she did.

She leads the way out of the Aurelia, tucks Zara safely into a cab, and starts walking. Eli needs to give the police one more chance, even though they haven't earned it. Ten minutes later, she reaches the precinct, a gray slab of a building where they make her wait for hours. She spends the time in limbo scribbling equations about voltage. The Aurelia's master electrician will help her wire whatever she needs, but first she has to show him that she's not just some girl Roscoe took a chance on for no reason.

"Can we help you?" an officer finally asks.

"It's about Roscoe. Gregory Roscoe."

The policeman takes Eli to a little room where she waits in an even less comfortable chair. Another policeman comes in and faces her across the desk. She tells them about Roscoe's final words. The angels on the ceiling. The details of the hidden walkway. "Did you *see* the hidden walkway?"

The uniformed man nods, but she doesn't know if that means yes or I'm-nodding-so-you'll-stop-now. "Thank you, Miss Vasquez. We'll let you know if there are any new developments."

Eli keeps trying to talk, but the officers are already leaving the room.

She spends the rest of her day collecting newspapers from various stands, even though she's supposed to be on a train to Stamford for her niece's dance recital. She sends a quick e-mail to her parents and brothers: *Have to stay in the city. Mi trabajo. Tell Lia I'm sorry and give her un abrazo fuerte.* Eli reminds herself that her parents believe in hard work, they're proud she landed this job. And this is part of the job: caring about Roscoe.

Guilt knuckles down. It turns every step into a crush of

regret. She should have been there when he fell. Why did she leave him alone?

When she gets home, she stacks up the newspapers and adds every online article she can find. There's a surprising amount of coverage. Eli does her best to look past the staging for some new piece of truth. Around one in the morning she settles onto her bed, coffee in one hand, laptop balanced across her knees. She wades into the sewers of the online comments. That's when she finds a mention of a man caught on CCTV outside the Aurelia and confirmed by witnesses — an older man in a dark-blue suit, with a mane of wild gray hair.

It's quiet in her apartment. Too quiet for Washington Heights, which is always throwing sound in great big handfuls.

What if Leopold pushed Roscoe and paid off the cops? Leopold had access, but even a director as intense as Leopold Henneman wouldn't kill someone over a bad lighting design.

Eli looks down at her *own* bad lighting design.

That night, she doesn't get anything that looks or feels like sleep.

The next day is Roscoe's funeral, and everyone from the Aurelia is at the wake — everyone but Zara and Leopold. No family. Roscoe didn't have one, which makes Eli their stand-in.

The company mills around in little groups, reminding her that she barely knows these people. They're surrounded by cheap fake flowers, the kind that smell like dust. The arrangement of lilies her family sent sings out in comparison. The funeral home's soft lighting makes everyone look like wax versions of themselves.

Roscoe's casket is closed.

Eli walks up to Toby. He's the friendliest of the actors. They've never really talked, but he gives her that quick look of understanding that comes when you can tell someone else is a member of the Rainbow Club.

They trade hellos, and Eli plunges right in. "I'm putting together a memorial piece. Can you tell me how you spent Roscoe's last day?" she asks, completely aware of how weird that sounds.

"Oh, love," Toby says. "That day. I was upstate. Leopold said he needed time to think over the production, and I offered him my cabin. I have a little cabin, you know. You can find it on Google Maps and smell the pine trees. It's lovely."

Eli feels her stupid theory wither. "Thanks." She crosses Leopold and Toby off her mental list. She walks over to the nearest group of Aurelia people. As long as Eli is prying, she might as well pry hard.

She asks everyone what they were doing *that day.*

Enna was in her high-end apartment building, complete with doormen who would know if she was lying. Carl went to a matinee at another theater. He even has the ticket stub in his wallet, which he offers to give her if she's collecting mementos. Meg sat in on a series of meetings about *Echo and Ariston* merchandise. Kestrel was waiting for her new roommate, which she says as though Zara Evans is some exotic disease she picked up. Eli grits out a thank-you and moves on to Barrett, who spent Roscoe's final hours sleeping with some girl he met at a bar. He provides the information with glee, like they're both people who sleep with girls and therefore she should be proud of him: gross.

Everyone has a story.

Eli goes home and turns on all the lights in her little apartment. Roscoe never got a chance to see it, but without him this place wouldn't exist. Eli would be back in Connecticut, her career over before it even started. She was going to invite Roscoe over here someday, for sandwiches and café con leche.

She sits down on the flowered couch that her mom insisted on and her brothers wouldn't stop laughing at. She gets back to work on the lighting design. Because Eli can't lose all this. Roscoe would hate to know, from beyond the grave, that she'd messed up the chance he gave her. Even if, when she closes her eyes and pinches them tight, Roscoe's death is still the wrong color.

Gray: like a bruise. Like a storm gathering under the skin.

XV

A day passes, then two, and Zara is hoping that Eli will text again. On the third day, she lets it go. It's probably for the best. She'll be in rehearsals soon, and thinking about Roscoe won't help.

That's the only reason Eli wanted to talk to her, anyway.

When she eventually returns to the Aurelia, Zara follows the signs on the wall to the meeting place Leopold picked. They're not in the studios. She checks every door to see which leads to Storage Room Two. That's what her call sheet says. *Storage Room Two. Evans, Ward.*

She's going to meet Adrian tonight.

Ariston.

But Zara's call time is a half hour earlier than his. A half hour with the director — doing what? Zara feels a sick wash of nerves and excitement.

Storage Room Two is as tall as a warehouse, with the same concrete slab floors. Every inch of space is packed tight with props. There are no neat aisles — as Zara picks a direction and walks, she realizes there are no aisles at all. She passes trunks of age-stained photographs and artwork in a strange array of styles. Daggers drip from the walls. She bumps her hip on an old-fashioned painted carousel horse.

Leopold is supposed to be here, but Zara doesn't even know where to start looking for him. It would be easy to lose a person in this mess. Does the props master — Barrett — keep it this way on purpose? Zara tries to picture him, with his dark hair and his perfectly sliced smile, stuck in this room all day and night, only props for company.

Zara makes four wrong turns before she clears an ornate paper screen and finds Leopold in a bare spot among the mess, like a clearing in the woods.

He is sitting on a bed.

A huge, rough-hewn bed with the sort of posts that must remember being tree trunks. Work lights have been set up around the space, throwing hard shadows. There is no script in sight. No stage manager or AD. Not even Leopold's assistant,

Meg. This isn't a traditional rehearsal. But after that audition process, why would she expect a traditional director?

Leopold pats the spot next to him, a patch of untouched white sheet. "Come. Sit."

Zara tells herself that this can't be what it looks like. She's heard about casting couches, but a casting *bed*? To wait until she already had the part is a bit of brutal genius. Leopold must know how grateful she is right now. How little she wants to loosen her grip on this role.

Zara puts down her purse. Takes out her script. She doesn't know what else to do.

Leopold sighs. "I suppose you don't have to follow the first direction I've given you."

Zara dismisses her worries. They're just a product of the strange room, the surprise of finding him here alone. Leopold is her director. She has no reason to think that he's doing anything other than directing her.

"Have you forgotten how to use your voice as well?" Leopold asks, teasing her. "A lack of words will give us some difficulties in rehearsal."

"No," Zara says. And then, because the sound came out much too small, she tries again. "No."

Leopold changes, like a wind hitting her from a new direction. "You look beautiful down here. Something about the broken light." Zara can feel his eyes taking a slow path up and down her body. She crosses her arms. His attention is making her awkward, twitchy. She should be used to it, though. Being an actress means people take stock of every inch of her.

"Is this the bed for the love scene?" Zara asks. She's trying to keep her head in *Echo and Ariston*.

"This is my hope," Leopold says, touching the sheets. His smile is edged with boyish charm. "If Barrett can make it look like driftwood. He'll have to bleach it to that special bone color, *if* he can manage." There is a scrape of disgust in Leopold's voice. Zara stands up a little straighter, a prickle at the base of her spine. She never wants to give Leopold a reason to talk about her like that.

Zara walks into the bright circle cast by the work lights. "Why are we meeting down here?"

"Questions instead of trust," he says. "Is that really how you want to start?"

Zara's worries gust inside her, gathering force, changing direction. All of a sudden she feels desperate to prove herself. "A studio is a blank page. This bed gives an actor more to work with — right?"

"A bed is more than just a prop," Leopold says. "This is the center of the story. The focal point of Echo and Ariston's passion for each other. I thought you, of all people, would be able to see that."

Zara can't let Leopold find out how little she knows about love. She has to keep this part of herself away from him. Safe.

She edges onto the bed.

They're not sitting any closer than they were at the read-through, but there is a soft shock in this closeness. Maybe because they're alone. Maybe because Zara still has the faintest worry that he might touch her.

But no touch comes.

"Was that really so hard?" he asks, and the teasing is back. But he drops it quickly, putting on his most brisk and professional manner. "Now before we begin, you and I have something important to talk about."

Zara nods. She is sitting in profile, his face at the very edge of her vision.

"There's very little I can do about Adrian Ward and his movie-star ways. The production schedule is a disaster; we've had to carve around his promotions and events. This play cannot thrive, it cannot be anything close to perfection, unless you are different. I will have to depend on you in a way that I can't depend on Adrian. And so I need to know that you have no outside commitments. No distractions."

Yes. This is what Zara wants. This is why she's here. To throw herself into this role.

To drown in it.

"Of course," Zara says, turning to face Leopold. "I'm here to work."

His hand falls on her wrist. She forces herself to stay perfectly still. Leopold smiles, and she can see pores in his skin, dark hairs running wild through his gray waves, and pinpricks of light in his eyes. "Good girl."

xvi

Adrian Ward is back in New York.

(Finally.)

There were shoots and reshoots, events and interviews, parties that had to be partied and clothes that had to be packed. Private planes and sleeping pills and his personal assistant telling him it was time to leave for the theater. Now Adrian Ward is at the Aurelia, in something called Storage Room Two.

He almost bumps into a fake horse.

There are voices a little farther off. One of them sounds girlish, and he knows that it has to be the new talent he's playing opposite. Adrian reminds himself to smile. (People like it when he smiles.)

He shouldn't be nervous. He should just breeze into this rehearsal like he's done this a thousand times before. But that's the thing. He hasn't. Here is what they've been saying online, as if Adrian is not an actual person who can do a Google search: *They cast Adrian Ward because of his fans. They cast Adrian Ward because he demanded the part. They cast Adrian Ward because his abs are more famous than anyone else in the show.*

Adrian turns a corner and sees something that brings his thoughts to a stop. There's a monstrous bed, with a girl and a somewhat old man sitting on it. They're talking in quiet, excited voices. Adrian already feels left out. Although he's not really sure that he wants to be a part of whatever is happening on that bed.

The girl leaps down. The old man turns to Adrian.

It takes him a second to recognize the director, Leopold. They met once in L.A. He had looked out of place there, like a slightly European vampire. Here, he looks perfect. Like part of the scenery.

"Hey," Adrian says. "Sorry I'm late."

The girl is staring at Leopold. (Most girls would be staring at Adrian. Not that he needs the attention. He just can't help but notice the difference.)

"Adrian," Leopold says, gesturing around the bizarre room. "Welcome. You understand, we have only a short time together, so I'm going to skip the pleasantries. We'll begin with act three, scene four."

"Oh." Adrian pulls his script out of his leather bag. "One thing. I'm not really —"

"Off book?" Leopold asks. "Not to worry." He plucks the script from Adrian's hand. "I want this exercise to be about emotion. It's about meeting each other in the same place." Adrian nods after each sentence. (Directors love it when he nods. It shows that he's really paying attention. That he gets it.)

"Echo, please find your way to the bed," Leopold says, waving a hand from where she's standing now to where he wants her to be.

The girl mounts the bed as quickly as possible.

"Again," Leopold says.

She climbs down and circles the bed, climbs on from a new angle.

"Again."

Leopold makes her repeat the movement not once, not twice, but fourteen times. He won't explain what she's messing up. Which is a little harsh. But directors do whatever it takes to get the performance.

The fifteenth time, Leopold says, "Brilliant."

And the girl glows.

Leopold turns to Adrian. "Ariston, if you will join Echo on the bed."

"Right." Adrian rubs his hands together, tosses his shirt aside, and tiger-crawls across the sheets. The girl looks horrified.

"No," Leopold says. "This is not a one-night stand in some godforsaken motel. Ariston, you have run away from your kingdom, your family, a future you believed in. All to find *her*." Leopold nods at the girl.

Adrian seriously considers turning around and leaving. This part should have gone to a real actor. But that's what Adrian wants to be, so this is his big chance — right? That's what his agent told him.

Adrian forces himself to calm down and really look at the girl. She's bigger than the girls in Hollywood. (It's not like Adrian *cares*. It's just the truth. If they were casting a movie, she would play the best friend, the sassy one without much screen time. Or the loyal one who dies tragically to remind you that the main character knows how to feel.) It's not that she isn't pretty, but prettiness is just the price of admission. Adrian gained four and a half pounds once, and everyone talked about it for weeks.

"What's your name?" Adrian asks.

The girl looks at the director, like she needs his go-ahead to speak. "Do you mean Echo, or . . ."

"Your real name," Adrian says.

The girl's posture perks up. "Echo *is* my real name," she says. "But people have been calling me Zara for some reason." Color rises into her cheeks, heats up her whole face. It suits her.

"Zara," Adrian says. "I like it." He takes the sheets inch by inch. Zara's body shifts, like a knot being undone.

"Yes," the director says. "Much better, Ariston."

This is one thing Adrian is really good at. All the reviewers say so. Okay, maybe not *all,* because some people only care what he's doing with his hair this month. But *real* reviewers say two things. One: he has so much natural presence that he basically pushes other actors off the screen. Two: he is utterly convincing when he falls in love.

(Adrian likes that. *Utterly convincing.*)

And just when he is starting to get his confidence back, that's when it happens. The director crumples to his knees.

"Hey, you okay?" Adrian asks, leaping down off the bed. He kneels next to Leopold but doesn't touch him. Touching might give the impression that he has any idea what to do. He should probably run to get help — but Leopold is holding up a finger.

Wait.

It's like the director is ripping each breath out of the air. *Riiiiiip. Riiip. Rip.* When Leopold's breath is mostly normal again, just a little rasp at the end, he stands up. "Let's continue."

Zara goes right back to where they left off, climbing back into the moment on command. It's not that easy for Adrian. If something like that happened on a movie set, doctors would be brought in. Everyone would at least get some cold water and take five. "Should we maybe —"

"Dear boy," Leopold says, setting a hand on his arm. "It's nothing, really."

82

Adrian is too shocked to let it go. "What was that? A migraine?"

"A vision," Leopold says.

Adrian doesn't know what to say to that. So he just nods and nods.

xvii

The night wakes up, the city filling with people who are beginning their second act, the dark echo of whatever they have done during the day. This is a time of guilt and shame and secrets.

Leopold loves it.

He could order a car, but on most nights he chooses to walk the twenty blocks from the Aurelia to the glass box of his apartment. It gives him time to skim over the next days, to anticipate.

But right now, he can't think past the knocking inside his head.

He tries to hold it off, at least until he can get home. The visions don't care about where he is. The visions won't wait.

He needs Meg. She knows how to handle him when he's in this state. He needs her voice, above everything. Leopold takes out his phone and calls her.

She doesn't pick up; she must be in a tunnel.

The knocking, again. These days he feels as though his body is just a door for the visions to come through.

"Meg," he breathes, leaving a message of one word. She doesn't call him back. It must be a very long tunnel.

Leopold finds a doorway and sinks down to his knees. In any other town, people might notice. In New York, he's just part of the scenery.

The visions used to visit him only in the theater. Now they are with him any time they please. They strike viciously in the middle of the night, or fell him as they did in rehearsal. They used to be less painful, almost polite, delivering inspiration and then leaving him the hell alone.

He closes his eyes

The first thing he sees is Roscoe.

And he is afraid.

Leopold is watching Roscoe die. It's not a memory; it's a moment, lived over and over.

Leaves clatter over his head — applause. But not much. The city is stingy, as always.

He stands up, not even bothering to brush the grime from

his knees. He considers hailing a cab so he can have the rest of this horrible vision in peace. But Leopold doesn't like taxis. The dense smell of them, the cracks on the seat like old skin. Everything ugly. This night is unbearable and cold, but at least it is beautiful. Leopold needs everything to be beautiful right now.

Even his pain. Especially that.

The picture in his head begins to darken and shift, and when the lights come up, a new scene is waiting. An actress in a small room, mirrors and bright lights. Leopold has wasted time hoping that this one is a mistake. But his visions have always found a way to come true.

xviii

Zara finds herself back in the studios for her next rehearsal. The intimacy of the storage room unsettled her, but now she almost misses it.

Kestrel runs to join the chorus members. She laughs the loudest. Hugs everyone the longest.

Zara warms up alone.

Leopold and Meg sit at a folding table with their heads together, whispering. Zara has never known a director with a personal assistant before. What does she do, exactly? She stays close to Leopold, within reaching distance. The looks he gives her are tired, the frayed opposite of the energetic presence she felt the other night.

Zara tries to catch his attention from across the room. All he does is mutter something to Meg.

Brilliant.

That's what Leopold called Zara.

Brilliant.

The word has a spotlight shine to it. Now that she's felt its warmth, all she wants is to feel it again.

The stage manager tells them it's time to begin. Echo doesn't have much to do in act 1, scene 1 — just wander around the marketplace as the chorus tells Echo's tragic story. Kestrel is the chorus leader, so she does most of the talking. Her voice has a metallic ring to it, cold and bitter.

"Ariston refused a love
To find a love.
Echo refused a love
To find a path,
Not knowing that it would lead
Past love, to death."

The chorus lays out the entire plot before the action even starts — that's how Greek tragedy works. It's never bothered Zara before, but all of a sudden it feels bizarre. The audience knows at the beginning that Echo and Ariston are going to fall in love. They know how bad things are going to get. People sit there riveted and watch things unfold, inch by beautiful inch. Until the beauty shades into pain.

Is that part of what people want? Zara has only ever cared about the love in Echo and Ariston's story. But the pain has been there waiting. Inevitable. It's right in the prologue, mocking her.

Leopold watches with bored eyes, shouts out blocking. Zara scribbles down her entrance, her crosses. The second time they run the scene, she sets down her script. Now she can really start acting.

Leopold leaps up from his chair and walks with her.

He puts a hand on her back. "Stand up straight." He pushes her upright. "An arch in the foot, please." His fingers brush up and down her neck. "More length here. And stop breathing like Zara Evans. You are not Zara Evans." He puts a hand to her stomach, which makes her feel soft and exposed, but she doesn't stop walking. She waits with empty lungs, until Leopold tells her that she can take another breath. "Slowly. Control it. Echo is not like you. Never forget that. Echo is better. Pull in your fat, please. No one is coming to the Aurelia to see a modern slob. Don't look at Megi who can't help you. Listen to me." He leans closer to her ear. His voice is a single drop of cold water. "Listen."

This goes on for an hour. Zara is wrong and wrong and wrong. But that's how she's going to get better, right? By knowing just how bad she is? Other directors she's worked with have given her some idea of what she's good at, but she's never known if she could trust the praise. Was her performance *really* good, or just good enough for a school play or summer stage?

This must be what making art feels like. This must be what it means to become a true artist. Zara must learn to second-guess, not just everything she's doing but everything she is.

Leopold holds her waist as she walks forward. "Yes," he says. "Yes." They're trembling on the verge of something good. The spotlight comes back, and the rest of the world is lost in the dark.

And then the scene ends and Leopold lets her go with a sigh. He pinches the bridge of his nose as if he is trying to keep his disappointment contained. "We have so much work to do."

So Zara works.

All week, she pushes herself. Day after day, Leopold is in her ear, whispering. The other actors keep their distance. There is no time to make friends, anyway. There is barely time to become Echo. On Friday, the actors' day off, her fear drives her to the studio so she can get in more time with her script, make up for years of training that she doesn't have.

She weaves her fingers into a knot and pushes her hands up, up, into the spot below her ribs where her voice lives. It leaps out, carrying farther each time she tries, but the sound is still breathy, weak. She stretches herself until her muscles make it clear that one more inch would be the snapping point.

And then she stretches a little bit farther.

This is what Zara wanted. To be bigger than herself. To do more than she ever could in her tiny life at home.

She says the first monologue until her voice turns into raw ribbons.

When she closes her eyes, she sees Roscoe on the ground, bleeding, but the blood is red curtain fabric.

Zara opens her eyes. She sees herself in the long mirror but she doesn't want to be that girl, the one who isn't good enough. She thinks of all the actresses in the greenroom, the ones who weren't cast. The ones with real résumés and the bodies that people want to stare at, to worship.

Zara hits her script again. Harder.

She runs the lines. Louder.

The edges of what she can do are invisible, but they're always there, and she slams into them so many times. She needs to be better. She needs to be *more.* Zara works until the sky — cut up into squares by the tall windows — goes watery red. It's only the middle of the afternoon, but a winter night is closing in.

Maybe she'll stay here until dawn. Maybe she'll live at the theater.

Zara is stuck on act 1. She can't get past the part where Echo runs away from home.

"There is no life here,
Only cold walls . . ."

Zara hears footsteps coming down the hall. For a single moment she is sure that Leopold is coming to berate her — or worse, tell her that she should give up now and leave the theater.

Zara doesn't notice a new fear taking root in the dark soil

of Roscoe's death until it's planted firmly in her mind. Roscoe failed at his lighting design. Zara is failing at Echo. What if someone wants to stop her? *Really* stop her?

Zara walks on her bare feet and tucks herself into the corner of the studio. Tense, each muscle in perfect suspension.

And then Eli peeks in. Everything about her looks tired, except for her eyes, which are fever bright.

They haven't talked since their trip to the balcony.

"I was over in the offices with the stage manager and I thought I heard your voice," Eli explains. "You okay?"

"Why wouldn't I be okay?" Zara crosses her arms over her chest.

Eli takes a long look at Zara in her tight-fitting rehearsal clothes, which only makes it worse. There's a sort of calculation in that look, like Zara is a tricky math problem. "How long have you been in here?"

Zara's brain feels broken. "Four . . . five? Hours?"

Eli twitches her head toward the door.

"I can't leave. I told Leopold . . ." *No outside commitments. No distractions.* "I have to keep working."

Eli nods as if she gets it. "This will be Echo-related, I promise." Eli points at the puddle of dark fabric in the corner of the studio. "Come on. We're leaving. Put your coat on."

Zara takes the first step. Despite Eli's promise, Zara feels that following her is against the rules. Exactly what Leopold told Zara to avoid. But she takes another step, and soon she's rushing down the hall, calling out, "Where are we going?"

xix

Eli leads Zara down Fifth Avenue, the wall of Central Park running along one side, the cobbled sidewalk under their boots. It's a medium-freezing day, but the sun is shining like it's got something to prove before it goes down. Eli is not looking forward to full-blown winter. She hates the cold, and how by January it feels like there's only one color left in the entire city, gray from street to sky.

Right now there's a red sliver of sun, turning the world pink and yellow and orange. There are jackets in bright colors, which will soon be replaced by dark wool and long puffy coats like trash bags.

Eli turns to face Zara, braving the wind, as a few curls make a jailbreak from under her knitted hat. Zara is painted in beautiful colors, but the look on her face is still furtive, as if Eli has stolen her from the Aurelia. Maybe she has.

"Where are we going?" Zara asks again.

Eli hasn't answered the question yet. She's learned a thing or two from doing theater, like how to build the suspense.

The park breaks open and there is a building: huge, classical, stunning. Zara's eyes pretty much triple in size. The Met is one of the only places in the city that can hold a candle to the Aurelia. As Eli leads Zara up the wide, shallow steps toward the arches and pillars, she gets a stretched-out feeling in her heart. A hopeful ache.

She needs this as much as Zara does.

The light plot is done, but Eli has no idea if Leopold will like it. And if he doesn't, she's done. Her job at the Aurelia, her dream career, gone in the time that it would take to hit a single cue. And then there's Roscoe, and the questions that hang over Eli's head like dark, gray clouds.

Eli leads Zara into a large room where they purchase tickets. Eli says, "Hey, let's check our coats."

"Why?" Zara asks.

"Why?" Eli repeats. "I'm afraid if I turn my head, you'll run back to the theater at full speed."

Eli hopes for a laugh, but Zara looks pained.

It's not her job to make Zara Evans feel better. And it's

definitely not her job to flirt. Zara helped Eli when she needed it, so she's doing the new girl a favor in return. This has nothing to do with Eli's crush.

She tells herself that so many times that she almost believes it.

They step into a courtyard with a high ceiling that feels like it's open to the night sky. Dark blue swims down through squares of glass. There are no paintings in this room. It's a lot of statues in grim bronze or glittering white marble. Everyone is Greek and Roman and gorgeous.

Almost everyone is nude.

Zara looks around, but Eli can tell that she isn't really seeing anything. The girl is completely in her own head. Eli's had that kind of week, too. But sometimes a person has to step outside of that and really see the world again. You can't make art if you have nothing to make it out of.

Eli circles around a trio of women. Their dimpled backsides shine like beacons. "The Three Graces," Zara reads off the card on the base of the statue.

"These ladies are nice," Eli says. "But they're not what we're looking for."

She winds a path around the pedestals. Zara follows so close that she's like Eli's impatient shadow. Eli stops in front of a girl. She has one hand at her naked breast, the other clenched tight at her side. At the base of the statue, small waves lick at the girl's feet, hungry as flames.

"Echo," Zara whispers, and looks up at Echo's stubborn body, her beautiful face.

That's what Zara looks like. Not every detail, but the general idea is the same. Eli doesn't say that out loud, of course. There are limits to how much truth she can tell a girl who probably doesn't even like other girls.

Also: the nudity thing.

"How did you find her?" Zara asks.

"Hannah," Eli says, and it comes out bitter as black coffee, like her ex broke her heart last Tuesday. The logical part of her knows that it happened a year ago and she should be over it by now. But here's the real truth: time doesn't work in neat, predictable ways. It doubles over on itself. Finds new ways to hurt you. "Hannah was at Tisch — acting major, but she took all these fine-art classes. We would come up here on Sunday mornings after an ungodly stack of pancakes. I mean, when we were dating."

There it is. The ex-girlfriend, the outing, all at once. Eli can't always tell how much people guess. How much they assume.

Zara nods and swallows. The brightness of her cheeks does not escape Eli. Is she embarrassed? Flustered? Does thinking about girls that way, *together,* make her confused or excited? "Was she pretty?" Zara asks.

"Sure," Eli says. "She was pretty and then we broke up." She doesn't mean to add more, but she's terrible at keeping her mouth shut around Zara Evans. "It was a big deal when I moved away from my family, to the city. To be with her. It was for her as much as the work. That's ridiculous, right?"

She waits for Zara to agree, but instead Zara shakes her head emphatically.

"I couldn't go home after Hannah broke up with me. I loved it here too much. So I asked my family to give me a year to make it work. And to put away money for school. That was always part of the plan. But the thing that made it all harder was Hannah never wanting to see me again. You'd think, in a city this big, it wouldn't be a problem. But we'd been living together. I worked at *her* theaters. I hung out with *her* friends. That was . . ." Eli uses her fingers to scatter imaginary dust. "Gone. I went six months without a gig. I didn't have anything saved up for school, and I was sneaking into theater classes at NYU just to get that feeling."

Now Zara's nodding. Because here's the thing: once you start doing theater, it's impossible to stop. Once you make room for it, there's this empty, echoing space inside you that absolutely needs to be filled with late-night rehearsals and sweat and motion and lights and people.

"One of the kids there hooked me up with a bottom-feeder job. *Echo and Ariston* at an experimental theater. Doing the world's most heartbreaking play while I lived through my own love-shaped catastrophe. I was crashing with people I didn't know, sleeping on Ikea futons, living from ramen to ramen. That's when Roscoe found me." She still remembers the day she met him. How he showed up at the stage door with his heavy-lidded eyes and his fairy-godmother plan.

"Light-board operators kept quitting on him," she says. "But it wasn't because he was mean. Just hard to figure out. Talking to Roscoe was like learning another language." Zara cocks her head. More words come out. "I've always had to do

97

that. Change how I talk to people. English or Spanish, electrical wiring or artsy art stuff. Queer, not queer." She cuts her eyes to Zara. "How am I doing with Zara-speak?"

Zara laughs, looking down at her shoes. "Ummmm." Her straight brown hair waterfalls over the side of her face. "You're almost fluent."

Eli has always been good with colors, so it's easy to name the one that quick-blooms inside her: red.

Bright red.

"When I was having a hard time with Echo, I would visit *her*." She nods up at the statue. "Watch the sunlight move across her body."

That wasn't what Eli meant to say, but Zara doesn't seem to notice. She stands up and circles the statue. Takes a deep breath — and starts to change. Her chest strains forward, her feet searching out the right places.

"What are you doing?" Eli asks.

"Playing the statue game," Zara says, like it's a thing everybody knows about. "When I was little, I thought it would turn me into someone else, but only if I got it just right." Zara checks the statue, makes adjustments. The clenched fist. The proud cast of her mouth. She closes her eyes, because that's what Echo's doing.

Eli lifts a hand and lets it hover for a second. "Is it okay if I . . ." Zara seems to understand, because she gives a tiny nod. Her eyelashes are so dark, her eyelids so delicate. Eli puts a finger to Zara's chin, tilts it a fraction of an inch. "There."

A smile spreads across Zara's lips. They're covered in clear gloss, which lets the true color, a brownish pink, shine through. She has a little freckle trapped inside her top lip, just left of center.

"You're almost making me like this play again," Eli says.

Zara's eyes snap open. "How can you dislike *Echo and Ariston*?"

Eli knows that this play is Zara's life. But that doesn't mean she can hold back her own truth. "Look at those waves." She nods at the water rising to cover the statue girl's feet.

"So?" Zara asks, looking full-on betrayed. As if Eli has the power to hurt her that deeply.

"Why does Echo have to die?" Eli asks, reaching for her Leatherman, stopping just short of flicking the blades. "Because she fell in love with the wrong person? Because she did it on her own terms?" Eli's hands feel dangerously empty, but playing with knives would be a good way to get kicked out of the museum.

Zara stays quiet, like maybe Eli asked her something she's never asked herself before.

"I don't hate the play," Eli admits. "I hate the ending."

The next day, costume fittings begin. Cosima dreads this part, because it means she needs to see them up close — the actresses, the ones who remind her.

The red-haired girl comes into the shop first. Two seasons ago, her hair was dull brown with only a hint of copper, but the girl is trying to make herself stand out. It only makes her harder to dress. She tries to argue about the circumference of her chest, and leaves with a scowl. She has been in plays here since she was a small thing. Cosima knew her name once.

She has decided not to remember.

The new girl enters next, a curious bird, her head peeking forward, then tilting. She's looking at the papers. Cosima's designs are everywhere in the costume shop, on loose pages in vivid colors of ink. When she draws, it's as if the characters are coming alive. But the sketches on the tables and the floor are old — leaves shed in some other season.

Cosima has a difficult time getting rid of things.

The new girl alights on the edge of the table, which is covered in thick, pale wood for drafting and cutting and tacking down pins. "We met at the read-through," the girl says. "I'm Zara Eva —"

"Arms out," Cosima says. Her voice used to be soft — she remembers that. But she doesn't care if it seems harsh now.

Better this way.

She takes the measurements — around the bust, the waist. Bad numbers mean costumes that sag or pinch. Bad costumes mean a show that no one believes in. A show that no one believes in means that the one thing Cosima still cares about is ripped away.

Around the hips now.

She cannot help but notice how broad this girl is, how soft. It sets a small fear to flaming in her chest.

There was another girl, years ago. A girl like family. That is what people do in this place, in theaters. They choose who to call their own.

Hat size next. For this girl, who is playing the lead, Cosima takes twelve extra measurements. Echo's costumes must be perfect above all others. If a button is out of place, Leopold Henneman will smell it.

Cosima summons fabrics from all corners of the room and drapes them around the girl. She tries Mediterranean-blue chiffon and the white organza that Leopold demanded. She adds gold braid and flicks it away. Black makes the girl look sallow — what to use for the death scene? Deepest purple? Yes, that will complement the ocean water.

The girl watches Cosima work with too much admiration. Against all of her rules, a warning leaps out.

"You look wrong," Cosima says.

She drops the fabric on the table. The girl is left standing in her blue underwear with the minuscule border of lace. She doesn't clutch to cover herself. The bird-girl stays perfectly still.

Her bones will prove brittle. Easily snapped.

Even though they're alone in the shop, Cosima waits until her work brings her close to the girl's ear to mutter, "He says that you are beautiful. He says everyone will love you. Don't listen."

This actress has eyes that are wide and ever growing. Her lashes are dark and long, the perfect accent to her emotions.

That, too, is just like Vivi.

That name, that name. Cosima hasn't gotten rid of it, even though she should. She picks it up, turns it around in her mind. Puts it back in a drawer, like some pretty fabric that will never be used again.

The girl in front of Cosima swallows, a lump trailing

down her long throat. Cosima has measured it — she knows how many inches from the point of the chin to the soft hollow between the bones.

The girl stands up and pulls on her clothes, looking as if she wants to stay awhile. Even Cosima's assistants know they are not welcome in the shop. Not during this play. But this girl is new.

Cosima calls her back for one final measurement.

She takes hold of some muslin and slings it over the girl's shoulder, and when it's in just the right place, she stabs it with a pin. A thin line of silver, through fabric and skin, to keep her from getting too comfortable.

The second week of rehearsals starts, and Zara can't look away from Leopold.

He moves through the studio as if he is on a mission to find all the air in the room and breathe it before anyone else can. He wears a gray suit, which feels strangely formal for the rehearsal process, but Zara has seen him in it so often that by now she has a hard time imagining him in anything else.

He smiles at her. There is nothing in the rest of his face or body that agrees with the smile.

"Shall we?" he asks.

Zara walks away from Carl and Enna, the actors playing Echo's father and mother. Today is a family rehearsal. On the floor, red tape outlines a space the same size and shape as the one they'll have to work with onstage.

Red tape spells out Echo's home.

The stage manager measured and laid out the tape before rehearsal. She sits patiently now, taking notes. Meg is next to her, watching Zara's every move.

Zara shakes out her shoulders, trying to rid herself of the worries that are piling up, making this worse. She feels the ghost of Leopold's hands on her waist. His voice, telling her *again*. All she has to do is get through a blocking scene. She closes her eyes and tries to find neutral. But neutral isn't enough anymore. She has to find Echo, the way she did with Eli at the Met.

You are not Zara Evans.

Enna flutters from Carl's side to the edge of the red tape. Echo's mother is a nervous, ragged butterfly in a dress that looks more like a dirty nightgown. Carl tosses out Echo's cue and she starts across the hardwood floor.

Leopold rushes to cut her off. He blocks her path with his body. "Walk," he says.

Zara can't.

Leopold flourishes both palms, inviting her. *"Walk."*

Zara takes a step, her chin up, stride deliberate. Leopold doesn't budge. Zara catches herself a few inches from him, holding her entire body like a breath.

105

"Why aren't you walking?" he asks.

Anger charges her in a sudden wave. Zara pushes into him. It's a mess of sweat and muscles. "This is Echo," Leopold says. "Stopped by her parents at every turn. Trapped but fighting."

Zara knows this feeling—what it means to be stuck in a small box that someone else labeled *home*. She never even tried to tell her parents about that kiss at the *Peter Pan* cast party. Maybe not the kiss, specifically, but what it meant. She could see how they would react as if it were already happening. They would nod and look at her with thin, concerned mouths. They wouldn't push her out of their red-tape-defined *home*. They would continue to love her, *of course*. But it would be one more thing they couldn't get their minds around, mostly because they wouldn't try.

Like theater.

Like abandoning her senior year of high school.

Zara can't even think about going back to their tiny world without suffocating.

In a final rush, she breaks past Leopold and into the red-tape box with Carl and Enna. Panting. Pushing. Alive in her own body.

"Yes!" Leopold says. But the approval is gone in a blink. "Now. We can't have every entrance take this long to block, can we?" He snatches the small victory away from Zara so fast that it makes her dizzy.

"You know how little time we have to rehearse," he says in a voice that is louder, meant for all the actors, not just her this time. "That means we must push against our own boundaries. Safety is not a word that has a place here. Life is not safe, therefore our theater cannot be."

Meg is looking at Zara exclusively. Enna is staring out the window as if she's seeing something other than the skyline. Carl is staring at Enna.

The scene moves on.

Zara may need Leopold to teach her how to walk, but at least she can show him how well she knows her lines. These are the same words that carried her away from the too-small box she was raised in. They wrenched the world open. Wrenched her open. "*I have done your bidding these many —*"

"That sounds *memorized*." Leopold treats the word like mouthwash, rolling it around, spitting it out.

Zara doesn't know what to say. ". . . It is memorized."

Leopold throws his hands into the air. He waves at Meg, who rushes to fill in the charged silence. "Echo doesn't know what she's going to say until the moment she says it. She's not reciting lines. You have to feel what she's feeling first, and let that lead you to the words."

Meg is so precise, so prompt, that it slows Zara's runaway heartbeat. "Okay," she says.

Zara goes back to her mark and starts again, not even waiting for a nod from Leopold. She's going to show him how well she understands. Zara doesn't have to reach far to find a girl who knows love is important enough that she's willing to trade her life for it. It's always there, just under the surface of her minutes, her days. She's wanted to fall in love like that ever since she found this play. Or maybe the wanting came first, and the words gave it form.

"I have done your bidding these many years,
But this I will not do."

The scene speeds on and soon Zara forgets that she's in a studio, forgets that she's in a play. She lets herself think — maybe this is it. The moment when she turns from a normal girl into a true actress.

And that's when Leopold takes her by the wrists and guides her gently to the floor. He doesn't hurt her — he doesn't push. Still, he makes it clear that he wants her to lie down, and then he sets his own body over hers so that it blocks out the lights coming from above. Zara doesn't know what to feel, so she doesn't feel anything.

"Yes," he mutters. "This should work."

He gets up. Zara waits there — afraid to move, afraid to stay.

Leopold snaps his fingers at Carl and then points to Zara.

Carl doesn't budge. From her strange angle on the floor, Zara can see him cross his arms. "Is this really —"

"Necessary?" Leopold asks. "Yes. I need you to help a fellow actor."

Carl frowns as he takes Leopold's place. His body is even larger than Leopold's, and his face looms over hers like an eclipse. She can see his stubble, a hundred tiny points of darkness. There is a minty aftershave layered over the harsh smell of his body, which is covered in the kind of sweat that comes from rehearsal. From exertion.

108

"Lower," Leopold says. "Get close to her."

Carl holds himself over Zara. She wants to close her eyes, but she knows that Leopold will take it as a sign of weakness. She wants to scream, or stop breathing. But that's what an amateur would do.

That would get Zara sent back to her red-tape box.

Home.

It would help if Carl looked at Zara instead of focusing his livid blue eyes on a point just to the left of her face. It might help if she felt like they were in this together. Actors working on a scene. If she could find some connection there, it might feel safe. But then she remembers that it's not supposed to feel safe. That's the whole point.

Leopold crouches down next to Zara's head. He drops his voice low. "*Now* you are trapped. Say the lines again."

"I have done your bidding these many years,

But this I will not do."

Carl's body over hers changes how the words come out of her mouth. There are only two choices. When she stays perfectly still, she feels panicked and desperate. When she moves, Carl moves to contain her. Cages her body with his. Zara's voice fractures and then builds into strength.

"I have no reason to stay here

And a world of reasons to go."

The emotions coming out of her are strong and true. With a tight ball of sickness at the back of her throat, Zara realizes — Leopold's technique worked.

Enna pulls the ingenue aside after rehearsal.

The hallway outside the studio smells like feet and chalk — has *always* smelled like feet and chalk. It's one of Enna's least favorite parts of the Aurelia, tucked in the back, one floor up from the theater offices. Every time the elevator carries her past those offices, a reminder prickles. Theater is a business. And she's not young or fresh or bankable anymore.

"We should talk," Enna says to the ingenue. Her grip on the girl's arm might not be strong, but it is commanding.

The ingenue looks up at her with an enormous stare. She still appears to be shaken by what happened in the studio. By the weight of the director and Enna's ex-husband. Or perhaps she is just shaken in general. Enna remembers her first production at the Aurelia. *Hamlet.* Ophelia. It felt like every time she took a step, every time she spoke, the world was about to tremble and change.

By the time she played Gertrude, twenty years later, it was a very different story.

Enna sizes the girl up and finds only one real mark against her. "Do people really think those are pants?" she asks, pointing to the stretchy black things on Zara's legs.

"You're wearing a nightgown," the girl answers, a touch too quickly.

"I like you, little fish," Enna says, curling a smile. She hasn't used these muscles in a while.

She heads down the hall, beckoning for Zara to follow.

"Where are we going?" she asks.

"Our dressing room," Enna says.

They take the elevator down. Enna knows that you have to stab at the ground floor button three times before it will light. The dressing rooms are off the same hall as the greenroom. That knowledge is less like a map in Enna's mind than the feeling of her own body when she wakes up in the morning. The backstage, the studios, these are her muscles and bones and blood. The stage is her beating heart.

She leads Zara through the women's dressing area and opens a door.

111

The mirror with its bright round bulbs welcomes her. Her hairpins sit in a row under yellowing snippets of her best reviews. There is a picture taken after opening night as Ophelia—laughing and bright and painfully young—tacked to one corner of the mirror.

This was Enna's sanctuary. A place to laugh and cry and be alone with men when plain old alone wouldn't do. But a few seasons ago, Leopold informed her that it was time to be generous. Five or six ingenues have shared the space with her by now. Most have stared at Enna like she is a vintage curiosity.

She knows the truth. They are afraid of her. Of *becoming* her.

"Now," Enna says, patting the single chair until Zara sits down. "Tell me about your time at the Aurelia thus far."

Zara tells a perfect little story about winning her dream role. It spikes Enna's worries, like a shot of whiskey poured into a drink that was plenty strong to begin with. "Has anything happened that you haven't . . . expected?" Enna asks the ingenue. Most people would have asked if she'd been made to feel *uncomfortable,* but Enna knows there is no such thing as *comfortable* at the Aurelia.

Zara's voice wobbles for the first time, as if she's standing on tiptoes, reaching for a difficult truth. "You mean Roscoe dying?"

Enna doesn't. She was so steeped in her own memories that she hadn't even thought of Roscoe. The sadness in this theater is so thick, she thinks, like perfume, or smoke. A person could choke on it. "I need to know if anyone has talked to you in a way that worried you. Hurt you in any way."

"No," Zara says, but it comes out slowly.

Enna nods slowly in return. She's given the girl a chance to tell her. And now she'll keep an eye on things.

"You're . . . different than I thought," Zara says.

Enna bursts out with a laugh that surprises both of them. She knows what *that* means. "Yes, well. I kept your expectations low. Everyone here thinks I'm a drunk and that I have to take fourteen different kinds of pills to stand up in the morning. Do you know why?"

Zara shakes her head.

"Because I *was* a drunk. I took the pills. Now when I pull something decent out of my sleeve, it's a surprise. Everyone gets to love me again." The smile that she gives is a showy flourish — a card player flashing a winning hand. "That sort of thing won't work for you. You started at the top. It's a long way to fall."

Enna shouldn't have been so honest. It makes the ingenue grip the arms of her chair, looking sickly. "So," Enna says. "Advice. *Don't leave. No matter what, don't leave.* That is letting them win. And don't let them see you crack. Crack if you must. But choose the people you cry in front of more carefully than the people you screw." She expects the girl to startle, but the ingenue keeps her wide-wide eyes on Enna. "Oh, and don't fall in love with anyone in the theater. Another piece of my own advice that I forgot to take."

A battle plays out on Zara's face, between curiosity and politeness.

Enna shed her politeness when this girl was still learning how to walk. "Carl and I were married once. You wouldn't know that. It was a long time ago." It doesn't feel so very long, though. Enna has to staunch memories of the marriage like blood from a fresh cut. The way Carl used to look at her, the way they used to kiss. One time, she tried to scramble eggs and turned them a frightful brown. Carl laughed as he dragged her away from the stove, into their bedroom, and hours later he made her perfect eggs for dinner. Sometimes Enna remembers this story and she is useless for a whole week.

She can't afford that now. The ingenue needs her.

"All right," Enna says, her voice cheerful on top, strained underneath. "That's enough chitchat for today."

Zara gets up to leave, but she spins around in the doorway. "Why are you being nice to me?"

Enna's smile feels broken. "That's what theater people do, little fish. We look out for each other."

xxiii

The next morning, Zara waits until Kestrel has used the bath-room, and then she subjects her body to the hottest shower it can stand. Her brain thickens with steam. She stays in there forever, telling herself that she just needs to warm up — that winter got too cold too fast.

But when her mind wanders, it goes straight to the Aurelia. And she knows that she's standing here, pulling in breath after breath of steam, because she's afraid to go back. She doesn't want to face Leopold.

Zara gets out of the shower and throws on her rehearsal clothes, which, as Enna pointed out, are flimsy and ridiculous. Old yoga pants. A T-shirt that she loved to death. Socks that she hopes don't smell, since she hasn't quite figured out the laundry situation in Kestrel's building. None of it is good enough for the Aurelia, but this is what Zara owns. She tells herself that she'll buy new clothes as soon as she gets her first paycheck. She's actually getting *paid* to do this — to stand on a stage and be Echo.

This is the dream. Zara has to make it work, no matter what.

Enna told her not to leave. Not to let them win.

When she opens the door, Kestrel's settled in on the couch. Waiting. "Hi, roomie." She picks up a tall glass filled with bright-green sludge. "Do you have Thanksgiving plans?" Kestrel asks, brandishing a smoothie at her.

Zara takes the glass. The green liquid inside smells like rotting innards. "I'm going home," she says. As much as she didn't want to leave after the audition, that's how much she's craving home right now. She'd put up with any amount of dry turkey and college talk just to sit there with her parents. Her mom will end up talking about boyfriends, like they're nice and somehow inevitable, and even that seems worth putting up with. "What about you?"

Kestrel shrugs one shoulder. "Mama and Alec have been in Europe so long they forget Thanksgiving even happens. I usually have plans with Carl. But he's been acting distant."

"I didn't know you two were close," Zara says.

Kestrel puts a hand to her collarbone in fake shock. "I don't see how you could have missed it." Zara doesn't bring up the fact that she's been a little busy. "Carl is more of my father than my father is. Or my stepfather. Or Alec. Anyway, Carl is the one who actually cares about me."

Zara thinks about what Enna said, about theater people taking care of each other. That's part of what pulled Zara into this world in the first place. "What about Enna? Are you close to her, too?"

Kestrel sips at her smoothie. "They had what's known in the parlance as a *bad divorce*. I didn't spend much time with Enna after that. She was too busy entertaining gentlemen callers." Kestrel tilts her head, as if she can see her memories better from this angle. "Actually, that started before they got divorced. It was hard to stay close to both of them after the shit hit that particular fan. But I never could get myself to hate her. Not like Carl did."

Zara sits down on the couch and tests her drink. It leaves a cold, bitter trail all the way to her stomach.

She goes to put down her glass, but the table is filled with a spread-eagled newspaper, a pot of glue, and jars of paint. "What's this?" she asks. But Kestrel doesn't need to answer, because as soon as Zara drinks in the details, she knows what this is. Roscoe's face stares up at her from the thin white page.

"They interviewed me!" Kestrel says brightly. "I'm putting it into my collage."

"You have a collage of Roscoe?" Zara asks, more than slightly unsettled.

"Of course not," Kestrel says. "It's for anytime my name or likeness is in the papers. Mama says I should keep one. To look back at when I'm older."

Zara picks up the paper and, against her better judgment, starts to read. It's a tabloid article about Roscoe's fall, plumped out by information about *Echo and Ariston*. They would have stopped reporting a normal accident weeks ago, but this death is connected to Leopold's play. The press loves Leopold Henneman.

"I had to talk to them," Kestrel says, voice glistening with pride. "I didn't feel like it was right to keep information to myself if it had anything to do with Roscoe's death." Kestrel gets up and heads for the kitchen to pour out the dregs of her glass in the sink. "Besides, if it really is the curse, it's going to happen again."

Zara goes back to the page in front of her, looking for the first place where the curse is mentioned, where Kestrel is quoted. *The curse is almost as old as the Aurelia. It started with a production of the Scottish play in 1912. There are undeniable patterns. It always ends on opening night.*

Kestrel picks up the bottle brush next to the sink and attacks her glass. Zara goes back to the article. *"It always comes in threes."* She looks up at Kestrel. "You think two other people are going to die?"

Kestrel shrugs, like that isn't up to her.

Like that's up to the curse.

"Can I keep this?" Zara asks, getting up. Her hand, which was clean only a minute ago, is already turning gray and tacky from the newsprint. She must be sweating. She must be nervous.

"That was my copy." Kestrel narrows her eyes until they look as thin and blue as the sky between window blinds. "What do you need it for?"

Zara wants to show this to Eli. She has no idea if Eli believes in the Aurelia's curse. What she *does* know is that Eli is still thinking about Roscoe. At the Met, Zara could feel how hard it was for Eli not to talk about him. Like he was right there among the statues and they were both ignoring his presence.

She asks herself:

Do you really think this will help Eli?

Or are you just looking for an excuse to talk to her again?

Apparently Zara has been sitting there with her mouth slightly open and nothing coming out of it for too long, because Kestrel's face sours. "Oh," she says. "I get it. You're too important to tell me things. Because you're *Echo*."

"No." Zara leaves the paper on the table. She'll find a newsstand, even if it makes her late for rehearsal. She abandons her smoothie, ignores her usual yogurt, and heads for the front door. "I don't think I'm better than you. You know that, right?" She slips on her shoes and her coat, her mind sliding back to rehearsals, to how Leopold always seems to want something other than her. Something *more*. Self-doubt hits again, so hard that she can barely stand. "You probably would have made a better Echo."

Zara grabs her purse and leaves. She's almost to the elevator when a voice shreds the quiet. It's Kestrel, screaming.

119

The hallway seems longer on the way back. Zara can't find her keys, and then she can't remember which one fits in which lock. By the time Zara has it sorted out, the screaming has stopped. Zara opens the door. Kestrel is sitting cross-legged in the middle of the living room, breathing deeply. If Zara hadn't heard the sounds, if she wasn't absolutely sure that Kestrel had been the one making them, she would say that Kestrel looks calm.

"Are you all right?" Zara asks.

Kestrel looks up at her, red hair bright and eyes unblinking. "I have no idea what you're talking about."

xxiv

Zara Evans is distracted. (Adrian can tell.) He sees it in the way that she keeps forgetting to blink. He can feel it, too. Standing with her in the hallway outside the rehearsal space is like hanging out with half a person.

"You good?" Adrian asks, touching Zara's arm. (Girls love it when he touches their arms.)

"Yeah," Zara says, still looking completely distracted. "Good."

Meg, the director's PA, walks toward them down the hall. Her honey-blond hair is slick in the lights. Her pretty face almost makes up for the khakis and standard-issue cardigan. Each step is more brisk and pissed off than the last.

She holds out a box. Plain cardboard, nothing inside.

"This is for your clothes," Meg says.

"Are my pants really that bad?" Zara asks, looking down. Adrian doesn't say anything. (Because, yeah, they are.)

But he doesn't want Zara to be embarrassed. He wants this rehearsal to go well. And if that means taking off his clothes, he's not going to ask questions. He moves fast, a whirlwind of fabric, until he's down to his boxers. "You can stop there," Meg says, shifting her eyes away.

"Oh," he says, leaving his fingers hooked in the elastic waistband. "Cool, cool."

Zara Evans stares at Adrian like he isn't real. (He's pretty much used to this by now.) It's true his muscles aren't exactly a natural asset. He works out twenty hours a week, sometimes more. People want these muscles when he takes off his shirt. People expect them.

Meg shakes the box in Zara's direction. "What is this for?" Zara asks.

Bad move, Zara Evans. "Just go with it," Adrian says. It's easier that way. And it makes directors want to hire you again.

"This is for act three, scene two," Meg says evenly.

"That's not one of the love scenes," Zara says. "In act three, scene two, Echo and Ariston have just met."

"This is a rehearsal technique," Meg says. "It goes back

to the method acting studios of the 1960s. Actually, in that case the actors were fully nude." Meg's eyes go to Zara and stay there. "Leopold thinks the two of you need to work on intimacy."

Yes, Adrian thinks. This is what he can offer the play. This is why they cast him.

Zara twitches a look up and down the hall. "Where is Leopold?"

"Not feeling well," Meg says. "He needed to lie down." Adrian remembers the vision that hit Leopold in prop storage and adds it to what Meg just told him. It doesn't take much work to find the connection.

Zara peels off her shirt, and all of a sudden Adrian is looking at her bra. It's black. Her underwear, on the other hand, is bright pink and cuts into the skin at her hips. She seems aware of it in a painful sort of way.

Adrian covers his eyes and puts out his hand. He lets Zara lead him into the studio. Her hand is warm in his and — can a hand be grateful? Her hand feels grateful. Meg must be staying outside because he hears the lock clunk behind them.

"Ummmm," Adrian says, opening his eyes slowly. "This is embarrassing."

"At least you have that body to be embarrassed in," Zara says.

Adrian had already forgotten about being semi-naked. "Yeah, what I meant is . . . I'm still not *really* off book. It's hard enough with movies, when I only have to remember lines for the day. I memorize them when I'm sitting in makeup."

"Really?" Zara asks with a nervous laugh. "I memorized these when I was twelve."

What does she want from him — an award? It's not that easy for everyone.

"So how do you do it? For the movies?" she asks.

"I think the ritual is what makes it work," he says, thinking it through one step at a time. "I can remember a line because it matches up with the way a brush hits my cheek. Or that tugging feeling of an eyebrow pencil. But this play is made up of monologues. Long ones." He goes to put his hands in his pockets and then remembers that his thighs are bare. "You can only put on so much makeup, even in theater."

Zara Evans is frowning. "When do you think you'll be off book?" she asks.

"I'm working on it," he says with his best apology smile. He's lucky that Leopold isn't here. Although it's possible it wouldn't even matter. Adrian is famous enough to get a certain number of passes.

Zara is looking at him like she knows that.

She holds her arms around her middle. It's hard to tell if Zara is shy or self-conscious or just freezing. The studio has an old heater and icy wooden floors. "I have Ariston's lines memorized, too," she says. "Maybe I can feed them to you for today."

"Hey," Adrian says, ignoring the bitter hint in Zara's voice. "You know this play backwards and forwards and inside out, right? Maybe you can do more than just feed me the lines. You can help me learn them." He has a dialogue coach that he meets with on a weekly basis, but that's not enough. Dyslexia, ADHD, a bad breakup, and a dead Greek playwright have combined forces to ruin Adrian's life. "I'll help you, too. With—I don't know. Whatever you need. Intimacy, right? We're on this ride together, right, Z? Can I call you Z?"

Zara sighs, then thinks, then nods and marches over to him, which means she has to stop hiding her body. He tries not to stare at her. "This is act three, scene two," she says, her voice moving in waves of confidence he's never heard before. "Echo and Ariston meet at the market, and they're already in love. But they don't know that they've fallen in love with the exact person they were supposed to marry before they ran away."

"Seems kind of silly, doesn't it?" Adrian asks.

"Silly, how?" Zara asks, crossing her arms over her chest again. (It only reminds Adrian she *has* a chest.)

"They could have just stayed where they were and ended up married. Popping out little Greek babies. It seems pretty obvious."

Zara frowns. "That's not the point."

"Oh." Adrian puts a hand to the back of his neck, which is suddenly hot. "Yeah. Probably not. So what do I say first?"

Zara feeds him lines. Adrian vomits them back up.

"Now say it again," Zara instructs.

When Adrian goes looking for the words in his head, he finds a thousand other things. Boring ones. Exciting ones. Some of them leap and demand his attention. Others whisper and whisper and won't stop. And then there's the scene that's

125

always playing out in his head these days. A car in a driveway in the middle of the night. Bags, everywhere. A barefoot girl on the pavement, not kissing him. Staring at him with the kind of sadness that you can't fix, not even with a perfect kiss.

Adrian's lines are gone.

He shrugs and smiles (people like it when he smiles) and says, "I guess we're doomed."

XXV

*D*oomed. Zara stares at Adrian Ward and his infuriating smile. They can't be doomed. She has to fix this. "We're supposed to be working on intimacy, right?"

Adrian nods.

It's strange to be this close to him, even now, almost two weeks into rehearsal. Zara has seen Adrian Ward in a dozen movies. When she stands next to him, when a cross brings her into contact with his gray-green eyes, there's a second where Adrian's fame sits between them like a glass wall. But then he does something normal — scratches his nose, or coughs, or nods for the hundredth time in a row — and the wall cracks.

He's just an actor.

"I have an idea," Zara says. "But you have to trust me." She thinks about what Leopold did at rehearsal the other week, how using their bodies in certain ways changed their performances. The memory of Leopold and then Carl climbing on top of her without permission still tightens her muscles, dries out her throat. But maybe she can take the same idea and use it on her own terms. With Adrian's permission, of course. "What if I touched you while you say the lines?"

Adrian stands there in his expensive-looking boxer briefs and fidgets. "That might be a little. Uhh. Distracting."

Zara shakes her head. Whatever Adrian is thinking is *not* what she means. "It's like when you match the lines to your makeup. When someone touches you, it changes your thinking, right? Helps you focus." She goes back to the last time someone kissed her. How all she could think about was his fingertip on the inside of her wrist. And the first time someone kissed her — she still remembers the moment when the girl fitted her palm to Zara's cheek, how she dove in with her breath held. "You say a line, and I'll touch your face. And then the next time . . . your arm." That way they can both get what they need out of this rehearsal.

Intimacy. Words.

"And if you get uncomfortable, take one step away and I'll stop," Zara says. She doesn't need Adrian to feel unsafe for this to work. Even if it was a shortcut to the feeling, it would be a

128

dangerous one. She doesn't have to hurt Adrian to get what she needs.

Leopold didn't have to hurt her to get what he needs.

"You really think that could work?" Adrian asks. His eyes are so wide and eager and adorable that she can see how he's made an entire career out of looking like that. But Zara doesn't have a famously beautiful face to fall back on. If she can't make this story work, no one will blame Adrian Ward. He's the one the ticket buyers are paying to see.

She's nobody.

"You suddenly look like you're about to throw up," he says. "Is the idea of touching me really *that* bad?"

She shakes her head and loosens all the doubts. When she steps forward, her underwear shifts, which reminds her that she's not wearing anything else. She catches a glimpse of the screaming bright pink in the mirror.

This will never work.

She tries it anyway, running her fingers along his shoulder. The muscle is bigger than she expected. Practically a continent. Adrian's looking at her expectantly instead of talking, so she whispers the first line to prompt him. "*I have seen things base and I have seen wonders.*"

He announces in a loud voice, "*I have seen things base and wonders.*" He looks like he just stubbed all his toes at once. "That's wrong, isn't it?"

They try it again. This time, Adrian gets it right, and Zara smiles for him. But she doesn't feel anything when she touches his shoulder. She tries again, just in case she needs more time to warm into being his Echo. Adrian says the line again, correctly, but nothing happens.

Maybe intimacy is hard to call up in this studio because it's so blank. It's a box of wood and Zara needs to paint something over it. A memory. But she used up her best ones just coming up with this idea. The truth is that she hasn't had many moments that have made her feel *intimate*.

"Do you mind if I close my eyes?" she asks.

"Go for it," Adrian says.

Zara runs through her best kisses one by one. She tries to pour herself into them, but nothing pours back out. Those moments were nice. She needs something bigger than nice. Something more.

Zara tries to forget the kissing and focus on what goes into it, what makes it so memorable in the first place. When was the last time she felt something so big her body could barely hold it? Something so bright she couldn't stand to look away?

Spilling down the steps of the Met with Eli, into a New York City night.

Grabbing Eli's hand on the secret walkway.

Not letting go.

Zara sets her fingers to the sides of Adrian's face. *I have seen things base and I have seen wonders.* She rakes her nails through his hair, tugging at the ends. *I have walked an entire world.* Zara trails her fingers down his neck. *Only when I stepped past the edge of all maps did I find you.* Adrian is saying his lines, and Zara is drowning in a rush of feelings. Strong ones. Drunk and dizzy ones. But she's not thinking about

130

Adrian Ward, or even *Echo and Ariston*. She's thinking about Eli's dark curls, her dark eyes, the force of her stare.

Zara goes up on her toes and kisses Adrian so hard that she sees every color breaking against the inside of her eyelids. She crushes herself against him, and he grabs for her, his hands on her back, skin everywhere. His arms give her a safe place to go breathless. She is kissing him with the crushing force of feelings she hasn't even known she was holding back.

Adrian steps away.

"Whoa," he says, touching his lips as a little smile trickles onto them. "I don't think I know the line that goes with that."

Their time must be up because the lock thunks. Meg comes in with their clothes and places the box on the floor.

Adrian jogs over, picking up his jeans. "That was brilliant, Z." He tosses her yoga pants to her, but she doesn't even move. She's still in shock. They land, with a flutter, on the floor. "Do you want to keep working?"

"I . . . umm . . . can't." She grabs her pants and shimmies into them fast. She's glad that they're making progress, but Zara has plans. When she left Kestrel's apartment in the morning, all she could think about was showing Eli the newspaper clipping about Roscoe. "I'm supposed to meet with the lighting designer. You know, Eli Vasquez?"

"Oh, right," Adrian says with an absentminded grin, tugging at his zipper. "Girl time."

"Right," Zara echoes, that kiss still numbing her lips. "Girl time."

xxvi

Eli has company in the lighting booth.

Leopold Henneman dropped in to make her life extra hellish, just for fun. He leans over the board, his body crowding the equipment, the notebooks, all the things she's started to think of as hers.

"Show me again," he says.

Eli's hand slides in from an angle to work the buttons, because now Leopold has taken her seat. In front of them, the stage pulses with light. Cue after cue — orange, crimson, gray fog, blinding white, blackout.

Leopold whispers, "Roscoe would be so disappointed."

Frustration makes a home for itself in Eli's chest. She can't keep down the argument that's rising. "You saw the light plot. You *said* you wanted to keep elements of Roscoe's design."

"I want to honor his creative intent," Leopold corrects.

"So . . . change it?"

Leopold grabs a lightbulb from a crate and throws it against the back wall. The movement is compact, his arm strong. The lightbulb is there one second — thin glass on a breathtaking arc — then gone, splinters vanishing.

"Artists don't wait for permission," Leopold says calmly.

Eli goes stiller than Zara pretending to be a statue. She thinks Leopold might throw something else. But then his eyes close and his shoulders melt downward. It's like he's not in the booth with her anymore.

"Are you having a vision?" she asks.

Leopold's lips flatten. "Only a daydream. A very nice one. In which I hurt you as much as you are hurting my show."

If the lightbulb was enough to fire up her worries, Leopold just added a splash of gasoline. But Eli *can't* be afraid of her director. She'll never get any work done. And that's what she's all about, the work. Leopold is just an aging director who's taken too many shots of privilege and is staggering around drunk. Apparently his brilliance comes with a Get Out of Being an Asshole Free card.

Eli is vaguely aware that her brain is making jokes because it's too paralyzed to do anything else.

133

Leopold takes one more deep breath, opens his eyes, and looks at her with fresh attention. "You'll fix it," he says. "All of it." When he leaves, Eli's anger trails him like a long shadow.

"Fuck," she says to the lighting board. "That's fucking impossible!" she yells at Roscoe. It doesn't matter if he can't hear her or not: the yelling helps, either way. She sweeps up bits of glass, and the swears keep coming, a constant lineup in English and Spanish.

"Is this a bad time?" asks a voice — a girlish one.

Eli remembers Zara's text this morning. They made plans to meet, but Eli isn't prepared: for how soon Zara showed up, how many plastic containers of leftovers are strewn through the booth, or how pretty Zara looks right now.

She's flushed. The kind of pink that comes after a good dream or a hard run or a long kiss.

"You can come in," Eli says, aware of how long she's been staring. Zara moves into the booth and perches on the arm of the couch that Roscoe called home. The last traces of ugliness that Leopold left behind are gone. "So what was the thing you wanted to talk to me about?"

Zara goes digging in her bag. "I brought something for you."

Delight settles over Eli like sunshine. She loves gifts: giving them, getting them. Zara hands Eli a newspaper article about Roscoe. It's not what she expected, but in a way it's the nicest thing Zara could have brought.

It means that Eli's not alone in this. Even if she never

figures out what happened to Roscoe, at least one other person will remember that he mattered.

"Thanks," Eli says. "I thought I had all these. But this one's new. So — thanks." Dammit. She already said that part.

She skips like a stone over the article, not wanting to sink in deep. That would mean taking her eyes off Zara for longer than a few seconds, and who knows how often she's going to come up here, searching for Eli? "I'll read the rest later," she says, setting the scrap of flimsy paper next to her enormous stack of notebooks. "Right now, I have to hit my head against this desk for an extended period of time until a better design leaks out."

Zara's eyes are big and shining, like she's trying to beam Eli the strength to keep going. "Can I help with something?"

Eli laughs. She can't seem to shake this girl. "Yeah. Sure."

Zara claps her hands and stands right in front of Eli, tosses her hair back, tilts her chin up. Eli swallows, remembering what it felt like to angle her chin up a little bit more, to help match Zara's body to Echo's. "Where do you want me?" she asks.

Dangerous question.

"On the stage," Eli says.

Zara bounds out of the booth. It feels smaller when she's not there. It feels *less*.

"Fuck," Eli adds under her breath.

Zara takes center stage. Eli turns on the microphone, the one that lets her talk down from the booth like some fuzzy-voiced goddess from on high. Ever since they went to the Met,

Eli has been aware of how much she told Zara about herself. And how nonmutual the sharing was. "Tell me your story," Eli says.

"*I was born to inherit a kingdom . . .*" Zara recites.

"No Echo!" Eli says, warming up to the task of lighting Zara. She can feel it in her hands, the prickle of skin coming back to life after it's been out too long in the cold. "I don't need Echo. I know her already."

Zara shifts off her mark. Shadows scribble in at her edges.

"If you won't tell me about yourself, I'm going to have to start making stuff up," Eli warns.

Zara looks vaguely terrified. "Ummm . . ."

Eli brings down a few dials, brings up a few others. Bright blue rains over Zara. It's a decent imitation of twilight, the time of day when a person is most likely to pour secrets. Zara wavers.

"You were born in a commune upstate," Eli says. "Your mom's name is Star of the North. Your dad believes in the healing powers of goat cheese. You have three sisters, Peace, Love, and —"

"No!"

"Peace, Love, and No?" Eli does some fancy finger-work on the board, and the blue light is replaced by a friendly apricot color. "See, that's interesting."

"Eli . . ."

"I'll stop, I'll stop." She can feel her smile growing devious. "Once you tell me who you are."

Zara's throat tightens. "I —"

136

"You have a tragic past," Eli narrates into the microphone. "You've already been married. Twice! You're one of those women who makes up young-people personas to get roles. Does Adrian know he has to kiss a thirty-seven-year-old?"

Zara's laughter is nervous around the edges. "Eli."

"You're right, he would think that's even *more awesome.*" Eli's hands move without her having to think about it, like a musician at the high point of a song. "Come on. You're making me do all the work here."

Zara pulls it together. But she doesn't speak.

"All right," Eli says. "You —"

"I was born to inherit my father's weird knees and my mother's quiet nature. Other than that, I don't want to be like them." She takes a deep breath. "They had a baby, before me. I think he lived . . . two weeks? My grandparents, my mom's parents, say my mom and dad were different before that. *So in love.* I never knew them like that. There are these other versions of my parents that I'll never meet." Eli can see that Zara wants to stop, but she struggles her way through it. "What would they be like? Would they still be *so in love*? I think that after it happened, they sort of shrunk in on themselves, tried to feel less. Or maybe they didn't try. Maybe it just happened." Zara pauses, like she doesn't know where to go from there, and then dives in a new direction. "I used to play the oboe! God, they loved that. They hated it when I started acting. Even though they were the ones who took me to plays when I was younger, and my dad used to tell me about his relatives who were in the theater."

137

"Really?" Eli asks.

Zara nods, eager gulps. "A long time ago. Yiddish theater. There was a whole district in the Lower East Side." She rushes forward to the edge of the lit circle. "Did you know that the first kiss between two women on Broadway was in a Yiddish play in the 1920s?"

Eli clears her throat, and the sound crackles through the auditorium. "Uhh. No. That's . . . interesting. What play?"

"God of Vengeance."

"Okay, based on that title, I'm gonna take a wild stab and guess that the girls don't get a pretty ending."

"No." Zara winces. "And the whole cast was arrested on obscenity charges."

Eli pauses to consider. "That's pretty badass for the twenties."

Zara looks up, cutting a path through the house, straight to Eli. "And think about how good the kiss must have been."

Is Zara trying to tell her something? Is Eli reading way too much into this? Zara probably only brought it up because she knows that Eli is queer: it's a little rainbow-wrapped present for her.

That's all.

She looks down at her fingers on the board. Walks the conversation back to a safer topic. "So why do your parents have such a problem with it?" Crap. That made it sound like she was talking about girls kissing. "The acting thing, I mean."

While she waits for the answer, she tries out Roscoe's favorite lighting cue, the one that Eli nicknamed Wrath of

God. A rain of golden fire falls around Zara in a curtain, her own personal meteor shower.

"I think it scares them. They stopped wanting to feel all the time. I get on a stage and I feel *so much*." Zara's fidgeting gets more intense. The glow coming through her movements gets brighter. "I have this theory . . . I think that acting is about finding keys for whatever is locked up inside the play. So I'm always looking for things that fit just right. Once you start paying attention, you see that most of life is a wrong fit. And then it's hard because you want this thing that you don't have, this thing that might not even exist. I never told my parents about that. I probably shouldn't have told you."

"Right," Eli says. "Because. The *oboe*."

Zara doesn't laugh, but she does look up at Eli in a tight-lipped, well-teased kind of way. Zara dapples with gold, but Eli can still see the blush that takes her face over slowly.

Eli stops the godly precipitation, leaving Zara in the dark. This feels like the best choice she's made so far. The blackness has a texture like heavy cloth. It makes Eli want to lean in so she won't miss a single one of Zara's words. Of course, they can't do the whole damn play in a blackout.

But it feels like Eli is on to something. "Thank you," she says.

In the darkness, Zara's voice is everything. "For what?"

"Giving me so much to work with."

Zara gets back late.

The apartment is quiet — no blender whirring in the kitchen. No late-night TV. The white-noise machine that does its best to cover up Kestrel's snoring is missing, and so is the snoring. It looks like Zara's roommate has gone out.

Zara doesn't remember crossing the living room, but here she is, hovering on the line between the common space and Kestrel's bedroom.

On the subway ride, Zara was still in the soft comedown from standing onstage, Eli's voice filling the air and her lights warming up Zara's skin. But now that she's back in the apartment, alone, her head fills with Kestrel's screaming. That bright, raking sound.

If Kestrel's not a safe person to live with, Zara needs to know — doesn't she?

Zara crosses the threshold. The carpet gives way with a spongy sort of feeling. Zara can see Kestrel's face plastered on the wall, over and over, a hundred times. This must be her collage. There are cutouts from newspapers and magazines mixed in with old family photos. Hundreds of photos. Some of the Kestrels are dancing, some are singing.

All of them are smiling.

Zara skims through a few drawers in Kestrel's dresser and finds expensive versions of the usual things — makeup, perfume, stacks of bras in sultry colors and silky fabrics. She would have done much better than Zara at the underwear rehearsal.

The closet is deep, filled with hangers of matched outfits, rows of whimsical shoes. Zara should be jealous, but somewhere deep she knows — this isn't beauty. Zara's spent enough time aching for beauty to recognize what isn't here. There is always an imperfection in beauty, some flaw or surprise to remind you it's real. Kestrel's room is a place where imperfection doesn't exist. It's a small world of gloss and shine. A spell to keep away the dark.

Zara is so caught up looking at the clothes that she almost

trips on something underneath. It's an old dance bag, a long one with double handles. When Zara tries to lift it, she feels more weight than she expects. It's an odd, lumpy shape.

The fear that visited her when she was alone in the rehearsal studio comes back. It's like standing at the edge of the stage again, knowing that something has gone wrong in the darkness just in front of her, but she can't see it. She can feel it, though: it feels like a body.

These things come in threes.

Zara works the bag out from where it's wedged, hunts for the zipper. At the first glimpse of what's inside, she lets go of a breath that's been curled up in her chest.

It's a dress form. A cloth torso, covered in Grecian drapery. Not as good as Cosima's work, but still, it's lovely. Zara can picture Kestrel in it. Kestrel, speaking Echo's lines instead of her.

Did Kestrel wear this to auditions, or just in the apartment, alone, as she prepared for a role she thought would be hers? Underneath the dress form are copies of *Echo and Ariston*, with Echo's part highlighted. Zara touches everything with cautious hands, as if Kestrel might find her fingerprints on the scripts, or smell her on the delicate white fabric of the dress — but still, she can't *not* touch.

Unlike the rest of the room, it is beautiful.

Across the apartment, a lock rattles. Because this is New York, there are four locks on the door, each with a different key — Zara guesses she has about thirty seconds until Kestrel gets the door open. She shoves the dress form down, makes sure the scripts are all back in the bag. Kestrel starts in on the second lock as Zara puts the dance bag back where she found it. A key whines in the third lock, the one that sticks when it turns. Zara runs out of the closet, past Kestrel's smiling faces, across the living room.

Kestrel's down to one lock as Zara swings her bedroom door into the frame, then gentles the last inch. She almost trips over her suitcase, packed for Thanksgiving. Zara leaps into the bed, still in her clothes. She pulls the sheets up to her chin.

She thinks about anything but Kestrel.

Echo. Echo. Echo.

The name that used to be her escape now leads her straight back to reality. To the fact that Kestrel wanted this part so badly that she made a shrine to it. And now Kestrel has been forced to live with Zara, the girl who was given the coveted role.

She can hear Kestrel moving through the apartment. Dumping a purse on the floor. Opening the door to her room. Will she notice if something is out of place? Zara feels guilty that she thought Kestrel was dangerous when she was just painfully disappointed. Zara's dream come true was basically her roommate's nightmare.

Echo. Echo. Echo.

Her mind slides to a cold memory of the studio. Leopold climbing on top of her. Leopold demanding a perfection she can't seem to give him. Leopold asking for her *full commitment.*

Zara thinks her way to the last good thing that happened. Sitting on Eli's couch in the lighting booth. Standing onstage with Eli looking down at her, drawing Zara's smile from out of the shadows.

Eli. Eli. Eli.

xxviii

Zara takes the train back to Pennsylvania for Thanksgiving. The world outside blurs and slows. Blurs and slows. She passes from brick and cement to dead grass and the exposed bone of winter branches.

Zara stares down at her hands, thinking about how they touched Adrian Ward with tenderness and then with a white-hot energy, as pure and stripped down as the wire at the center of a lightbulb. All while her mind was on Eli.

She gets out her phone.

Are you headed home?

The answer comes in less than a minute.

Yes. Metro North is my pumpkin carriage. Don't tell anybody but I just turned back into a teenager from Connecticut.

As long as you keep my secret, too.

Which is???

Zara can feel her heartbeat in her fingertips.

I intend to eat an entire cranberry pie WITH crumble topping.

Deal.

Zara stares at the little screen. It was supposed to be a joke, but Leopold really *wouldn't* approve. She remembers him, his hand on her back, *no one is coming to the Aurelia to see a modern slob.* Cosima, shaking her head over Zara's body, *you look wrong.* Zara has never wanted to be the kind of actress who doesn't eat, even if eating costs her roles. She's always known that plenty of directors default to skinny girls, but it's never really shaken her before. Things feel different now. Zara doesn't know why — because more people will be watching? Because she's playing opposite a boy whose muscles are the definition of perfect? Because this is Echo, and she's always secretly known she isn't beautiful enough for the role?

She thinks of Eli, whose arms are like summer branches, whose waist is a long, smooth slope. Whose last girlfriend was an actress.

Zara's parents hug her at the train station. Her mom even cries a little. When they get home, she helps her dad prepare green beans and sweet potatoes while her mom focuses on pie, and they don't stop cooking until noon the next day, even though it will only be the three of them eating. Zara loads her plate. When she gets to the table, it takes less time than she expected for her parents to bring up boyfriends. Apparently her old one called to see if she has time to hang out.

"No," she says, automatically. She hasn't thought about him in two months. She's thought about Eli twelve times in the last minute.

"Have you met anyone new?" her mom asks, treading carefully, like it's a minefield and not an ordinary, everyday conversation. "Anyone . . . nice?"

She thinks about Eli's dark eyes, her easy bravery. Zara wants to bring back a story to make her smile. "Yeah," she says. "There's this girl who's doing the lights for the show. She's about my age. She's"—Zara can't help smiling as she echoes her mother's word—"nice."

Her parents exchange a confused look.

That's it. No follow-up questions. No awkward congratulations. No *we love you no matter whats*.

"How are rehearsals going?" her dad asks, changing the subject with the most obvious question in the world. It's also the question Zara wants to answer the least. She pushes food from one side of her plate to the other and thinks about how Leopold pushes her around the studio, whispering in her ear.

"Good."

She looks out the window, at clouds that ache with snow. Zara had no idea how easy it would be to lie. It's not the same as acting, even though it would look the same to anyone on the outside. If acting is a key to some kind of truth, this is locking the truth up tight.

Her mom made the cranberry crumble pie just for her, and Zara knows that if she skips it, her parents will assume something is wrong. She takes the world's tiniest splinter and a single dollop of whipped cream, excuses herself, and goes to her room.

There are all of her favorite plays lined up on the hand-painted shelf over her bed, the bite-size paperbacks waiting for her to flip through them. And there are her most-loved plays, her *Echo and Aristons,* covered with margin notes, little shreds of herself that she left at every age from twelve to eighteen.

Zara sits down gingerly on the edge of the bed.

It feels like a stranger lives here. A ghost.

A girl who doesn't exist anymore.

Zara takes out her phone. She wants to tell Eli that she just came out to her parents but she doesn't think it worked. They'll probably go to bed tonight talking about how it's nice that she made a new friend.

Hey.

She wants to say more than *hey,* but every time she lets herself keep typing, it gets too serious. Too fast. Soon she'll be telling Eli that she wants to spend every minute with her. That they should probably have babies.

Eli's text shows up a few minutes later.

Hey. Have you OD'd on family time yet?

Zara laughs and writes back.

Bone-dry stuffing and relationship talk for dessert.

Ha! My family doesn't ask me those questions anymore.

Why not?

I only brought one girl home, and let's say they did not fall in love with her. They just assume that will happen with my next girlfriend.

Zara folds onto the bed, holding herself tight across the stomach. *My next girlfriend.* Of course Eli will date someone else, maybe soon. The idea is perfectly reasonable, and it makes Zara feel perfectly sick. She polishes off her pie in a few bites. She gets in her pajamas and stays in them for the rest of the trip, eating nothing but plain turkey and soup. She spends her time with *Echo and Ariston,* worrying about how she'll impress Leopold when she gets back.

At night, she dreams about Roscoe and wakes up screaming.

Her mom insists that she's come down with some kind of flu and shouldn't go back, but Zara reminds her that this isn't school or a regular job   she can't just call in sick. Besides, Zara's not actually sick. She's terrified.

Of course, she doesn't tell them that.

Her mom insists on sending the rest of the cranberry crumble back to the city with Zara. After one more stale-smelling train ride, she rushes to the Aurelia. She doesn't even have time to stop at Kestrel's because the trains are running behind schedule. Zara shows up for the run-through exactly on time, which she knows is considered late in the theater world. The stage manager gives her a hard glare. Zara feels the

149

right amount of guilty, but she's also glittering from too much coffee and the fact that she gets to see Eli again. It only takes a second to spot her in the corner of the studio. Eli's black curls hang down in perfect spirals over a gray sweater. Her jeans are still ripped, but it's gotten cold enough that she layers black tights underneath them.

Zara walks up to her, and it feels like she's back on the train. The rest of the room blurs. Slows. Zara has never felt this way about a girl before — which is immediately overshadowed by a larger truth. Zara has never felt this way about *anyone*.

Eli holds out her arm before Zara can even greet her. "Leftovers. I wish I could say I made them, but my mom and my brother did most of the cooking. I pretty much sat around and acted like a human armchair for my cousins and my niece to climb on." When Zara doesn't say anything — because she can't find a single word that's good enough — Eli fills the silence. "There's macaroni and cheese in there, and plátanos. We only had side dishes left."

"Thanks." Zara takes the little plastic container. Suddenly, her appetite floods back into her. She rushes to her bag and comes back with an aluminum tin, holding it out in both hands, turning the dreaded pie into an offering.

"The famous cranberry crumble," Eli says, pulling it close and taking a closed-eyes whiff. Zara can smell it, too. Cinnamon and tart berries. "How was your trip home?" Eli asks. "Did things get better?"

"They stayed the same. Which is pretty much the problem. I think I'm going to skip the day off for Chanukah." Zara had to fight to get that day off in the first place, and now she doesn't even want it. She'll tell her parents that Leopold needs her for rehearsal. They won't understand, but they won't be able to stop her, either.

"Holidays in the city," Eli says with a warm smile. "Sounds good to me."

Part of Zara wants to say something, and part of her is happy just to stand there. To feel the strange combination of stillness and rush that comes from being near Eli. To run her eyes over those blue-green tattoos for the first time in weeks and learn them like lines in a play.

But then she sees the rest of the actors finishing warm-ups, which she hasn't even started. She gives Eli a quick, lopsided grin and finds a spot in the corner to do a few stretches. Eli joins the rest of the designers where they've lined up along the far wall. Cosima with her pins, Barrett with a props list and a smug look. He's going over something with Leopold when the director simply walks away — and all heads turn.

"This marks our last rehearsal in the studios, before we move to the stage and take our rightful place," he says. "This is also the designers' chance to watch before we slip into tech and they have to make everything work. The path to a perfect opening night begins here." Zara expects more of a grand speech, but Leopold stops. He stands there in utter silence for a moment. Then he winces, as if he's touched a hot stove that no one else can see.

"Let's begin," Meg says. "Shall we?"

The stage manager tells them to take their places, and

Leopold returns to the long table, where Meg holds out a chair. She is so careful with him. So caring. She makes sure that he has water. Her pale-blue eyes are slicked with concern as he buries his face in his hands.

"Where's Enna?" Toby asks.

Everyone turns around in circles, and a few people check the hallway, but no one can find her. The rest of the actors trade looks. No one seems terribly surprised. Zara remembers what Enna told her about low expectations.

The assistant stage manager goes to look for her.

Even with the ancient radiator clanking, the studio is shiver-worthy. They work through the first act without Enna. The stage manager reads her lines flat, which drags the energy down. Leopold is barely watching, anyway. His hands never stray far from his face. He downs his glass of water again and again, Meg refilling it over and over.

The mirror is a cold reflection of act 3, scene 2. The lovers meet.

Zara wants Leopold to see what she's capable of. That she has something to bring to a love story. Adrian and Zara form a dance with their lines, their delivery smooth and seamless. That rehearsal before Thanksgiving must have worked because Zara can feel the difference. Adrian is more than off book. He's right there with her, inside the scene. He holds out a hand to Zara's face. Where before there was nothing — a crackle of brightness.

But Leopold is silent, a thumb and a forefinger pressed to his forehead as if something inside is trying to get out.

152

"I was a girl who owned greater than half the world," Zara says. *"I am a girl who has given that up."*

"Which world did you own?" Ariston asks. Zara has always imagined this line as playful, but Adrian is serious. He sets his nostrils wide and crunches his fists in readiness. He's an action hero, ready to save Echo — not realizing that she's already saved herself.

"None that was worthy of the sacrifice," Zara says.

Leopold won't look at her. He doesn't care that she's acting with her whole body, that she's pushed herself through walls that she could barely see a week ago.

"You will be in need of a new world, then," Ariston says.

"It is here," Echo says, and Zara lightly touches the soft spot between her collarbones. Leopold still isn't paying attention, but these words stir up something new. He isn't the person that Zara needs right now.

Her eyes catch on Eli.

Look at me, she thinks. *Please.*

Eli's eyes move from her notebook to Adrian and back again.

"You are what I have wandered for," Zara says.

This is for Eli. Only Eli. *"Those nights in the woods, you were with me. It would be safer if I cut out my tongue and lived the rest of my days in silence. But I have met you and I must speak."* The words are two thousand years old, but somehow Zara feels as if she's inventing them. Meg told her that would happen when she was really acting. These words aren't just Echo's now.

They're hers.

Zara used to listen when people in her drama classes called this scene *too easy*. *Insta-love*. Like what Echo felt for Ariston was as cheap as a cup of bad coffee. But there's more, hidden in the fabric of the scene. Echo wants Ariston so quickly and so completely because she's already fallen in love. She's been hollowing out a place inside herself for years — and he fits.

Zara plays the statue game. She casts her arms back, clenches her fist, remembers Eli's finger tilting her chin to just the right angle. She doesn't close her eyes. *"I have learned that fear is a kind of death."*

Eli looks at her as if she's just woken up from a muddled sleep. Watercolor pink spreads across her cheeks. Zara looks straight at her. It breaks the fourth wall. It shatters the rules.

Zara doesn't care.

And Leopold doesn't notice. Whatever is happening in his head must be awful, because when Zara shifts her eyes away from Eli he is grimacing, his face contorted in a sort of frozen howl.

What is he seeing that's so much more important than the play?

So painful?

Zara makes her exit, and Eli watches her all the way off-stage. Zara only has a minute before her next entrance, but she leaves the studio.

In the hallway, Zara slides down the wall until she's sitting on the linoleum. She holds that look on Eli's face like she would hold water in cupped hands.

Meg slides out of the studio and looks down at Zara. She waits for the door to click quietly shut.

"Zara," Meg says. "The performance you just gave was . . . interesting."

Zara can't believe she was so careless, that she didn't think about Meg noticing what she was doing with her lines. Who she was delivering them to. The part of her mind not on Eli was so focused on Leopold, on what he was watching or ignoring, that she didn't even think about anyone else.

Meg might be quiet, but she notices everything in this theater.

She crouches next to Zara. Everything about her is mild, soft. Her cardigan and khakis are so boring that when she's not speaking, she almost disappears. Up close, she even has an inoffensive smell. Lavender soap. "I wanted to ask if, at the start of rehearsals, Leopold asked you for a promise."

Zara nods. Slowly.

"What was it?" she asks. Meg's not quite whispering, but her tone is low and careful.

"Commitment," Zara says. "No distractions."

"And you agreed?"

Zara nods again as the thought cracks and runs over her, making her cold. Meg is calling Eli a distraction.

"I'm going to tell you something," Meg says, her voice a little hoarse. "Whatever you do, don't forget. Leopold Henneman doesn't take broken promises lightly." Zara hears an echo of Enna's words, like far-off footsteps.

Don't fall in love with anyone in the theater.

"Now," Meg says, standing up, back to her perfectly brisk self. "I think you have an entrance?"

Zara follows her back into the studio. She doesn't know where to look, but she avoids glancing at either Eli or Leopold as she takes her place. Zara feels a sort of vertigo that sometimes comes before an entrance, but it's worse than usual. As if she is standing on the highest story of a skyscraper, past the railing, and the wind is singing through her.

You started at the top. That's a long way to fall.

She closes her eyes and tries to get back to that place where her breath is round and her heart is ready. But in the dark, all she can hear is screaming. She thinks it's a memory of when she found Roscoe.

She wonders if they will ever leave.

But when Zara opens her eyes, the screaming is real and everything falls away. The door flies open.

"Stop."

It's the assistant stage manager. Her breath is ragged, hands on her knees. She would never cut off the run-through like this. Unless.

"It's Enna."

ACT II

i

The day of Enna's memorial, Zara starts to file into the theater with the rest of the company, but Leopold gently detaches her from the group and puts a hand on her back, steering her away, toward the greenroom. He's been busy for the last six days, bringing Enna's understudy up to speed while Zara has been floating from rehearsal to apartment to rehearsal. She's afraid that Leopold wants to say something about how off-kilter her acting has been, even though she's not the only one who's been pitched sideways by a second death at the Aurelia.

Leopold closes them into the greenroom together, even though there's no one left in the hallway outside. The building is silent and vast and impossibly still. Zara has never been on a boat in dead water, so far from land that the safety of shore is only a memory, but she imagines this is exactly how it would feel.

Leopold is wearing a tasteful black suit, perfectly tailored and obviously worth more than everything she owns put together. It only highlights how ragged Zara is in the knee-length black skirt she bought at the mall. The director's hair is untamed, his presence giving off the faint electricity that always makes Zara think that touching him might involve a shock.

Leopold tells Zara that he doesn't want her at the memorial.

"Let me explain," he says. "I don't want you to be seen before the gala."

"What do you mean?" Zara asks, struck by a vision of herself locked away in Kestrel's apartment. Not able to come out unless Leopold says so.

"No large public events. Not yet. I want the press to love you," he says in his most practical tone. "If the press loves you, the world loves you."

Zara still wants to be out there with the rest of the company. "Maybe it would be good if the press sees me now. Gets used to me." She likes that idea — it takes some of the pressure off the gala and the previews and opening night.

"You're worried that you aren't what they want," Leopold says, pinpointing her fear so easily that it makes Zara feel transparent. Leopold shakes his head, soft and understanding. "You're not the first actress to feel that way."

He doesn't tell Zara she's wrong, though.

Leopold waves her toward a couch. He touches her shoulder, the spot where it shades into her neck. It's strangely intimate, and she wants to swat him away. But she can't *swat* Leopold Henneman. "You're underestimating how much people love stories about girls like you."

"Girls like me?" Zara repeats in a dark, empty voice. A shadow voice.

"Lifted from obscurity. As plain as plain can be. You will be everyone's dream, coming true," he says. "But we have to follow the rules." Zara is highly aware of him stroking her hand. "This is not a process we want to rush."

Zara blinks hard. This feels wrong. She shakes her head, clearing away the nervous debris. The conversation has gone so far in one direction that she's lost sight of what today is about.

"Enna—"

"Will have plenty of people to mourn her," Leopold says. "She was loved, once upon a time." His lips spread. His smiles have sharp edges, like they're trying to pry things out of her. "You and Enna hardly knew each other. Is there some other reason you want to be out there today?"

Eli.

Zara has been doing her best to avoid Eli since Meg talked to her—but Zara's best is getting worse by the minute. Zara lives in a fever dream between Eli's texts. They call each other sometimes — not in the middle of the night, like Leopold used to. In the morning, when the light is still coming in pink and soft. They wake each other up.

Leopold is still looking down at her, and Zara gets the feeling that she needs to say the right thing in the right way. It's like rehearsal, but worse. Zara is living the actor's nightmare, where she steps out onto a stage and the lines have scurried away from her. No amount of fumbling or fear will bring them back. How is she supposed to keep talking to him, being as open as he wants her to be, without mentioning Eli?

If she did, would it really be as bad as Meg made it sound?

She wipes sweat off the back of her neck and immediately regrets it. "Enna and I were in the same play, and that means something." Zara brushes the sweat from her palm to her knee. "It's intimate."

"True," Leopold says.

But there's more to it than that. Enna's death has been a tricky knot in Zara's chest since the minute she found out. There is sadness tied up in it, and a dark thread of guilt, like she could have done more to stop this. She was right there in the dressing room with Enna, days before she died. Shouldn't Zara have noticed something was wrong?

There's also a fear that keeps visiting her.

These things come in threes.

"Enna was my friend. At least, she was friendly with me. Before she died." Zara hadn't realized how important that had been to her — another actor treating her like she belonged at the Aurelia — until it was gone.

Leopold is studying Zara with deep concern. "I think we should be meeting much more regularly. There is so much happening right now. We mustn't lose sight of one another."

Zara nods before she can even think about what that means. How they could possibly be meeting more regularly. More rehearsal? Just — talking? Will the phone start ringing at two in the morning again?

Leopold gets up and switches on the monitor mounted over the door. "You can watch in here, if you like."

She is left alone with the grainy TV. It's up there so actors can keep track of performances. Kestrel told Zara that one year Toby attempted to rewire it so he could watch the Thanksgiving Day parade, which he called *gayer than Pride,* but the monitor stubbornly refuses any other stations.

It's all Aurelia, all the time.

The stage has been cleared. They should be moving into tech tonight. Instead, hundreds of people have gathered to say good-bye to Enna. Over the podium a spotlight appears, bright as a splash of pain.

Leopold comes onto the screen.

It doesn't feel real, seeing him out there when he was just in here, sitting so close. But the audience breaks out in clapping and cheers, so it must be him. They love Leopold Henneman. They always love Leopold Henneman. Still, applause feels out of place. Is that what actors are supposed to want, even when they die? Flowers tossed at their cold feet? A standing ovation?

Leopold pours out words with ease. "Enna brought brightness to a grim world." This doesn't sound like the sharp-minded woman that Zara shared a dressing room with, or the nightgown-clad butterfly that wafted in and out of rehearsals. It's like Leopold invented a perfect actress so he could praise her.

As soon as Leopold finishes, Carl takes the stage. The image on the TV is black and white and wavering. But Zara can see his eyes, bright blue, hovering a few inches over her face.

Carl clears his throat.

"When I met Enna, she was twenty-two. When I found the courage to speak to her, she flipped me off." The audience gives a surprised, grateful laugh. This Enna makes sense to Zara. This Enna, she can imagine. Carl clears his throat, as if the rest of his speech has gotten painfully stuck. "When I found the courage to speak to her again, it changed the world."

Zara remembers what Kestrel told her.

I could never get myself to hate her. Not like Carl did.

Either Kestrel was lying then, or Carl is now. He could just be an actor putting his talent to use, but this is the not the voice of a man who hates his ex-wife. It vibrates with honesty, a string plucked at just the right pitch. Carl goes on and on about their life together, sticking to the early years.

So far, no one has mentioned the version of Enna that Zara met a month ago. No one is talking about how she died. *An overdose.* The full autopsy still needs to be done, but there's no real question.

Enna told Zara that she didn't drink anymore. No pills, either.

Zara's breath is fine one moment, and then it's not. She can't stay in the greenroom and listen to the rest of this. She pretends to be calm, walking down the backstage hallway, the monitor still leaking words about Enna's talent. Zara's feet carry her toward the dressing room. She's only been in there once. When she talked to Enna. It's where Enna felt like a real person — unpredictable, imperfect — not like some pretty lie they were all making up together.

The outer dressing room is an explosion of costumes in different colors, rows of shoes that stand empty and waiting. The open door to the little dressing room is covered over with a line of yellow police tape.

Even if Zara has been telling herself that Roscoe's death was an accident, that he fell and wasn't pushed, Eli has given her doubt, and that doubt is like a crack in her mind — prying it open with possibility.

She puts one leg over the tape, careful not to touch it. Every crime show she's ever seen tells her she needs gloves. With so many costume pieces lying around, she might be able to find some, but that seems too much like admitting that she's really doing this. She pulls her sleeves down over her hands instead.

The little dressing room would be upsetting even if someone hadn't died in it. Chairs are upturned, the mirror cracked at one corner. And there are words — slashed in bright-red lipstick and smudged with eyeliner.

HAS-BEEN and IMPOSTOR and SLUT.

Zara turns a full circle. She's struck dizzy by the truth. If

165

she told people the awful thoughts she has about herself, it would look something like this. Different words, but the same ragged scrawl of fears. Zara doesn't think she'd be able to write straight onto the Aurelia, though. She doesn't think her worries are important enough to merit the wall space.

Zara takes out her phone. The shutter sound clicks again and again as she takes pictures of each wall. She gets on her knees to capture a few close to the ground. Down there, with the dust-and-spice smell of old costumes, Zara finds tiny, cramped words on the underside of the makeup table.

I PRAY YOU, PARDON ME.

Zara knows these words.

It's not an obscure line — any theater person would know it. *I pray you, pardon me* is what Gertrude says in the final act of *Hamlet,* right before she drinks from the poisoned cup.

Right before she's killed.

ii

Zara carries those words around like stones in her pockets.

I pray you, pardon me.

Days crowd into each other, rehearsals bleed together. Zara talks to Eli more and more but says less and less. One morning before she gets out of bed, Zara plays a game. She picks up her phone, opens her texts, and types in everything she wants to tell Eli. Everything she's afraid to say.

I found something in Enna's dressing room.

These things come in threes.

I'm not exactly straight.

She erases the words as quickly as her thumbs will allow.

That night, when rehearsal is over and people are flowing down the hall, Zara lingers near the greenroom. Kestrel and other chorus members — a dauntingly beautiful group of people — are preparing to go out for the night. Adrian Ward should be the center of attention, but he looks lost, plunked down into someone else's life and trying to make the best of it.

Eli comes down the hall, at the back of the crowd. She looks the way she always does: black jeans, a tight black T-shirt, boots loud and hands busy. Her Leatherman is out, and she whisks through the blades one by one. Zara has cataloged Eli's nervous habits: opening and closing the Leatherman, dancing a finger over her silver rings, rubbing her tattoos with a thumb when she thinks no one is looking.

Zara takes off down the hall, moving against the tide. Adrian pulls her to one side before she can make real headway. "Hey, are we running lines?"

"Not tonight," Zara says. "Tomorrow?"

"Yeah," he says. "Great. You know I need to keep running them to keep them fresh. That technique you came up with is amazing."

"Thanks," Zara says, thinking about that kiss — the one that she pressed onto Adrian but meant for Eli. Zara is picturing it, *feeling* it, at the exact moment when Eli passes them in the hall.

She turns bright red and hopes that Adrian doesn't think the flashburn of color is for him.

"Yeah, seriously brilliant," Adrian says, keeping her trapped there for another long moment. "You should patent it or something." Zara nods, as if the movement can speed up what Adrian is saying.

As soon as she's been released, she runs to catch up to Eli. Leopold and Meg appear at the far end of the hall — together, like always. Zara doesn't think they're watching, but she would rather be careful. Just in case. She doesn't say anything to Eli. Instead, Zara focuses all of her attention on Eli. Like magic, Eli looks straight up.

Zara twitches her head toward the wings. Eli follows, her face brimming with question marks.

Zara makes another sudden turn and pulls them into a closet.

She figures it will be filled with set pieces, maybe sound or lighting equipment, but instead the shelves are crowded with mannequin heads. There are crowns of braids and curls in every shade of black and red, brown and blond.

"Why are we in the wig cage?" Eli asks with a laugh.

Zara is back inside the actor's nightmare standing on a blank stage with an unwritten script. Eli watches her in that studying way. Soon she's been waiting so long that she starts to frown, and Zara notices that Eli's mouth has crinkle spots at the edges. Not quite dimples.

Zara opens her mouth to say *I think I'm falling in love with you.*

What comes out is, "Enna's death is the wrong color."

iii

Eli doesn't have to tell Zara they're leaving the Aurelia: they do it without speaking. They stride through the stage door and down the alley, their shoulders absurdly close to touching.

Zara and Eli don't say anything for blocks, as if the theater might be able to hear them. Eli keeps catching the tail end of the looks that Zara is giving her. Nervous, wispy looks. Then they are down the stairs to the subway, flashing through the darkness in an overbright train car. No one has ever looked good in this lighting. It's one of the small evils of the world: at the beginning and end of every day people have to see each other in, literally, the worst possible light. But when Zara hugs the pole and examines the list of stops, Eli has no desire to look away.

They wordlessly agree to get out at Union Square.

Eli gets a dose of Christmas lights, a double dose of holiday shoppers looking for sales.

She pulls Zara through all of it, to the Strand. This would be perfect for a date, and as a bonus, it's a place Eli never came with Hannah. Eli's ex-girlfriend preferred the kind of things that were more fun to post pictures of online than actually fun to do. But this is Eli's idea of dately paradise. The store is filled with books to huddle over, to cherry-pick sentences from and read out loud.

A couple of beautiful boys hold hands by the new fiction tables, their winter coats touching, then everything touching. Eli whips up a daydream involving her lips, Zara's neck, and the history section.

She takes off her hat and does her best to cool down. She turns into the YA section, leaving Zara's neck untouched. "So. Enna."

Zara rocks back and forth on her boot heels, hands in her pockets, coat swishing. "Yeah."

"You really think . . ."

Zara gives a flustered nod.

"But . . . I mean . . . *actually* . . ."

If they want to do this, they're going to have to start filling in the blanks. It makes Eli think of the first time she achieved nakedness with another girl. They kissed and tore things off each other like they were so experienced, then fumbled around for hours. It all came down to whether they were brave enough to start using words. Asking specific questions. Of course, there's a world of difference between *Does this feel good to you?* and "You think someone killed Enna?"

"I don't know. *She* thinks someone did," Zara says, keeping her voice low.

"No one's going to hear us," Eli says with certainty. "The employees just want to shelve things."

"What about the customers?" Zara asks, eyeing a clutch of hipsters with slouchy hats.

"Nope." Eli inches her voice louder to prove her point. "Too busy with their own problems. That's one of the good things about living here. Nobody cares."

"That's *good*?" Zara asks.

"Look," Eli says, not able to deal with this particular brand of innocence right now. "Sometimes caring gets in the way. My parents cared *so much* that they couldn't let me pick out my own shoes when I was sixteen. They love me. But they think that means getting to have a say in everything. Like dating. Let me give you a hint: girls were not their first choice."

Zara looks sorry for her, and Eli doesn't want that.

"They got used to it," she says. "And even if they hadn't, I would date whoever I want." Well — that last part's not really true, because if it was, she'd be with Zara by now, standing four steps closer, hands in a borderline inappropriate place.

Eli forces herself back to the original topic. "We can shout about two deaths in a cursed theater, and it won't be the weirdest conversation I've heard in Manhattan this week. It won't even rank."

"Really?" Zara's eyes go luminous with interest. "I want to know the other things you heard."

Either that husky glory is Zara's flirting voice or Eli has completely lost her grip. It's true that Zara has been standing closer than she used to, sometimes so close that Eli can feel every micromovement of her body. And yes, there's been a certain amount of hand touching. But girls touch each other all the time. Girls have intense friendships that have nothing to do with wanting to tear each other's clothes off.

"Tell me about Enna," Eli says, hoping that last thought didn't leave a mark on her voice.

Zara gives Eli the facts about the dressing room, shares her grainy cell-phone photos, and explains the Gertrude line. Eli stacks it on top of what she knows about Roscoe. Two deaths. An accident and an overdose.

"They found alcohol in Enna's system," Eli says. "Drugs, too."

"Yeah," Zara says. "I know."

"So you don't think she just drank the drinks and popped the pills and then got a little . . . dramatic with the walls?"

"Enna told me she didn't drink anymore," Zara says. "Or do drugs."

"A fact that nobody has ever lied about in all of history," Eli deadpans. Her thoughts swerve in a new direction. She starts to walk, because all of a sudden she can't stand still. Book spines flash as she goes up one narrow aisle and down another. "What about that article you gave me?" she asks. "Kestrel's theory? The curse?"

"You believe in that?" Zara asks.

"When you call something a curse, it takes on a life of its own," Eli says. "Broken bones, accidents, backstage fights, these happen at theaters. Besides, it can go both ways, right? What if someone is *using* the curse, the idea of it, to cover up normal murders?" Eli looks back at Zara, who doesn't even bother to hide her disbelief: it explodes from her expression. "It sounds like something theater people would do," Eli adds. "Smoke and glitter to distract from the nitty-gritty of a set change. It's like when the stage door was left open. The police called Roscoe's death an accident, but what if they hadn't? That door changes the story. If it's locked, Roscoe could only have been pushed by someone in the theater. If it's unlocked, it could have been anyone in Midtown."

Without meaning to, Eli has led them straight to the theater section. Next to Ibsen and Chekhov is a shrine to *Echo and Ariston.* There are face-out copies of five different translations.

Eli picks one up and ruffles the pages. "No escaping it, I guess."

"It's still safe to be at the Aurelia, right?" Zara asks quickly, looking at Eli like she's qualified to give this answer. To save her from leaving. Eli doesn't say anything right away, and when Zara grimaces, Eli has to push down the desire to reach out and smooth away that pained look.

"Of course," Eli says extra softly to make up for the too-long pause. "We'll keep each other safe."

Zara gives her one of those wild stares, like she did at the read-through. The one that gave Eli hope. She puts down the copy of *Echo and Ariston* and heads out of the bookstore into the holiday-drunk night.

Eli loves it: the whole bright season. In her family, Christmas isn't really a day. It's six weeks of presents and food stretching from Thanksgiving to Three Kings Day. Leopold stormed all over the best part of the year with his production schedule and didn't even apologize, like nothing could possibly be as important as his play. At least Eli has a little tree in her apartment and she has lights everywhere and it *feels* like Christmas. She glances at Zara. "Does this Christmas stuff bother you?"

"I'm used to it," Zara says, but it feels like an automatic answer. Then she slows her pace and presses her lips together, really thinking about it. "I guess it still makes me feel . . . lonely. That's not the right word. There are millions of people around. But that's how it feels."

Eli looked up the dates for Chanukah a while ago. Now she stops in the middle of Union Square, right there on the bench-lined walkway, and even though the timing is less than ideal, she reaches into the silky lining of her deep coat pockets. One hand stays down there. The other pulls out a little box wrapped in silver paper. It looks like a tiny moon, sitting between them.

Zara takes it, looking straight down at the box. Like it will disappear if she looks away.

She pulls up the tape, eases the box open. Eli is nervous — she has no idea what Zara will think. If she'll act like it's strange that Eli got her a present in the first place. Zara lifts out a leather cord with a key hanging on the end. Eli found the key at a secondhand store in a cut-glass bowl. She probably could have stolen one from the Aurelia's prop storage, but it wasn't worth risking Barrett's creepiness. Besides, she likes that she had to go out into the world and find it. She likes the way it looks sitting in Zara's palm. Weathered, like it had to travel a long way before it found her.

"For your imaginary locks," Eli says.

Zara stares up at Eli. Like *she* might disappear if Zara stops looking. "No one's ever gotten me something like this."

"Well, good," Eli says. "Because you're about to get seven more somethings exactly like it." She has the rest of the keys in her bag. She's been carrying them around for days, clinking as she walks, a reminder of the feelings she can't seem to get rid of.

She hands them all over, because she just can't wait.

Zara sits down on a bench to string the keys. She ties the cord around her neck. Eli wants to ask if she can help, but she keeps her words and her hands and her feelings to herself. If this is something Zara wants, she'll have to make the first move. Possibly *all* the moves. Eli just stopped feeling alone for the first time since Roscoe died. She needs a friend, not another hopeless love story.

"What do we do now?" Zara asks, looking up at her, eyes gone golden in the streetlights. The eight keys slide into each other and tug the necklace down, chiming softly. It settles against the soft valley of skin at the opened top button of Zara's pale-blue sweater.

Eli swallows hard. "We keep our eyes open."

iv

Zara expects Leopold's office to feel like Leopold does—intense and claustrophobic—but it's a blank room in the administrative portion of the building, one floor up from the studios. Zara takes a quick inventory. A long metal desk, a few skeletal chairs, an assortment of show posters. *Macbeth, West Side Story, Arsenic and Old Lace.*

The stage manager sent an e-mail telling Zara that she was called for a private meeting with the director—which sounded strange until Zara remembered that she agreed to it. She can't remember why. Probably because Leopold was touching her knee and saying yes to whatever he asked for was the quickest way to make him stop.

She gets up and paces, reaching for the keys around her neck. She hasn't taken them off since Eli gave them to her. Not to sleep. Not even to shower. She had stood bare-skinned this morning, warming up slowly. Thoughts of Roscoe and Enna dissolved into the steam, replaced by much more welcome thoughts of Eli. She had touched the keys, playing her fingers back and forth between the circles, tugging at the teeth. Then one of her hands followed the path of the water — down, down.

Zara can't think about that now.

Not in Leopold's office.

Even though Leopold is missing. Maybe he's caught in a vision. Not for the first time, Zara wonders what he sees. Has he changed his mind about her? Will her Echo ever be good enough? Back when he was just a voice in her ear, she asked about the visions. Now she knows better. Zara Evans doesn't get to ask Leopold Henneman questions.

That's not how it works.

She checks the little square of glass in the door. No one's coming down the hall from either direction. She takes the seat behind Leopold's desk — where he sits when he's alone, thinking about the play. There's a buzz in Zara's skin. A blankness in her brain.

Zara knows this is a major trespass. But Leopold is always

179

the one telling her to push the boundaries. To be less polite. To follow her instincts. She wants to prove that she's safe here. She pulls the loose metal handle of a desk drawer. The whole tray slides out eagerly.

There is a gun inside.

Zara moves back quickly. She doesn't take her eyes off the gun. It looks heavy, the metal as dark as the moment before sleep.

Zara slows down her breathing and pulls the rest of the handles until the desk bristles with open drawers. Most hold paperwork, office supplies. The deep filing drawer at the bottom is filled with knives.

Zara picks one up. It's strangely light. She puts a finger to the blade, expecting pain, and feels only plastic. Zara presses the blade slowly against the skin of her arm. The shiny plastic clicks slightly and disappears — not into her arm but back into the hilt of the weapon.

It's a prop.

It can't be for *Echo and Ariston*, though. Wrong time period. Leopold must be looking at props for his next production.

Zara flips open the calendar on top of Leopold's desk to see what show he's doing next. December is crowded with *Echo and Ariston*— tech, gala, previews. When they open on the twenty-ninth, Leopold can leave the Aurelia and start rehearsing a new show. January stares up at Zara, perfectly white, completely blank.

So do the months after it.

180

Zara hears someone coming down the hallway. She flips back the calendar and quietly slides back the drawers.

Leopold strides in, snow still clinging to him from the bitter world outside. "My dear." He gives her a hug, which lasts longer than she expects, and she melts into it a little bit. Leopold gives off a sense of calm that Zara hasn't felt in weeks. There's been an anxious buzz around the director for too long, like a swarm of flies.

This is a moment of relief she didn't even know she needed.

Leopold sits down at his desk. Zara hopes he can't feel her imprint on his chair. Her warmth, lingering.

"I think it's time that we talked openly about the challenges of this production," Leopold says. "Two of our company have died, swiftly and unexpectedly." Zara sighs, and tension drops from a hundred small places in her body where she's been holding it tight. She's thankful that Leopold mentioned Roscoe and Enna. The silence around the deaths has started to feel like a bruise. A tender spot that no one wants to touch.

"I'm not blind to how difficult things are at the moment," Leopold says. "And if you ever need someone to talk to, please remember that I am here. Come straight to me if you need anything."

Zara nods, but she can't help thinking:

She didn't go straight to him.

She went straight to Eli.

Leopold stands up and paces, even though the room is tiny. "Despite these difficulties, you and I still have a love story to tell."

"What about Adrian?" Zara asks. His absence feels strange all of a sudden. It's true that he breezes in and out of rehearsals, that Zara barely sees him except when they're face-to-face in a scene, because the whole production schedule has been designed around his movie star needs. But if they're talking about Echo and Ariston in love, shouldn't he be here now?

Leopold gives her a knowing head tilt. "Adrian Ward is here for his pretty face and his ability to pull in ticket sales."

Zara blinks, startled. She didn't think Leopold would be so blunt about it.

What does he say about Zara when she's not in the room?

Leopold stops right in front of her, demanding Zara's full attention, but the all-knowing director is gone. His expression is stripped of the usual charm. Leopold looks almost — nervous. "I want you to know that I am sorry if there have been moments when *I've* made things difficult for you, if I've been less than perfect in my role."

"No," Zara says. The words rush out of her without any real thought. "You're just doing your job."

"This play must be perfect, above anything else I have done," Leopold says. "I'm sure you understand that feeling." Zara does. This is her one chance to be Echo. Every other thought she's had recently scatters like leaves before a strong wind. "So how do you and I tell the world's greatest love story when you have never been in love?"

Zara feels the storm hit.

She doesn't answer — what answer can she give? That she

182

was afraid he would notice? That she *has* fallen in love, but Meg told her to forget it because Leopold wouldn't approve?

Zara made a promise. *No distractions.* She can't tell him that she's already broken it. That she plans to *keep* breaking it.

"I've never been in love," Zara says woodenly. "It's true."

Leopold smiles, clearly pleased that he was right. The delight rises off him in waves. "You have nothing to draw on, which puts a stranglehold on your performance." He sets a hand on her shoulder, and it's heavy there, keeping her in place. "We will have to do something to help you find those feelings." He draws a circle around her with his steps. "I want you to close your eyes."

Zara does as she's told.

He's here to direct her. She's here to act.

But she won't tell him about Eli. There's nothing to tell. They haven't kissed. They've barely touched.

"Imagine that you are perfectly in love." Zara's mind stays blank. She's afraid to even *think* of Eli. "Imagine that you have known another body stacked on top of yours. Bearing down. Heat. Pressure. Imagine that you have no breath, and the words fight to come out of you."

Leopold moves behind her. His breath is warm, stirring the fine hair at the base of her neck. "Imagine that you are holding nothing back." She can feel his fingertips creeping onto her waist. His lips close to her ear.

She can feel a tremble, and it's fear, but she's not sure where it's coming from.

How much she wants Eli?

How little she wants Leopold to find out?

The little fact that she just lied to him, and she's afraid he can tell?

His hands on her waist?

Zara breathes and tells herself a story. She is safe. She is calm. She is in love. Nothing can touch her.

Leopold steps away and claps, a private little applause session. Zara opens her eyes to see him smiling broadly. "Zara. This is great work you've done here. Can you feel it?"

It's a good thing that she's gotten so much practice lately, because the lie slips out, unrehearsed. "Yes."

She tells herself that she can handle this — she can like Eli this much and keep it to herself. She can deal with the pressure of being a professional actress. She can banish her strange fears. She can be the perfect Echo. She can keep Leopold happy. She tells herself that everything is going to be fine. Better than fine.

Beautiful.

The cue-to-cue is killing Adrian. Standing onstage for hours, not even acting, while the designers run around and make tiny changes? It's a waste of his time.

"Hold!" the stage manager yells, and the actors freeze. Zara's hands are stuck to his chest.

The designers run around while the actors stay in place. "Why does it take so long for them to fix every single thing?" Adrian asks.

Zara's eyes flick around. Talking is against the rules. (But the rules are different for Adrian, and everybody knows it.) "This is the only time the designers have to make their ideas work," Zara whispers. "We had six weeks." She looks up at the lighting booth and then back at Adrian.

He nods like he gets it, but secretly he can't figure out why Zara would side with the crew.

Down in the orchestra pit, Leopold is talking to Barrett, the oil slick of a props guy. "That can't possibly be the right sword." Adrian waits for Leopold to rip into him, but Barrett just rolls his eyes and spends twenty minutes finding another rapier.

"See, he gives that guy special treatment," Adrian whispers to the top of Zara's head. "I mean, have you *ever* seen Barrett do something right? He's terrible with the props. Plus I heard him talking about one of his hookups in the dressing room the other day. It was bad, Z. Really bad. A page out of the creeper manual."

Zara makes a yes-Barrett-is-disgusting face.

Leopold turns away from the props master, and Adrian tries to catch his attention from across the room. But the director just keeps moving, looking for someone other than him.

Lately, Adrian has been feeling a little overlooked. (And that's not a feeling he's used to.) He shows up, does his scenes, leaves. He's not really part of what's happening at the Aurelia.

He can hold on to the words, even the long-ass monologues, thanks to Zara and her special technique. Adrian can get the words out now, but he can't really *act*. (Or maybe he can. Maybe he's better than he thinks he is. But then why hasn't Leopold told him so? Why hasn't Leopold told him anything?)

The director starts to shout from his table out there in the middle of the house. Zara tenses at Adrian's side.

But the anger isn't for her. Not this time.

The lights go from blue to some other shade of blue. Leopold spins around and shouts up at the lighting booth, "That can't possibly be the right cue. You can fix it, or you can leave."

Adrian feels bad for the lighting girl. Eli. Her boss just died, and she's got a pretty intense job at the moment. Leopold could cut her a break. "I guess *that's* not special treatment," Adrian mutters to Zara.

She looks bad all of a sudden. Paler than pale. Like she wants to break off the stage and run — where? Away from Adrian? Then he would be completely alone.

"Keep moving!" the stage manager yells. Zara gets out one line before the dreaded "Hold!"

The second Adrian has his lines down, they absolutely forbid him to speak.

It figures.

In Hollywood they do this stuff before he even steps onto the set. He has people to stand in place for him. An army of not-quite-Adrians. They go out for drinks sometimes and after a few rounds they let girls at the bar guess which one is the real Adrian Ward. He misses those guys. He misses those *girls*.

All he has right now is Zara — and he doesn't even have her. Not really. They kiss every day, but that's just onstage. There was that one time in the studio, but Adrian stopped it, stepped back right when things were heating up. He couldn't get Kerry out of his head. "Hey, Z," he whispers. "Maybe we should run away together at the next break. Ariston would love that, right? It's his sort of thing."

Zara whispers back. "I think I used up my running away on the Aurelia."

"Hey," Adrian says. "Me, too." He didn't even know that was true until it came out of his mouth.

He came here to get away from what happened with Kerry.

With the blond in her red hair, the sweet, scratchy voice, *those thighs.* Kerry, so pretty and not at all famous. The famous ones fall for Adrian, too, but they go back to their actor and director and music-producer boyfriends as soon as the movies wrap. Kerry was different. Adrian called her his Indie Darling, and she liked it. (Most of the time.)

He wishes she were here right now and then wipes the thought clean. Kerry was the one who said she couldn't be seen on his arm — couldn't *just* be Adrian Ward's Girlfriend. Adrian didn't get it. He knows his fans can be intense and his fame can feel like too much, but why should that stop them from being in love? Was that a bargain he made when he started acting — get too big and lose the person you want to be with? He doesn't remember signing that contract.

"Are you okay?" Zara asks.

Now he must be the one looking sickly.

The stage manager calls a break, and Adrian hops off the stage and walks right up to Leopold.

"I'm here to act," he says. "Not just, you know, stand. I was wondering if you have any notes for me." Adrian needs to know there's something he can do to be a better Ariston. He's supposed to be giving the performance of a lifetime. If he can pull that off, it means he didn't come all this way just to avoid an ex-girlfriend.

Leopold waves him away. "Nothing at the moment."

"I just need to know, if there's anything I can be doing . . ."

Leopold takes Adrian by both shoulders. He's stronger than he looks. "Don't worry. The press will be gentle with you. They love you. And the public? They go to sleep at night *hoping* to dream about you. It's Echo I'm worried about." They both look to Zara on the stage. She looks small up there, stranded. "I wish my reputation could protect her, but you must know that casting someone as your love interest is a high-stakes game. She must be perfect. If not . . ."

Adrian knows what he's talking about. It's happened before. Even to famous girls. If his fans think that someone isn't good enough for him, even in a costar capacity, she'll get eviscerated. He's been around long enough to notice that people can be seriously nasty when it comes to actresses.

"Zara is a good actress," Adrian says. And it's true. She gets nervous sometimes, but when she's on, she's very, very good. She blazes through their scenes.

She makes him feel so much.

But Leopold is looking at Zara Evans like she was a

mistake. "This girl has never been in the public eye. Never touched a real stage before. She's never been in love. She's far too innocent."

Adrian claps his hands together. "Right." He turns back down the aisle and strides toward Zara. She helped him once, and it's time to pay that back. Maybe Adrian's not the world's best actor, but there are things he can do to help this production. Whether Leopold knows it or not, he just gave Adrian a brilliant idea.

vi

Zara takes in the long makeup table and the clutter of shoes and bags opposite Cosima's tidy costume racks. The men's dressing room is so much like the women's that Zara feels like she's stepped into a mirror world — everything an inch to the left of where it should be, the colors muted, the smells sharper. Aftershave and deodorant instead of hairspray and flowers.

"Is there a reason you wanted me to see this?" Zara asks Adrian, who led her in with a huge smile and no real explanation.

Then Zara notices something at the end of the long table, and it feels like a reason to stay put.

Carl's bag.

Rich brown leather with brass clasps. It's sitting on a chair right at the end of the makeup table.

Enna's death won't stop bothering her, and she doesn't know how to let it go. Maybe it's easier to worry about Enna's death than it is to worry about Echo, about Leopold. Maybe this is just another way that Zara's paranoid brain is distracting itself. It tells her that this is an opportunity she shouldn't ignore.

We keep our eyes open.

"All right," Adrian says, clapping. He pulls out his phone. Bounces lightly on his feet. "You and I are going to take a picture."

"What?" Zara asks.

Adrian grins at his phone without answering. He seems thoroughly distracted. Would he notice if Zara stuck a hand into Carl's bag?

"You stand over here," Adrian says, waving one of his hands, directing Zara toward the best lighting.

She walks, her steps sticky with self-consciousness. As much as Zara loves standing in front of hundreds of people at a time, cameras are different. They demand little slices of perfection. What happens onstage is beautiful, but it's also messy and breathing and real.

Zara fiddles with the hemline of her shirt. "What's this for?"

Adrian looks so beautiful and sure of himself. "Leopold wants us to do it."

"Did he say why?" Zara asks. She thinks back to his office, the director's body so close to hers. He's famous for pushing his actors.

She shouldn't let it bother her.

Adrian shrugs. "Just a marketing thing. You know. Get your face out there."

Zara snaps back into the present. "He said he didn't want anyone to see me until the gala."

Adrian is getting frustrated now. Which he also expresses by shrugging. "He must have changed his mind."

That sounds like such a small thing, but it makes Zara go incandescent with worry. Why does Leopold want to change the plan now? He must be desperate. She made a little bit of progress in their meeting, but it wasn't enough.

"Wait," Adrian says, hopping next to her, his arm going around her shoulders. It feels like a rash spreading. Adrian holds his arm out, making the muscles on his forearm hop out. "Put your head on the boyfriend shelf," he says.

"The *what*?" Zara asks.

"Right here," he says, patting the smooth place just below his collarbone. Zara laughs, surprising herself with the warm sound.

"Like this?" she asks, tilting her head into place. Adrian's chest rises and falls. The moment gives Zara a forceful shove of déjà vu. This feels the same as taking pictures with every boy she's dated.

He hugs her tighter. "We have to make it look couple-y," he says, the corners of his smile curling as the phone makes the fake shutter snap.

Couple-y. It hits Zara all at once. If Adrian posts this online, two million people will see it by morning.

"Don't put that up," she says. Adrian's fingers rush over the buttons of his phone. He is a hurricane of social media. "No worries," he says. "You look really good." He thrusts the phone out between them and shows Zara — the entire frame is taken up by the two of them, her hair falling in a soft curtain, her T-shirt dipping at the neckline to reveal contours of her chest that she would rather not have two million people staring at. She's wearing her necklace strung with eight keys, not that anyone besides Eli will know what that means. And then she notices Adrian's caption — *Love this Echo.*

"Oh God," she says.

"Why do girls always hate the pictures you take of them?" Adrian asks, already off in his own little realm, muttering and focused on the screen. He pushes a button. "Look. A thousand people liked it already."

A *thousand*? How is that even possible?

Hot panic-prickles spring up on Zara's neck. *Eli.* What will she think when she sees it?

Maybe that Zara doesn't feel anything for her. Maybe that Zara will do anything for Echo — even pretend to date someone famous. Maybe that Zara is desperate for attention, for closeness, for love.

Maybe nothing at all.

They're stuck in the Aurelia all the time. Eli flirts with Zara, but she probably doesn't mean anything by it. Zara's just *there*. As far as Zara knows, what Eli is experiencing could be the same as when Zara leaned her head on Adrian's chest. An almost-feeling. An empty replica.

"You all right?" Adrian asks. "Do you want me to get you something from the snack machine?" Oh God. One picture and now Adrian is being sweet and solicitous and acting like her boyfriend.

Zara almost says no, but she has less than three minutes before they go back onstage. She still needs to look through Carl's bag.

"Yeah. I could use a ginger ale." Her stomach is a mess, so it's not even a lie.

Adrian sends a smile back over his shoulder as he leaves the dressing room. Zara waits a beat. Closes the door. Waits another beat.

Then she crosses the room.

She's not sure she should be doing this. Any of this—staying at the Aurelia, hiding things from Leopold, spending so much time with Eli, pretending that she belongs with Adrian Ward.

The brass clasps come undone with a sharp flick and Zara's hand slides along the opening of the bag. The leather has a thick, musty smell. It gives her the right feeling, so she plunges her hand in. She finds a few loose mints, a change of shoes, a copy of *Murder on the Orient Express*, a wallet, a phone.

What did she expect? A bottle of pills with Enna's name

on it? Secret messages that spell out *I killed her*? Anything, she realizes with embarrassment, as long as she could show Eli. Zara wanted to go back to her triumphant and glowing and all she came up with were purse mints.

The door swings open.

"Thanks for the ginger ale," Zara says, dropping the bag at her feet.

But it's Toby, not Adrian. She didn't think any of the other actors would come in during break — they usually flock to the greenroom.

Toby scolds her with expertly furrowed eyebrows.

"Adrian brought me here," she says. The words are true, but they sound as convincing as a set built out of cardboard.

"Of course," Toby says. "Adrian Ward, with whom you have as much chemistry as a cat and a cold bath."

Zara's relieved. She doesn't want to be Adrian Ward's fake girlfriend. But what if he can see how she feels about Eli just as easily? What if *everyone* can? Toby is old friends with Leopold. He could tell the director about her feelings without having any idea how much damage he might be doing.

"That's not *Adrian's*, is it?" Toby asks, nodding at the puddle of leather sitting at her feet.

"This? I. Ummm." Zara picks the bag up gingerly, pats it back onto the chair. "I was walking by and it fell." The open clasps sit there, calling her a liar.

"Oh, sweetie, sweetie," Toby says with music in his voice. It would comfort Zara if she wasn't so firmly in the clutches of her nerves. "You know I'm going to have to tell Carl about this." He looks at her appraisingly. "Unless . . ." He draws it out, makes her wait. "I want you to come out with me tonight. To the bar. There hasn't been any time for us to bond in this horrid production."

The threat of telling Carl should be enough, but Zara can see another reason to go out with Toby — and it's not to bond. *We keep our eyes open.* Toby knows everything about the Aurelia. He can tell her more about Carl and Enna.

There's only one little problem. "I'm not twenty-one."

Toby sticks a hand to his chest, as if the words have fatally wounded him. "We're going to the Dragon and Bottle! It's a hundred-year-old theater bar. If you're Aurelia, you're family."

vii

Toby remembers the first time he gusted into the Dragon and Bottle on a cold wind, high on his own hopes — and probably other things. He's slowed down a considerable amount since then. Now, instead of sitting at the bar and making friends with every pretty boy who walks in, he takes up one of the dark wood booths near the back.

Zara's face is kissed with shadows from the hurricane lamp. The waitress slaps two beers on the table and gives Toby a hug so handsy that it might be scandalous if they weren't both quite so gay.

Toby nudges one of the pints — unnecessarily frosted on this winter night — toward the nervous girl on the other side of the booth. She looks into it like it she's staring down a dark fate.

"Drink up, my dear," Toby says, polishing off most of his pint in one go. He needs the *oomph* of courage. When he found Zara pawing through Carl's bag, he should have told Carl straightaway.

This isn't part of the script.

"I want to be very clear with you about something," he says, wagging a finger at Zara. It's his best I'm-a-wise-adult-so-you-must-listen gesture. "Carl is my greatest and truest friend. Our friendship is antediluvian. Do you know what that means? When the world flooded, Carl and I were already close." He stops long enough to finish his pint, noting how bitter it always gets toward the end. "If you're digging around in the hopes that you can find something bad about Carl, you're going to be disappointed. He wanted only the best for all of us. Including Enna."

Zara lifts her eyes — large, bitten with dark lashes. "Kestrel told me they hated each other."

"No, no, no," Toby says, feeling his inner pendulum swinging from sober to tipsy. It takes so little these days. "Kestrel has it backwards and upside down. Carl worshipped Enna. It hurt him so much, to see her like that." Toby takes a long draught from Zara's pint since she doesn't seem interested. "*I* hated her sometimes." He shouldn't have admitted that — but oh well. No taking it back now.

The look Zara's giving Toby is a bit strange, so he tries to explain himself. Possibly also a bad idea. "Enna was a cloud — gentle and lovely until she was storming all over you. And then there were the drugs." Toby looks around at the bar, layering it with other nights, other people. "Enna and I used to come in here for a friendly pint or twelve, but she had stopped. Same with the pills. Xanax, Oxy — she used to gobble them like cut-rate candy. And when you go off such things, your tolerance is destroyed. Getting clean can be more dangerous than staying dirty. Enna must have had a little drink, a pill or two to relax — nothing that would have hurt her five years ago — and the way things were, it tipped her over the edge." Another round of drinks appears. Another kiss from the sweetheart waitress. As soon as Toby and Zara are alone again, more words fly out, as if the truth is a glass he's accidentally backhanded off the table. "In the end, what happened to Enna wasn't really her fault."

"What do you mean?" Zara asks.

"Oops," Toby says, burying himself in the second drink. "I've said quite a lot, and I won't say any more."

"Toby." Zara tugs at his name. "Please."

He doesn't want her to look at him with those big, bruising eyes. There's no reason Zara shouldn't know this — in fact, it might save her life. "Enna went off the cliff, but there was someone right behind her. Pushing."

"Who?"

"Leopold," Toby says evenly, to make up for his slight drunkenness. "That man is an art monster."

Zara pushes away the second pint. She's drinking in his words, ignoring the beer. "What does that mean?"

"An art monster is someone who gives his entire life over to creation. Leopold Henneman doesn't give a shit about the people he uses, or the problems he creates."

Zara is silent.

"And he's brilliant," Toby plows on. "We don't think we're supposed to stop brilliant men. We think we're supposed to worship them. We all play our roles *so* well."

Zara's phone goes off in her pocket. She does the thing that all young people do — takes it out without worrying that Toby might feel suddenly invisible. He is just drunk enough to reach out and pluck it from her hands.

"*Come back to the theater,*" Toby reads from the little screen in his most dramatic voice. "*I think I figured something out.* Now who is this from?" He looks all over until he finds what he's looking for.

Zara. Eli.

A smile spreads over his face, to see the names all snuggled up like that. Toby shouldn't love this idea as much as he does — not after what happened with Michael. They used to sit at this very booth, on this very bench, hip to hip, kissing when they thought nobody was paying attention, dropping whispers into each other's ears, drinking each other's Dark and Stormys.

If Leopold has plans for this girl, she shouldn't be foolish enough to fall in love. Not with another girl. Not with anyone.

But Toby doesn't have the heart to stop it.

"Let me tell you a story," he says. Their cramped little booth isn't much of a stage, but it will do in a pinch. "Let's start at the beginning. God created men and women and trees and snakes and it got very nasty for a bit. Skipping forward — I was a grocery boy here in New York. I craved the spotlight. It's an old story. Not quite Faust. Faust's gay cousin. Someone should have slapped me and said 'Go back to your cabbages!' But there are no time machines, and hindsight is a know-it-all prick." Toby holds for a laugh, but Zara is staring at him, solemn. He rushes on. "Leopold gave me a chance. A tiny role. Which turned into a larger role, which became regular employment. Soon enough I was kissing my cabbages good-bye. And that, young lady, is not a euphemism."

Toby runs a hand over the rough wood of the table. He wishes they could stay in the nice part of the story for a while.

"It might have been easier if Leopold thought I was out there kissing every lad in Midtown, turning myself into a scandal. But I did something worse, at least in his eyes. I fell in love." Zara holds herself across the middle, as if those words have stabbed her in a soft place. "Leopold made it clear that this, of all things, was a conflict of interest. I couldn't be 'committed to the Aurelia' if I was always running off to be with someone."

Toby can see Zara's breath rise in her throat and stay there. "Did you break his heart?"

"No," Toby says. "No, I tried to keep him. And it got very nasty for a bit." He wants to skip forward again, but this is the part of the story that Zara has been waiting for. The tragic ending.

"It was a particular time in the history of New York City, and Leopold chased away Michael by telling him — by *lying* — he said that I was sick." Toby won't use the *A* word. He doesn't have to; from the frozen-eyed look on Zara's face, she's got that much figured out. "Apparently Michael wanted to stay, stand by me and all that. He was a good man. It's likely he still is, somewhere. With someone else. Leopold told him that I didn't want to see him anymore. That I . . ." Toby breathes. "That I thought it was his fault."

Zara is staring at him, stricken.

Toby holds out the phone. He's been keeping it hostage this whole time. He's done what he came here to do — told her that Carl is a good man and she has nothing to worry about. Except for Leopold, of course.

"Go," Toby says, and Zara pulls on her coat. If these two girls are really in love, he won't be able to stop them. Nobody will. "Just take my word," he adds. "If you have anything to hide, keep it hidden."

viii

Eli is under the stage.

She's been down here for hours in the cavernous dark, searching for equipment. There's no time left to make this work. Tech is already halfway over, the lighting plan is set, and Leopold hates it.

The trapdoor in the stage above her creaks open. When it lands, the whole stage shudders.

There are Zara's feet, testing the thin rails of the ladder. She's wearing her winter coat, the one that Eli is getting attached to. It has an orange silk lining and a button missing from the cuff.

Zara hits the bottom of the ladder and looks around. "Could you have found a creepier place to meet if you *tried*?"

"The East River," Eli answers without hesitation. "Or the laundry room in my apartment building."

Zara whips to face her, several degrees more feisty than usual. "You shouldn't be down here."

"This is my job," Eli says. "This is where my equipment lives."

Zara shakes her head and corrects herself. "You shouldn't be down here *alone*."

Eli never feels alone when she's making art. It's a conversation she's having. *This is what to care about,* she tells people when she's lighting a scene. *Mira, esto es importante.* And they look where she wants them to look. They sit up and pay attention.

Zara's fingers twist up in her purse strap. "I'm worried about you."

Eli doesn't know how to process that kind of concern. When she lived at home, her parents *seemed* like they were always worried about her — but really they were worried about themselves. How she made them look. How she made things hard on them. She knows because they told her, almost every day, from the age of four or five until she moved out.

Eli is hoping Zara will drop it, but she goes from worry straight to scolding. "People are getting hurt. It's not safe."

"This is New York City!" Eli says, heat kicking up through her chest. "What exactly did you expect?"

"You told me that if I stayed, we would look out for each other. Well, that's what I'm doing."

Eli feels the tap of guilt on her shoulder and brushes it away. "I'm not the only one who takes chances. You were out with Toby. *By yourself.*"

Zara's face goes blunt. "He made me talk to him after he caught me looking through Carl's bag."

Eli has to beat back a smile. This is the girl she saw at auditions — the one who climbed onstage and tossed her feelings around with such force that everyone in the room felt it. Zara's been softening her edges lately. Making herself less. Trying to keep Leopold happy.

She should always be like this.

Eli's thoughts act like a spotlight on her own desires. How much more she wants. The things she hopes might happen between the two of them. Dios. She's being absurd again. This girl has been in love with Ariston her entire life. She dates boys. She's *told* Eli about dating boys. Not one mention of a cute girl in there. Eli would have noticed.

So then why is Zara doing the thing where she twists her fingers up like she's folding an invisible love note? Why are her eyes getting wider, their black centers turning huge?

Oh, right. Because she's an actress. She's in it for the attention, which Eli *keeps giving her.*

"The lighting design," Eli mutters. "It's still not right. Let me show you what I figured out." She goes around making a few last-second adjustments, the blades on her Leatherman flashing. Then she comes back and squares herself up to Zara.

"I need you to say a few lines." Eli's been waiting for this moment for hours and now she's too surly to enjoy it. But the surliness is doing an important job, keeping the rest of her feelings pushed back.

"Okay," Zara says, crossing her arms tight. "What part do you want me to —"

"Whatever," Eli says quickly. "A monologue. Just keep talking."

Zara nods, leaving her chin tipped slightly upward at what Eli is starting to think of as the Echo angle.

Eli gets a flash of that photo, the soft-eyed girl pressed up against Adrian Ward. For two whole seconds she worried that Zara had been messing with her the whole time, that she was just Adrian's girlfriend-in-waiting. But that's not the Zara she knows. That Zara's not even *real*.

Which is a serious problem. No matter who Zara likes or doesn't like, she's the star of a story that's being told by somebody else.

"Take off your coat," Eli says roughly.

Zara sheds it like a winter skin she doesn't need anymore. Eli watches her soft arms move, revealing the rest of her body: the proud sweep of her shoulders, the sweet pinch of her waist.

Zara's breath drops in that trained actor way. Eli's eyes trail downward, following the rise of Zara's breath as it moves from her chest to her stomach, where it pulses. Softly. Zara's voice spreads through the dark space.

"The gods have not given me leave to speak,
And yet I will,
For to leave this unsaid would be a violence
Against all things . . ."

This is Eli's favorite monologue. Whether she hates the play or not, there are some truths in life that can't be denied. This monologue is one of them. The words fill Eli's chest with bright-hot-white feelings.

"I love this part," Eli says. Zara pauses at the end of a line and mouths the words *Me too.*

Eli picks up the piece of equipment that took three hours to find. Zara takes a deep breath and continues.

Eli's hands explode with light.

This, too, is undeniable. The way this fire looks on Zara's face, her shoulders, her collarbones.

The keys that Eli gave her.

All through the basement, Eli has set up reflectors. Their shimmering skin grabs the light and throws it back. Zara looks around with a ferocious sort of wonder. Eli presses the lantern closer to Zara, and her curves take on exhilarating brightness. This is how Eli wants the whole show to look. Close and intimate. Candles and flame.

"Ariston should be the one lighting you," Eli says, trying to make it sound obvious, like she unlocked the answer when she was staring at her notebooks or remembering some talk she had with Roscoe instead of tossing in her bed at night, one hand pressed between her thighs. "Echo's normal life is going to be murky. Blues and charcoal, bruise-colored. And then, when you meet Ariston . . ." She holds up the lantern to illuminate Zara's face.

Pink and gold mingle on her cheeks. Her lips stand out, heart-stopping against her smooth skin.

"It's perfect," Zara says, holding up her fingers. She turns them slowly, drenching them in light. "I love it."

Eli's breath hitches. "There's more."

ix

Down here in the dark, Zara is brave enough to name what she wants. She is waiting for Eli to kiss her.

Instead, she hands Zara a lantern.

"You get to light Ariston," Eli says. "Only fair."

The small lantern is heavier than it looks, with a tiny switch on the bottom. When Zara flicks it on, yellow-white pours everywhere. She already loves the way the light clings to Eli's curls. The way it makes the black part of her eyes shine like searchlights.

"Can I try it out?" Zara asks.

Eli looks down at her not-even-a-little-bit boyish body. "I'm not a good stand-in for Adrian Ward."

"You aren't a stand-in for anyone," Zara says.

Eli looks at her like she's just said something necessary. Something terrifying. Something true.

Zara feels every word, every breath, moving them closer to a moment that already exists. Echo always finds Ariston. They always fall in love.

Zara holds up the lantern, painting Eli's skin with light. Eli holds hers up, and the light doubles. Zara's nerves pound, but so does every good feeling in her body. She asks herself — what does she want right now?

This.

More.

This.

She is breathless as Eli's hand meets her skin.

Her wrist first — then a seamless line up her arm and down her back. Eli's fingers leave an echo-trail. From her back to her stomach, she draws a circle around Zara's waist. Moving up, Eli skirts her breasts, pausing for a second before she moves on to the spread of bones in Zara's chest, the hollow at her neck.

"This is what I want the light to feel like," Eli says.

Zara closes her eyes. She expects Eli's lips — she lives for a moment inside that hope.

"*Now* look," Eli whispers.

When she opens her eyes, her skin is filled with white fire. Eli is holding the lantern so close that it looks like Zara is lit from the inside. Eli touches Zara's forearm with one careful finger. "This is what I want," she says. "For Echo."

Zara stands there, so bound up in waiting to be kissed that she forgets to blink. Forgets to breathe.

There's a final half step forward. A trade of breath, a tilting of lips.

Fear slides into the paper-thin space between them. Zara will ruin this just by having it. The world isn't going to let her keep Eli. It isn't going to stop Leopold from taking them apart.

But their lips meet, just the same.

Eli kisses her, one hand holding the lantern between their bodies so they won't crush glass into their skin. Her other hand touches Zara's temple, sweeping Zara's hair back as their mouths rush forward. Eli kisses with a softness that barely hides how strong she is. Zara pushes back against her, a slow tide.

When she's done this before, it's been mouths and hands and movement and breath. The blocking feels different this time, and it's more than just blocking — a new feeling that floods in, filling every space.

Eli shifts and puts down the lantern. Zara waits with her eyes closed, trusting that Eli will come back. Her fingers tremble slightly. She feels them stirring the air of the Aurelia.

This is Echo, she thinks. *This is exactly like Echo.* The smile that comes to her lips turns sharp. Zara promised herself that she would be able to feel this without putting either of them in danger.

But this is the story — this has always been the story.

X

The next day at rehearsal, Zara touches everything. She walks through the house, skimming her fingers along the backs of the seats, row after row, red so deep and soft that it makes her blush. The stage manager tells her to sit down, which makes her feel like a scolded child. Zara settles into the second row, perched at the edge of the aisle. She looks over her script for act 4, scene 2, but she can't focus. Her skin is shimmering with everything it felt last night. Her lips are fully awake.

Her body is a walking memory.

When she climbs onstage, what happened is right beneath her feet. Down there in the dark. Eli is up in the lighting booth running through the show with her new board op, and Zara is onstage, about to rehearse yet another love scene with Adrian Ward. The lantern-lit kiss has become one of the stories of the Aurelia, built up like the layers of paint and dust.

She wonders how many love stories are buried in this theater. How many secrets.

"Where are you?" Leopold asks from his spot in the front row.

Zara's head snaps up. She didn't even realize she was staring at her shoes.

"I'm ready," she says.

"Oh good," Leopold says in a voice ballooning with pretend delight. "Did you hear that, everyone? Zara Evans is ready. In that case, we can begin."

Adrian tries to sneak her a smile. He's always doing that — being nice to her when Leopold is at his worst. But Zara gets the feeling that Adrian will never know how bad Leopold can truly be. He gets the stage-ready version that the rest of the world sees. Zara is learning — from Toby and from Meg and from Enna, from Leopold himself — who the director is behind the curtain.

She trusted Leopold Henneman so easily a few months ago. She can't decide who she hates more — that old version of herself who wanted to stay up late into the night, impressing him? Or Leopold, staring at her now with a flinch of pain as

214

she says her lines, letting her know that she'll never be good enough?

"Once I had everything, and it felt like nothing," Zara says. *"Now I have nothing, and I am filled."*

"Lovely," Leopold says.

She can see it, how he flicks from bored to furious, how he calls her brilliant and then breaks her down. He keeps changing the story so she won't know what to believe — except for him. The sick part is, his compliment still made her glow for a second.

But not half as brightly as she burned last night.

Zara thought it would be easy, once she and Eli kissed. That they would slide into being together. That's how it worked for Echo and Ariston. They met, they kissed, they became inseparable.

When Eli and Zara left the theater at two in the morning, Zara kept a safe distance between them. No twined hands, no sides pressed together. What if someone was working late and saw them? What if one of the crew members told Leopold, not knowing what he might do?

Adrian finishes a monologue and Leopold twitches his hands, signaling Zara and Adrian to move closer together. They both jump to match his urgency, and she wonders if she's the only one who feels like a puppet. "Our play has the potential to be immortal or forgettable," Leopold says, getting up, mounting the rehearsal stairs, moving in close. "In the end, whether the audience believes in this love story lies with you." He circles Zara like he is a red pen and she is a word out of place. "You have shown us that you are capable of emotion. Feeling, however, is not enough. We need explosive potential behind each moment, danger in each breath."

Danger? Zara feels it every time she thinks about what happened to Roscoe and Enna. And a different kind, every time she stands too close to Eli.

Leopold slips behind Zara, his hand spanning the distance between her shoulder blades. He pushes her toward Adrian, until every part of her is crowded against him. Adrian's whole body feels like an apology. She can't tell if he's sorry that Leopold is pushing her into him, or sorry for liking it.

Leopold's voice is a thick whisper. "This is what we need, in the moments you are standing together."

"Kiss/kill," Meg adds from down in the orchestra pit.

"What's *kiss/kill?*" Adrian asks. He sounds eager to learn, and again Zara remembers her old, innocent self.

Leopold chuckles. "We use such different words in the theater, I know. Kiss/kill is the distance we use to show intensity." Leopold prods Zara in the back again, forcing her even closer to Adrian. "So close, the characters seem to have only two courses of action. They might kiss, or they might kill each other."

Leopold pushes Zara farther; every contour of Adrian's body is obvious now. Standing this close to him is part of the blocking, has always been part of the blocking, but the way that Leopold pushes her makes anger slide through Zara, burning at the back of her throat.

She doesn't step away. If two deaths aren't enough to make

216

her walk away from this role, and being kept away from Eli isn't enough, being shoved up against Adrian Ward is definitely not enough.

"Still wrong," Leopold says, studying their bodies like he's hanging a picture frame and it's just a fraction off. He adjusts her — a flurry of small touches — and she goes sickly hot everywhere his hand meets her skin.

"Come to my office tonight, before the gala," Leopold whispers to both of them, as if he doesn't want the rest of the company to know how much they're embarrassing themselves.

"Okay," Adrian says. "No problem. Right, Z?"

He tries to smile at her again.

Zara can't smile in return — not even a quick, pretend tug of the muscles. She can't say *no problem* back to Adrian. Leopold is the biggest problem she can imagine right now.

217

xi

Barrett calls himself the God of All Props, but sometimes he feels like the God of Broken Things.

He's still at work even though everyone else is running off to get ready for the gala. He's been here all day! He is only a tiny bit hungover! *Fantastic,* Barrett thinks. He should be given a trophy. Which he would then promptly lose in Storage Room Two.

It is a kingdom of crap.

"Have you found those chairs?" he calls to one of his assistants. Aubrey? Audra? One of those *A* names.

"Over here," she says from about half a mile away. She is knee-deep in furniture. He drinks in the sight of her in tight jeans, gray T-shirt, and dark ponytail, which swishes as she walks. When Barrett came to New York and hunted down Leopold to ask for a job, this was not the one he envisioned, but it has its benefits.

"Chairs!" he says, so loudly that the sound rings in the huge space.

Leopold has demanded a completely new set for act 1. He has rejected fourteen different types of chairs already. If Barrett were anyone else, he would have been fired over the chairs.

The girl bends down to retrieve an oak Craftsman. "What do you think of these?" Barrett can vaguely tell that there are more of them in the pile — maybe a whole set.

"Sure," he says, not really caring.

He settles down in an armchair covered in seventies avocado upholstery and watches as the girl power-sands and stains and polishes. They're not really supposed to do that sort of work in here — ventilation issues — but Barrett is in charge, isn't he? He hums in appreciation of the girl and her work. He, personally, has decided that he won't be working much until he gets a better job. The one his father should have given him in the first place.

In the meantime, he is determined to enjoy being the God of Broken Things. And Audrey or Aubrey is part of that. He's been too busy to talk to her yet, to find out what keeps her up late at night, thrashing with disappointment, what makes her sad to the point of disbelief. But as soon as he does, he will know just what to say. He is very good at broken girls.

"Have you ever blackmailed someone, Aubrey?" he asks, taking a stab at her name.

"It's *Abigail*," she says.

"That is so sweet." He runs a finger along a seam in the chair until he finds a hole. He plunges deep into the stuffing. "What a sweet name."

"Of course I haven't blackmailed anyone," she says, narrowing her eyes as she snaps a chair leg into place.

Barrett sighs. "It sounds like it would be fun, though, doesn't it?" He knows the truth, of course. Blackmail is exhausting. Soon the chairs are ready, and after a quick inspection, Barrett tells the girl—what was her name again?—that she can leave.

Leopold Henneman is on the floor of his office, imagining ways to die.

The fake gun has been held to his temple and inserted into his mouth, touching the roof. He has toyed with various knives. And then there are the many ways to asphyxiate. Leopold has held his breath, testing the limits of his mortality with the same calm as when he thinks about placing an actor for a soliloquy.

Meg opens the door and looks down at him.

"Vision?" she asks.

"No," he says, setting a hand to his temple. "But I had one earlier today, and it's still with me."

"Here," Meg says, holding out a small orange prescription vial. "You forgot to refill this."

Leopold is terrible at keeping track of his prescriptions, even though sometimes it feels like they are the only things keeping him human. His doctor, who does not believe in visions, nonetheless prescribed him something for the pain.

The little orange vial of Oxycontin is mostly hidden in Meg's hand as she taps out a pill onto her palm.

"You're an angel," Leopold says.

Meg's eyebrows lift slightly.

She takes the chair nearest to him as he lifts his head to swallow. He reclines, the back of his head dull against the carpet. He has spent so much of his life looking at Meg, but this is a new angle. It casts her in sharp absurdity, a Picasso — her fine arched nose and tart pink lips entirely in the wrong place. It reminds Leopold that the loveliness of her face will unravel soon enough.

Art is the one thing that lasts.

"Do you want me to help you up?" Meg asks. "Adrian Ward and Zara Evans are waiting outside."

"God, I told them to come here," Leopold says. "Private meetings, you know. To help her along." He climbs up from the floor as Meg places the weapons back in their drawers. It's easier not to think about them when he has the drug in his system. It is already starting to settle into his limbs, spreading looseness through his mind.

By the time Adrian and Zara come into the office, Leopold is as close as he ever comes to feeling content.

Adrian claps his hands to prove his readiness. "What did you want us to practice?"

"Oh, these meetings aren't a strict rehearsal," Leopold says. "More . . . inspiration."

Zara winces. It does not escape his notice that his lead actress hasn't been entirely delighted with his methods Leopold has chosen, after a great deal of work and effort and consideration, not to give a fuck.

This is how he gets results. And results are what matter. Coddling people has never resulted in a piece of great art. Letting everyone meander toward the point has never helped anyone find truth.

Discomfort. Pressure. A touch of madness.

These are what create perfect moments. And Leopold is in the business of perfection.

"Don't worry," he says. "I know you have to prepare for the gala tonight. I won't keep you long." He beckons to Meg. "They seemed to be having trouble with the idea of kiss/kill earlier. Shall we show them?"

Meg purses her lips. Leopold loves this — the moment when she resists. He loves watching as she agrees, bit by bit, that he has made the right decision. She slides across the small room, into Leopold's space. He draws her close, wrapping his arms around her with a stunning ease. The danger that

Leopold was talking about is there, passing back and forth between them, an electrical charge.

"Like this," Leopold says, breathing the words onto Meg's neck. "In the scene at the market. When you are making your home together. On Ariston's bed. As you fight. As you make love. As you wait for the soldiers to come. I want you no farther apart than this."

Zara and Adrian watch. They are pinned to the picture in front of them, unable to speak.

That is exactly what Leopold wants.

That is perfect.

224

xiii

Zara waits as Kestrel tests the heat from a flatiron with her finger. She sways in front of her vanity mirror, her firecracker-red dressing gown swishing against her thighs. Zara begged for help getting ready for the gala and then immediately started to regret it. What if Kestrel sabotages her first public appearance as Echo? Would she go that far — would she try to get rid of Zara if she had the chance?

"I'm so glad we're doing this," Kestrel says with an unnatural glow to her smile. Too many white strips.

She puts Zara in the makeup chair and goes to work with an array of steel instruments in tiny sizes. Zara knows what Eli would call them: *dollhouse furniture from hell.*

She checks her phone.

There are the messages from her parents. They ask the same things over and over again. *How is rehearsal? How is the city? Are your boots warm enough? Do you want us to come in for a night?* She sends them just enough of a response to let them know she's not dead, that she's doing fine.

That, no — she doesn't want them to visit.

"So, are you going to the gala *with* anyone?" Kestrel asks, her voice like dragging string in front of a kitten. Zara gets the message and puts her phone down. "Adrian, perhaps?"

"No," Zara says. She's spent enough time pressed against Adrian today. She thinks of Meg and Leopold trapped in their kiss/kill moment, and her mind goes slippery with discomfort.

"Aren't you curious if *I'm* going with anyone?" Kestrel asks as she swipes something cold onto Zara's eyelids.

"Oh," Zara says, picking up her cue. "Do you have a date?" She hopes that Kestrel has someone to go with. Someone to make her happy, after the disappointment of losing Echo. "Who is it?"

Kestrel is swaying, sending her robe back and forth with an electric shimmer. "I can't tell. It's a secret."

Zara's phone buzzes in her pocket. Her palms are lined with sudden damp, heart doing the clichéd thing that hearts do. Zara knows from movement classes that bodies aren't natural-born liars. And right now, her body is telling one simple truth.

She's been waiting to hear from Eli.

Zara waits as Kestrel curls her eyelashes and dabs on a clear gel, then layers it with matte red lipstick. She touches a cold spot of perfume to Zara's neck. As soon as Kestrel breaks for the walk-in closet, Zara goes for her phone.

It's Leopold. Zara's heart pauses for a single, painful second.

You're going to be glorious tonight, my dear.

Even though it's just a text, she can hear his voice, the way it caresses the words. He's decided to be pleasant with her tonight. Doting, even. She's starting to hate that more than the moments when he's cruel.

Another message from Leopold.

Where are you?

Zara doesn't want him to know. It's ridiculous — she's staying at Kestrel's, he's perfectly aware of that. It's not like she can hide from him. But she wants to. Her fingers rattle over the buttons as she texts back.

I'm getting ready.

She shoves the phone under her leg, but it goes off again, shuddering into her skin. She looks down. She lights up.

It's Eli.

Goddamn gala.

Zara rushes to respond.

I was afraid you weren't coming.

From inside the closet comes muffled shouting. "Do you like A-lines?" Kestrel asks. "Forget it. How do you feel about off-the-shoulder?"

Another text from Eli.

Leopold likes the lanterns slightly more than he hates the lanterns. Must bathe in champagne to celebrate.

Part of Zara is relieved — she wants Eli to be there tonight. Part of her is confused — why is Eli acting like nothing happened, like they've simply skipped back in time to before they kissed?

Zara's phone buzzes again.

Do you think I'll need a dress?

I'm not in charge of these things but probably yes.

Insert swearing here.

Zara lets out a small breath that should be a laugh. Talking with Eli like this feels good.

But Zara wants more.

When Kestrel emerges from the closet, any worries that Zara had about sabotage are gone. The dress Kestrel holds up is stunning — white silk, sheer at the shoulders, luscious and broad at the hips. It even looks like it might fit. "What do you think?" Kestrel asks, studying it with a critical eye.

Zara is in love.

People expect her not to care about pretty things. *She's* not beautiful — she can hear Leopold, telling her that in no uncertain terms — but Zara has always been lit up by pretty words, pretty art, pretty dresses. Her mind skims back to Eli.

Pretty girls.

"Go," Kestrel says, feeding off Zara's spike in happiness, pushing the dress into her hands. "Try it on."

Zara drapes the silk over her arm like a miniature waterfall. She heads for Kestrel's bathroom — because of course, Kestrel's room has an en suite bathroom. The tile is cold on her feet as she slips off her jeans and undoes the button-down that Kestrel insisted on so Zara's makeup wouldn't smudge. She pulls on the dress — the fabric is smooth, irresistible. It sits on Zara like a better version of her own skin.

She looks at herself in the mirror.

What would her parents think of this girl? She has the same straight nose as their Zara, the same complexion. But her lips spring up like roses, bright red, and her cheeks are perfectly ripe. The white dress sings the praises of her hips, her stomach, her chest — the parts of her body that she usually hides. Zara touches the snow-colored fabric around her middle. She can't hide anything now. She doesn't want to.

"Thank you," she calls out to Kestrel. "The dress is perfect."

No answer. Kestrel must be changing.

Zara opens the camera on her phone, takes a quick picture, and sends it to her parents. She wants them to see her like this. She wants them to understand. She doesn't want to put her phone back on the floor with her jeans, so she looks for a spot in the medicine cabinet to set it down.

Something tugs at her vision. Something hiding in plain sight, half-covered on one of the shelves. In the midst of all that lavender and pink and mint green, it's easy to pick out a single bright-orange prescription bottle.

Xanax.

Zara grabs the bottle and it gives a rattle. She pops the lid; there's a handful of pills at the bottom, small powder-blue ovals. She can hear Toby's voice.

Xanax, Oxy — she used to gobble them like cut-rate candy.

Enna was an addict. There's no reason to think that her death was anything other than a simple overdose. Still, Zara is already doing the math. The prescription count printed on the label is twenty. How many are missing? Five? That can't be enough to kill a person — right?

She's still holding the bottle when Kestrel breezes in.

"Ugh. Brilliant." Kestrel grabs the bottle in a stranglehold. "I know I'm supposed to enjoy these soirees," she says, twitching a pill onto her palm, "but they make me très stressed. It was better when Mama would come back from Paris or wherever and we would go together. Now she says that I can't be seen that way. It's *babyish*. And going with a secret date is sort of like going with no date at all, since you can barely be seen together. Still, it's better than nothing, right?" The words pinch at Zara in ways that Kestrel can't possibly understand. "Anyway, bottoms up."

Kestrel's smile is a flashbulb — bright, then gone. She tips her head back and dry-swallows the pill.

Zara steps into the Plaza. A man rushes to take her coat. She follows Kestrel's lead, pretending she's done this a hundred times before, but Zara is sure that something in her eyes, the twitchy corners of her smile as the coat-check man calls her *gorgeous,* gives her away.

She can't really be here.

There is nothing *real* about this.

The grand ballroom at the Plaza is impressive, classical, edged with gilt. It looks like it was ripped out of a little girl's dream and set down gently in the heart of New York. But it's not just the room — it's the people staring at Zara. Yelling, *Over here, Echo!* Taking her picture as she works against a well-trained impulse to hold herself tight across the stomach.

It's the thought of Eli, out there somewhere. Eli, who kissed her.

When the crowd parts, Zara thinks it will be Eli waiting for her, but it's not, of course. It's Leopold, smiling broadly. It feels like he's showing her what kind of smile he expects her to have on her own face all night. He hooks his arm through hers, and a little bit of the brightness in Zara's vision fades, even though the room is studded by the flashes of photographers.

The gala is like rich food — after a few bites, it's too much. At nine thirty, Zara loves it. By eleven thirty, her picture has been taken roughly ten thousand times. Her smile muscles are threatening to give out. Her sore feet claw for attention.

And there are other disappointments. Zara had thought that by this part of the production, she would be surrounded by new friends. But as she looks around the room, she feels further away from everyone than she did on the day of the read-through.

Meg is detached from Leopold for once, looking elegant but forgettable in a long black dress. Barrett oozes from group to group, flirting with every woman he can find. Carl is stone-faced, and Toby is drunk. Enna's understudy makes the rounds, smiling at everyone like this is just another production — like the woman she replaced didn't die only a few weeks ago. Kestrel moves around the room in an endless circle. No sign of her secret date. Zara can't stop thinking about the Xanax in the bathroom. She'll tell Eli about it — if Eli ever shows up.

Zara can't even escape to look for her. Leopold has been steering her around by the elbow all night.

Everything is wrong.

And the champagne isn't helping.

"Have another," Leopold says with a goading smile as the tray in the waiter's hand passes in a circle. Zara has already downed two glasses — more than she's had in her entire life.

She doesn't know why Leopold wants her to drink. Zara feels his attention like a hand at her throat. She has to do what he wants or he'll take Echo away. He'll hurt her career. He'll make Eli disappear. Like he did with Michael and Toby.

"This is my Echo," Leopold tells yet another group of patrons. His vaguely European accent is stronger than usual. Some days it's as thin as tissue paper.

"She's utterly charming," says a woman in a silver gown, as if Zara had said something and wasn't just standing there, hanging on Leopold's arm.

"Yes, she's a breath of fresh air," an old man adds as he openly stares at her body.

In the thick of rehearsal, Zara almost managed to forget that there will be audiences soon. They'll be there at previews, which Leopold says are just glorified rehearsals, but people pay money to see them. Those people will look at Zara however they want. After they've heard so much about the play and bought a three-hundred-dollar ticket, they'll feel like they own a little piece of her.

"Wait until you see the big reveal," Leopold says to the patrons. The champagne is harsh in Zara's throat. Maybe she's had too much. She coughs, holding the glass away from her. This is the first she's heard of a *big reveal.* "I'd say it's going to be brilliant, but that's for you to judge."

People are laughing, and the sound swirls in Zara's head. Leopold hands her another champagne flute. The crystal is breakable. It will shatter in her palm if she clutches it too tightly. "You know who's brilliant?" Zara asks. "The lighting designer."

She didn't mean to say that. The champagne did it for her.

"Of course," Leopold says. "Roscoe." He hangs his head down. He is very good at looking mournful.

"No," Zara says. "I mean, yes. But I was talking about the *new* designer. Roscoe's assistant. Eli Vasquez."

She *really* shouldn't have said that. But she hates that nobody knows about Eli. Zara almost tells everyone about the lanterns, how beautiful they're going to be. But the lanterns haven't made an appearance at rehearsal yet. How would she know about them if she hadn't been spending time with Eli, under the stage, alone?

Leopold is looking at her strangely now.

If she says one more word about Eli, Leopold will see the truth. She doesn't know how he hasn't seen it already — if he could tell she's never been in love, wouldn't he be able to tell that she is now? Because she can't stop falling in love with Eli, even when they're not in the same room. Even when Leopold

234

is in the room, watching her carefully. Feeding her drink after drink.

The woman in the silver dress turns to Leopold, puts on a kittenish smile, and says, "People have been saying that these accidents have something to do with a curse on the Aurelia. It's so dark and delightful." Zara watched Roscoe die. She doesn't know if she would describe it as *delightful*. "Is it true that the theater is cursed?"

That is a fantastic question.

"It's true that people say so," Leopold tells the small crowd in his most charming and enigmatic tone. "And what people say has a way of becoming true."

"Mmmmmm," the woman says, as if she's savoring Leopold's wisdom. The men in the circle nod like they know just what he means.

Zara wants to break free. She wants to find Eli and kiss her for an hour without stopping, then tell her the story of every moment they've been apart.

Leopold eases his link with Zara's arm, somehow making it look as if *she's* been the one holding on to *him* all night. "If you'll excuse me, I should see to our leading man." Zara sends a hunting look through the crowd, but Adrian is nowhere to be seen. Apparently he doesn't have to be paraded around like this.

Leopold walks away. He gives Zara one more glance over his shoulder, as if he wants to be sure of where he left her. He blows her a kiss — not for the onlookers — a small, private tap of fingers to lips. Another test passed. Another lesson learned. She has a hold on one corner of the truth, and she's peeling it back. Leopold loves her as long as she does whatever he wants. As long as she's willing to be whoever he wants.

You are not Zara Evans.

Her hand goes, absentmindedly, to the necklace of keys. Kestrel tried to tell her that it didn't match the dress.

Zara disagreed.

Eli makes her feel more like herself and more like Echo at the same time. How is that possible?

Zara makes one full turn of the room. No Eli. She checks her phone. It's devoid of messages.

She sends a quick one of her own.

I'm in the ballroom wearing white and drinking too much. Find me.

That was wrong. She shouldn't have sent that text. They can't be seen in front of all these people, together. In front of Leopold. But Zara can't stay away from Eli all night. It's not physically possible.

A hand comes down on Zara's arm, and for a second she thinks that she summoned Eli just by thinking about her. But the hand is wrong — large and bony. Too much sweat in the canyons of the palm.

Zara looks up and finds Carl staring.

For a second, the world tilts, and she remembers the force of his body hovering on top of hers. His eyes are as blue as a painfully bright sky.

"We need to talk."

XV

Carl tries to edge Zara away from the crowd.

The girl doesn't budge. "You want to talk to me? Now?" Zara shakes her head. The motions are larger than necessary, as if she's playing to a house of a thousand instead of an audi-ence of one.

Carl knows what that means. She's gotten herself drunk.

He lowers his voice. "This is about Toby."

He still can't believe that his good-hearted friend took Zara to the Dragon and Bottle. It was a poor choice. But then, Toby has never been known for his wonderful decision making.

Zara stands on her tiptoes, scouring the ballroom. "I'm looking for someone. Excuse me." She strides away, and Carl's first impulse is to grab her, to keep her with him until he can explain a few important things. But he doesn't dare touch this girl.

Instead, he follows at a close distance. "Please. This will only take a minute."

She looks back at him, her face as transparent as window glass. Even when she isn't tipsy, her emotions have a way of showing through. It's what makes her a fine actress. At least, when she's in control of herself.

He hopes, for a fleeting moment, that her career survives this production.

That *she* survives.

"Please," he says, his voice thinning. "We need to speak."

Zara lets Carl steer her toward the back of the room. Even here, the sounds of mingling are thick, tangled, hard to talk over.

"You need to stay focused on the play right now," Carl says.

"What is that supposed to mean?" Zara asks, her amber eyes narrowed.

"Whatever Toby said to you," Carl says, "forget it. He's an old drunk."

"He told me he was your best friend," Zara says.

"Who better than a best friend to recognize an old drunk?" Carl fires back.

Zara has the glare of truth about her tonight. Carl knows that truth can be a powerful thing, but only if people believe in it. They believe in lies just as often. It all comes down to presentation.

"Toby thinks that you're worried about what happened to Enna," Carl says in his most reasonable and reassuring tone. "It's a simple fact of life. We live at the theater. Some of us die here. Ask Cosima if you don't believe me."

Zara crosses her arms, turning from a polished actress into a teenager in one swift motion. He wonders if she has any idea how young she truly is.

"So you think what happened to Enna was *normal?*" Zara asks.

Carl breathes carefully. Otherwise he will stop being able to speak. He is partly to blame for the girl being here in the first place. He needs to explain this. He owes her that much.

When he sits down in the nearest chair, the glasses on the table bump and resettle with a shiver of crystal. "Leopold does *unpleasant* things to his actresses."

"What does that mean?" she asks in a numb voice, a close cousin to a whisper. Carl knows all the variations on whispering. He knows all the ways to speak, and what they mean. He has been an actor for so many years. It should mean that he reads people perfectly.

But he failed when it meant the most.

"When we met, Enna and I were so young," Carl says. "We were in love, and playing two people in love. You can imagine Leopold enjoyed that. He couldn't have orchestrated it better himself. But then a few seasons later, he cast Enna in the role of a ruined woman. And she became one. There were drugs. And men. Enna didn't hide her indiscretions. In fact, she shouted them from the rooftops." Carl's heartbeat takes over his body, drowns out the crowd. "For years, I didn't know the truth. I had no idea where it started."

Zara sits down next to him, and it's like everyone else in the ballroom vanishes. He's left alone with a story that feels impossible to tell, and a girl who needs to hear it. "Our happiness no longer suited Leopold. He forced her to sleep with him, did she tell you that?"

Zara tries to blink away confusion, then pain.

Carl is spitting the words now. "He did degrading things to her, all in the name of the play. He was her director. He told her it was the only way to make her believable in the role."

"She could have told someone," Zara says, but she doesn't sound as if she's convinced herself. Leopold was so famous, so well loved. His productions were intense and beautiful, and if he was known for being unorthodox with his actors, well, that was what they'd signed up for, wasn't it? That was the price of genius.

Who would Enna have told?

Who would have believed her if she cried rape?

Carl might have — he needs to believe that he would have — but Enna's ability to trust had already been destroyed.

240

She chose alcohol and pills as her comforts. Carl only learned all of this later, much later.

From Meg.

"Why did she keep coming back to the Aurelia?" Zara asks. She is trapped in this terrible story with him. It's a tiny room with no doors and no windows, a room that there is no real escaping from. "Why did *you*?"

"I didn't know. Not for the longest time. As for Enna . . . she didn't want to stop acting, and Leopold was one of the only directors who would still work with her once her . . . reputation spread."

Zara is shaking and shaking her head, as if that could make it untrue.

"Now he's pushing you," Carl whispers, the words a rumble in his chest. "And I never wanted that. But I had to save her. I had to."

Zara swallows. It sounds dry and painful. "Save Enna?"

"No," Carl says. "It was too late for that. It was like . . . she died years ago. I had to stop him from doing the same things to Kestrel."

Carl is the closest that Kestrel has to a father. He watched her grow up. Took her to plays and dinners, bought her presents. He nursed her through her first heartbreak. There was no way he was letting Leopold have her.

Carl watches as understanding comes over Zara in a fuzzy patchwork. "You . . . You're the one who stopped Kestrel from being cast as Echo."

And suddenly the rest of the world rages at full volume,

because they're no longer alone. Kestrel has circled all the way around the room and come over to see them. She hovers behind Zara, who said that last stupid sentence without knowing Kestrel was right there.

Her dress is a blaze of blue. She's gotten too thin. Carl can see her bones, like they're trying to cut their way out through her skin. "I thought it was so nice to see you two talking," she says in a shaky voice.

And then the screaming starts.

"Not here," Carl says. But Kestrel's mouth is stretched out, and her voice is strong. She has terrible nerves. Ever since she was a girl and her parents left for the first time of many, trusting her to the care of their ridiculous friends, she's had these fits. Carl grabs her by the upper arm. "Sweetie, please. Everyone is watching." The journalists gather, flies around a sticky-sweet spill. He doesn't want them spreading stories about her in the morning. "Talk to me," Carl says. "Just talk."

Kestrel nods, and breathes, and it's like watching a self pour back into her body. "I read for Echo five times. Leopold didn't want me. Something was wrong. I knew it. I knew I was born for that role. Mama says so. *Everyone says so.*"

Carl nods with sympathy as he pats her back. He hates what he did. But he did it to keep Kestrel safe from a man who would force himself on her. A man who would happily abuse her and then say he was only serving a higher purpose, his *art*. Carl hates what he did, but he isn't sorry. He's done much worse things to keep the people he loves from misery.

Kestrel gives him a murderous look, but Carl knows that it

242

will blow over. It has to. If it doesn't, he has nothing left. "You were the person I trusted," Kestrel says. She turns away, the razors of her shoulder blades moving up as she takes a breath. Holds it.

"Kestrel," Carl says. "Sweetie."

She picks up a glass from the nearest table. Zara tries to grab her, but Kestrel has gone white-hot, untouchable.

The glass flies.

xvi

She did *what?*"

Adrian is behind the little stage at one end of the ballroom, listening to the stagehands argue.

"Kestrel tried to take him out! Tumbler to the face!" one of them says, happy and merciless, like he's talking about reality TV. (Adrian has nightmares about reality TV—the shark-infested waters that famous people are tossed into when everyone else is done with them.)

"Yeah, but she missed," said another stagehand.

"Awwww," says the first one, like he's seriously disappointed.

Leopold asked Adrian to wait backstage. He did it with these apologies in his voice, like that would be a problem for Adrian, but Adrian likes it better back here. There are always people at parties who want to touch him, take pictures with him. Sometimes he loves it and sometimes it's exhausting, and both of those reactions feel wrong. Smarmy or ungrateful. Take your pick.

Leopold walks in through the side door. Adrian can sense one of his hugs coming on. He steps away before it can happen. There's always too much body heat and cologne involved.

"My boy, my boy," Leopold says. "Tonight we make the public believe in Echo and Ariston's love."

"I thought this was just about shmoozing," Adrian says with a nervous laugh.

"The photograph you posted online got people quite excited," Leopold says, and Adrian gets to bask in the fact that he did something right. (He hasn't basked in a while. It feels good.) But then Leopold's arm is around him and he's using his most urgent director voice. "You need to take things to the next logical step."

"There is no next step," Adrian says. "It was a picture. To make people excited about Zara. As Echo."

"We want them excited about the two of you together," Leopold says. And he whispers a plan into Adrian's ear.

Adrian pulls away, and he can feel the depths of his frown.

245

He was the one who wanted to tell Zara to go along with anything, but now he's not so sure. "Don't we want the audience to
stay focused on the play? How good it is?" Adrian came here
to impress people with his acting, not his ability to post a picture online and get hundreds of thousands of hits.

"Your Ariston, while perfectly adequate," Leopold says, "is
not enough to maintain this illusion. Not without a little help."

Adrian sighs and attacks his hair with a nervous hand.
"What about Zara? Does she want to do this? I mean, is she
ready?"

"The girl is more than ready," Leopold says. "She's . . .
eager."

Adrian thinks of Kerry, on the patio of the tiny apartment
she could barely afford, swigging blueberry lemonade straight
from the bottle, hollowing out avocados to make guacamole.
She won't know that he's doing this for the play, for the audience, for the marketing. She'll only see him acting, and she'll
think it's true, because that's the one thing Adrian is good at.
Utterly convincing.

And then he'll lose Kerry.

(Really lose her.)

Maybe that's good, though. Maybe that's exactly what he
needs so he can shove this whole thing into the past and get
on with life. Adrian rolls his shoulders and says, "Let's do this."

Leopold claps him on the back and takes the stage before
Adrian can rethink.

The lights in the ballroom dim, and the noise level goes

from shout-to-be-heard to a hushed whisper. "You are here tonight because you want to fall in love," Leopold says. He has a decent voice — not an actor's voice, but the kind that you could imagine telling a story around a campfire. "Perhaps you used to slip in and out of love easily, when you were younger. Perhaps some of you are finding love tonight." There are a few stray laughs. "I think you've waited long enough to see what true love looks like."

Leopold waves his hand toward the wings, and Adrian strides out onto the little stage. This feels like practice for the Aurelia — but it's also different, because during the play Adrian won't be able to see the audience. The lights will drown them out.

Tonight, he can see everyone.

"Here is your Ariston," Leopold says. "A young man who comes to us from a kingdom of plenty, which we've been battling for ages. I'm speaking, of course, about California." The audience laughs, full-on. Adrian realizes he loves this part. When he sneaks into movie theaters in disguise, people are always on their phones or muttering to each other or making out, regardless of what he's doing on the screen. This is better. This is *more*.

Adrian gives a bow, and the audience cheers.

"And here," Leopold says, "is your early Christmas present." He shades his eyes and peers out at the ballroom. "Echo? Where are you, my dear?"

A gasp rises as a little spotlight goes hunting through the

crowd. It finds Zara standing alone near the entrance on the far side of the room. Even from this far away, Adrian can see that Zara looks surprised.

She really is a good actress.

She works her way through the crowd, and Adrian watches her along with everyone else. He can't stop thinking about what Leopold said. (*She's eager.*) The room narrows down from hundreds of people to just Zara. Her dress is white. Her hair is loose. Her cheeks shine like moons.

She looks beautiful.

And nervous. When she arrives onstage, Leopold pulls her in for a kiss on the cheek and Zara goes stiff. When she takes her place at Adrian's side, he can feel her trembling where their arms almost touch. It reminds him of the first time he ever kissed a girl. He was eleven. It was for a movie, and he hated the idea that his first kiss would be fake. So he asked the actress, who was thirteen and a half, to practice with him in the studio lot. She pushed him against one of those little carts and his lips went numb, totally confused. Then her tongue was in his mouth.

He remembers how scared he was. And how grateful that she took the lead.

"Hey," he whispers to Zara. "You okay?"

She gives a blinking nod. It feels like some kind of Morse code that Adrian can't figure out. He puts an arm around her and the crowd cheers. Leopold is hovering behind them. Waiting.

It only takes one perfectly choreographed turn, and then

Adrian is kissing Zara. Her mouth is flat, which throws him off. Leopold said that she was ready. But maybe she just needs time to adjust to the new reality. Adrian's hand in her hair. Adrian's hips gently nudging hers. Adrian's, not Ariston's.

The audience is going insane. Adrian didn't think a room of old theater patrons and journalists could get this riled up. It's like nothing he's ever experienced. Adrian's blood rises to match the heat of the lights, the heat of kissing, the roar of applause.

xvii

The room grows furious with cheering — Zara feels it in her body, louder than her pulse. Every time it surges, Adrian drives the kiss deeper.

Zara has kissed him a hundred times in rehearsal and a hundred more onstage. This feels different — hot and smothering and breathlessly wrong.

This is her life. Not the Aurelia.

And Leopold is right there behind them for the big reveal. He knew about this. He *orchestrated* it.

And then, over Adrian's shoulder, she sees Eli standing in the wings. Not only is Eli wearing a dress, it's the perfect one. Dark, fathomless blue with tiny points of silver. With her hair down, she looks like a wild night spread out over the sea.

Zara draws back from Adrian. A furious red has settled over Eli's face. She rushes for the door, her combat boots peeking out below her gown.

In this moment, Zara doesn't care about Leopold. About what he wants or what he'll do to her.

She runs.

Eli slams through the backstage door, headed for the lobby. Zara left her coat at the coat check, and there's no time to get it now because Eli is already passing through one of the triple front doors.

Zara hurries under the shattered light of the chandeliers. She picks the middle door, which turns out to be a mistake, the heavy old-fashioned fins of revolving brass and glass barely moving as she pushes. In front of the hotel, the night smacks into her like a careless stranger. Cold slides down her back. Wind takes the hem of her dress and waves it around.

Eli disappears around the corner.

Zara pitches forward in her borrowed heels, balanced like a tiny boat taking on ten-foot waves. She keeps her eyes on Eli's gray coat as she steps into the street, crossing at almost a run, muttering under her breath — probably every swear she knows, in two languages. Zara has to stop at the intersection, where a stream of speeding taxis holds her to the curb.

"Eli!" Zara cries. "Eli!"

The taxis clear the intersection and Zara takes flight. Halfway across the avenue, she catches up.

Eli turns, a tight spin. "What?"

Zara wants to touch her, but she can tell it's not allowed. Eli's hands blink open with rapid fury.

"Why were you late?" Zara asks. As if that's what matters, as if that's why she kissed Adrian Ward.

"I couldn't find my invitation, and then I remembered Roscoe put it with his," Eli says, her words so heated that they're almost melting together. "So I went back to the theater — yes, *alone* — I found the tickets in the booth with this note Roscoe wrote to himself. It said get a corsage to match her eyes, but then he crossed it out and wrote they don't make dark-brown corsages, so just get something pretty. I spent half an hour crying on the floor. That pretty much catches us up."

The light changes and cars speed at them in a solid line, horns and headlights bearing down. Zara and Eli run. When they make the far side of the street, Zara reaches for Eli's hand.

"Look," Eli says, snatching her fingers away, not stopping. "I know that kiss was about the play. Your career. Whatever. I know this is how things work. So you don't even have to say it, okay?"

Zara doesn't know what to do. She's terrified of the Aurelia, and she's terrified of losing it. She's sick of *how things work*.

"Eli . . ."

"*No*," she says, and the word is so hard, but her eyes are soft and starred with tears. "You don't get to kiss me under the stage and then kiss Adrian Ward everywhere else. Maybe that would have been a good deal a long time ago, but I'm not doing it."

"I didn't know that was going to happen," Zara says, leaning forward, everything in her trying to get back to Eli. "I stopped it. I left."

"Too late," Eli says.

Zara gulps cold air. She's out of time. "I love you."

She finally said it — not in her head, not on a stage. The words slipped out and hit Eli, and instead of a smile or a kiss or an *I know* or an *I love you, too*, Zara gets the world's most frustrated sigh.

"Fuck," Eli mutters, hands clutched to the opposite arms, holding herself together. "This is *not* the time you tell someone you love them."

Zara feels a bitterness that has nothing to do with the cold. She messed this up in a single day. Ruined whatever could have happened between them. She can still see it — the beautiful possibility of them. *Together.*

She knows she should turn right around and go back to the gala. She could make up some story to keep Leopold from hurting her. Hurting Eli. Zara should tell him she needed to step outside, get some air. That would make sense to Leopold. What girl wouldn't lose her head over Adrian Ward?

But the feelings Zara has been chasing since the day she found that ragged paperback of *Echo and Ariston* are right here, in a girl who made herself out of tattoos and abrupt laughs and every form of light.

Zara takes a step forward.

"What are you doing?" Eli asks.

"Telling the truth."

When Zara kisses Eli, it starts as a little brush. One pass, then two. Eli's lips are so hesitant that it hurts. Zara puts her hand to Eli's face and tries another brush, a painter searching for the right stroke. She's not going to let Eli go this easily. All Zara has to do is find the right kiss — the one that changes the story. Her hands grasp at Eli's waist. And then Eli's hand is on the back of her neck, soft and gasp-worthy.

Eli's fingers rain down Zara's bare shoulders, stroke the secretly soft inside of her elbows, work their way down to her hands, curling their fingers together. It's perfect for a second, and then it's not enough. Zara tugs at the collar of Eli's coat. A hundred places on their bodies meet. Time melts, the way it does in the theater. The brightness behind Zara's eyelids grows brighter, the shadows take on a velvet depth. Eli lets out a low sigh. Zara kisses her harder. Everything is heightened, everything is *more*.

Eli pulls back, letting her lips hover. There's a tiny smile warming them. "What now?"

Zara sighs into Eli's shoulder. "I don't want to go back to the gala. And Kestrel's apartment . . ."

Zara sketches a quick update about Kestrel throwing the glass at Carl, about her screaming, about the Xanax. Before she can stop herself, Zara asks, "Can I come home with you?"

"Ha!" Eli's laugh is even better up close. It breaks things up — a moment away from the trouble at the Aurelia. An intermission laugh. "I was worried it would look shady if I asked you. But you asked me. So yes."

Zara rushes in for another kiss. Eli is right there, her lips already warm. People part and flow around the two girls. They've made an island, a safe place to stand for a few moments before the city pushes them down the sidewalk and washes them away.

As soon as Eli gets Zara back to her apartment, she goes into lighting mode: she can't help it. Good thing she already has candles scattered everywhere — clustered on every surface, turning them into altars. Eli grabs a book of matches. She only strikes enough for half the candles, the little white tea lights and the skinny pillar candles with their colorful pictures of saints. She doesn't want to shed *too* much light. There'll be plenty of time for Zara to see the crumpled graph paper on the floor, the pots of herbs on the windowsill, the ugly flower print on the couch. Right now, Eli wants to focus on the way that Zara is looking at her from the doorway as she lingers with one hand on the frame.

How Zara waits, so patient, until Eli holds up the last match between her thumb and finger and blows it out.

And then, how Zara isn't patient at all.

Eli was expecting to take this one tiny step at a time. So here's a surprise: Zara has her up against the wall. She presses into Eli like she's been waiting for this, like she wants to leave a mark so Eli won't forget she was here. It's hard to believe that Zara Evans is here. She wants to lower the window and shout it to the whole neighborhood.

"This is the first time I've had a girl over here," Eli says in the breathless space between kisses.

Zara's hands pause — one on Eli's waist, one caught in her hair. It felt good, the way she tugged at it when the kissing was involved. Now it's just damned awkward. "You haven't been with anyone since . . ."

"Hannah," Eli finishes for her.

Zara pulls back, just a little. "Did she break your heart?"

Dios, this girl isn't messing around.

Eli doesn't want to lie: that's a bad way to start. But she doesn't know how to phrase this particular truth. Not with Zara's breath so near, teasing her with the potential for more. "Hannah made me feel like I wanted too much."

"What did you want?" Zara asks, her eyes glistening in the half dark.

257

"Don't make me say it," Eli groans.

"What?!" Zara's face is all question marks and exclamation points. Eli doesn't stand a chance.

"Love. Okay? The ridiculous kind that people write plays about and then remember for the next two thousand years."

Zara holds a smile in her cheeks, tight, like she's trying not to break into a mad grin. "You're a romantic, Eli."

"Yes. In fact, I am. So when things got rough back there, I thought the whole damn thing was happening again. I thought, Zara Evans likes me, but not *enough*. And I worried that if we went too far and it didn't work, I would die. Nothing dramatic. I would just lie down and die and go hang out with Roscoe, wherever he is. And they would put a little marker on my grave: *Here lies Eli, the tragic queer girl.*"

Zara is laughing, her lips pressed together. Eli kisses that laugh right where it lives, in the base of Zara's throat.

Zara seems to enjoy that, but when Eli pulls back, Zara tips her head down, squaring her face with Eli's, suddenly serious. "You haven't said it back yet."

Eli shakes her head, curls flying. "You can't tell someone it's time for them to say it!"

"You have a lot of rules about this," Zara says.

"Yeah, well, as you just pointed out, I'm a romantic." Eli takes a breath. With one hand she reaches around Zara and pulls her close, her hand pressed against the perfect crescent line at the small of Zara's back. "You're beautiful."

Zara shakes her head, way too emphatically. She's been listening to whatever ridiculous things Leopold and her stick-insect roommate have been telling her. She's been thinking that she needs to match Adrian Ward's pretty-boy looks. Eli doesn't want Zara's head filled with that nonsense. "I noticed you at the auditions," Eli says, satisfied when Zara's eyes fly open. Eli runs two fingers under the sheer straps of Zara's dress. "I tried to stop noticing you. I *wanted* to stop. And I couldn't. And then I fell in love." Zara sighs. It's the warmest sound.

She dances away from Eli and sits down on the hardwood floor, ignoring the couch. She looks up, clearly waiting for Eli to join her. "I want you to tell me everything about yourself."

"Everything?" Eli asks.

Zara nods fiercely. "This is the good part. Nobody can take that away from us."

Right now, with that look on Zara's face, Eli almost wants to see somebody try.

xix

Zara feels the world shrink down to a circle of candlelight. Eli sits, knees touching hers, so close that every breath Eli lets out is the one that Zara takes in. She could rush forward just a few inches and close the distance.

Kiss/kill.

That's what Meg and Leopold would call it. But Zara questions those words. Kiss/kill. How could it be a real question, which way the decision would go? Echo would never hurt

Ariston. Zara could never hurt Eli. That's why she kept away as long as she did.

But they're here right now, in Eli's apartment. Safe.

"Okay," Eli says. "Story time." She smiles so wide that her cheeks imprint with the commas that Zara loves. She touches them, one at a time.

"Sorry," Zara whispers. "No more interruptions."

Eli takes a deep breath, like Zara does before she starts acting. The kind of breath that stirs truth out of its hiding places. "I was my parents' baby," she says. "Their only girl. Which was supposed to make me their princess, but I, uh, turned down the role. Everything was a fight by the time I got out of high school. The boots, the tattoos . . . everything." Eli reaches out and smooths the fabric of the couch. "I needed a change. Now that I'm here, I can see the good stuff again. Like, they're the ones who got me to the Aurelia."

"They wanted you to be a lighting designer?" Zara can hear the ripe jealousy in her voice.

"They like the arts. But it's more than that. When I was little, my mom was always telling me about growing up in Puerto Rico. About the sunshine. The light there, she said it was so much better. More. And when I was a baby, all I wanted was to be in the sun. She called me her Luzecita, told me I lit up every room. At some point I started to take it literally, you know? I would steal candles from around the house, find a lighter in my brother's stash and spark it a thousand times until the fluid ran out. When I was nine, I begged my dad to let me help him with the Christmas lights. Stood there on the roof and fed him string after string while Mom yelled at us to get down."

Zara is smiling now, so wide, so much, her face almost hurts.

Eli takes Zara's arms and holds them, her thumbs rubbing circles into warm skin. "I still can't believe this is happening," she whispers.

"Yeah," Zara says. Her words have had a shine to them ever since they kissed on the street, but now they go dull. "What if I told you we had to keep it a secret? For a little while?"

"A secret," Eli repeats slowly. "I don't think I've ever been good at those. I was the only first-grader with a playground girlfriend. Sometimes I think what I loved most about living in the city, about being with Hannah, was how damn free the whole thing felt. We got our share of weird stares because you get those anywhere. But I could touch her, kiss her, like there wasn't a different set of rules."

"I want that," Zara says. The words slip out — she doesn't even think them first.

Eli frowns, like she's trying to figure this out. "But you don't want people to know we're together."

This is the heaviest sort of truth. Now that Zara has given it words, she can feel it pressing down on the whole night. "Just one person."

"Is it Adrian?" Eli asks, her voice spun in a bitter new direction.

"No," Zara says, almost laughing.

Eli pauses. Softens. "Is it someone in your family?"

Zara curls up, the memory a blow to her stomach. "I tried to tell my parents. They pretty much ignored it."

Eli lifts her face in both hands and kisses her, and for just a second the entire world is the red-dark behind Zara's eyelids. And then Eli pulls back and says, "I'm sorry."

Zara nods. She looks down into the wavering flame of a candle. She can feel Eli staring at her. Hard.

"I need to ask you something," Eli says. Zara nods again, smaller this time. "Who's this person you're so afraid of?"

XX

The stage is empty. The gala ended an hour ago, and the last scavengers of hors d'oeuvres and gossip have gotten into cabs and spread like an opening fist, a finger to each of the boroughs.

Meg is the only one left.

Soon the hotel staff will come to whisk away the napkins, the crystal glasses with their slowly melting ice. For now, Meg has time and solitude and she can unfold the evening, moment by moment.

Zara and Adrian took the stage. There was a single, flawless kiss. Then Zara ran away. Meg could have killed her — what if Leopold had disapproved? Did she want to risk his anger?

But right now, he loves Zara Evans. Right now, everyone does.

The press thought the ending was something right out of a fairy tale. Leopold fed into their frenzy. He called her *my little girl from the woods*.

Right now, he loves her.

Meg laughs so hard that she starts to shake. She remembers that feeling. And the places it led. Her head is a dark forest of memory, where she could lose herself for days.

She grabs every glass on the table, silently thanking Kestrel for the inspiration. She flings them one by one. Onto the ground. At the wall. Inches away from her own feet. She considers taking her shoes off and walking through the shards, but Leopold would notice. She can't hurt herself so badly that he would see it, or she would have to stay away from the Aurelia.

Leopold is still having visions.

They're not out of the dark woods yet.

Zara stands on a small platform above the stage, looking down into an unexpected pool of water.

It is cobalt blue and perfectly still.

Leopold stalks through the orchestra pit. He's told Zara to climb up and await further instruction. She arrived at the Aurelia a bare second before rehearsal started. Usually, she gets there half an hour early to warm up — sometimes more. But Leopold hasn't said a word to her about what happened at the gala, and Zara wants to keep it that way.

The rest of the cast is assembled onstage. They're doing costumes tonight but not makeup; in the glare of the lights, faces lose their shadow. Zara is looking down on a company of ghosts.

"So far, we have held with the Greek tradition," Leopold says, "keeping Echo's death offstage. A messenger runs to tell us what happened. Echo is nowhere to be seen." Zara can feel his voice, like it's meant only for her. Teasing her with some idea he has. Some new way to make her life worse. "What if we make a different choice? What if we choose not to spare the audience this pain?"

There is nervous thunder in Zara's chest — and then she realizes it's someone running up the steps. Barrett joins Zara on her little platform. He's tall and broad and there's hardly room for both of their bodies.

Barrett smiles down at her, a smile she knows because she's seen him give it to other girls. It involves all of his teeth and two very convincing dimples, but his eyes are dead.

He holds two lengths of rope in his hands. "I'm going to show you how to do these binds," he says. "Ready?"

Zara wants to say no, but then Leopold will know she's causing trouble for the production, which is behind schedule in every possible way. Zara just has to keep agreeing for two more weeks. Previews will come and go, the show will open, Leopold will leave, and Zara will have everything.

Echo and Eli.

"So what I did," Barrett says, "is I tied each of your wrists with rope, and you have to keep your wrists together. Don't forget, that's your job. Keep those wrists together, no matter what. It will make your hands look like they're bound, even though you're essentially wearing rope bracelets." Zara breaks her wrists apart, puts them back together.

Like a magic trick.

"Good girl," Barrett says, and the way his voice curls around her makes Zara wish she was wearing an extra layer of clothing, just so there could be more between him and her skin.

Zara has a sudden flash of the night before that won't be held down. A dark room, a single bed, little mounds of clothes everywhere, like offerings. Eli's face bright in the shifting gray-white city light. Her hands all over Zara's skin. Her mouth, sliding down to Zara's breasts, testing the waters. Zara's body might be at the Aurelia, but really she's with Eli in the soft hold of those sheets, two girls batting their legs into each other, like they're learning how to swim.

"Are we prepared?" Leopold asks. He waits for nods from the stage manager, from the stagehands, even the costume girl. Zara tries to wipe the remnants of last night from her expression.

Leopold can't know.

Not how good it was. Not how Eli breathed warmth onto every inch of Zara's cold skin.

The water below is a frigid blue. Zara has no interest in jumping. But the words that come out of her mouth are "I'm ready to die."

"Messenger, downstage right," Leopold says, "and Ariston

will be held by two of the soldiers upstage right." The actors carefully find their marks. "Since Meg has been so instrumental to this staging, I'll let her explain the rest." Leopold pats his assistant on the shoulder.

Meg looks at the tableau with a brisk, assessing stare. "Here's how it will go. Zara, at the midway point of the messenger's speech, you jump from the block. As soon as you're in the water, there should be a certain amount of splashing, struggle. Keep it realistic, though. No need for hysterics. Echo lets herself go under, and as soon as that happens, we'll go to blackout and the hydraulics will lower the tank beneath the stage. The rest of the messenger's speech will be delivered in the darkness, while the stagehands reset." She spreads her palms, flips them. "When the lights come up, the stage will be whole. The tank will be gone."

"Echo will be a memory," Leopold adds. Because he can't possibly let someone else have the last word.

Zara shifts her toes to the edge of the platform.

"Meanwhile," Meg says, "under the stage, Zara will surface and a stagehand will help her out of the tank." Zara tries to imagine that far into the future — just a few minutes, really — but her mind is stubborn.

Stuck on the fall.

"Zara, as soon as we go to black, you're free to surface and breathe." Meg must be able to see that Zara is reluctant because she adds, "It's perfectly safe. We had several stagehands test it."

Zara didn't see any of those tests. The Aurelia's curse comes back to her all at once, a landslide of worries that haven't been able to touch her for so long because she's been too busy with other things. Too busy with Eli.

These things come in threes.

The first two deaths seemed like accidents — what could look more accidental than new staging that doesn't work?

Zara tells herself that she's just making up reasons to worry. She's found this pure, intense, white-hot happiness and she's afraid something is going to come and snatch it away — that's all. The play has conditioned her to expect it. But not all love stories end like that, in cold, blue silence.

In death.

The messenger starts in on his speech. *"I saw her on the cliffs above, and even from such a distance she was proud and held no hesitation."*

Zara has to look as if she's choosing this, even though every muscle in her body screams against it.

And then light moves over her — a web of shimmering blues and greens — a gentle reminder. Eli is up in the booth. Eli is watching her. Zara stands taller. Tonight, this will be just another thing they laugh about while they kiss each other.

And that makes Zara brave enough to jump.

A few weeks ago, if someone told Eli that she would have Zara pressed up against a decorative screen in prop storage, hands linked, lips one *yes* away from kissing, she would have laughed. And then secretly hoped they were right. And then laughed again. Now that she's here, her nerves are so deafening she can't even enjoy it.

"I don't want you doing that jump," she says. "There's no time to practice. It's totally unsafe."

Zara sighs, leaving behind a miniature frown. That just makes Eli want to attack her lips. To fix things with kissing. But she's started an argument, an important one, and she has to see it through.

"Remember that speech you gave me about doing your job?" Zara asks. "Well. This is mine." Her teeth clack, bone on bone. Zara has been shivering from jumping into the swimming pool of the damned. Eli is doing vigorous, nonsexy things with her hands to keep Zara warm.

"Maybe you can talk to Meg about it. I mean, you obviously can't talk to *him*." Eli doesn't want to say Leopold's name. It makes her as sick as the sweet garbage-y scent that rises out of random vents in the street.

Last night, Zara let loose the stories she'd gathered of just how *dangerous* Leopold could be. Lies, manipulation, rape. "He shouldn't be able to tell anyone what to do. Especially not you." She feels this inner spinning, this dizzy sickness. She wonders if it's what Roscoe felt like before he fell. "I want you safe. Forever."

Zara laughs, a short stab of sound. "Ariston tried that with the cave, and it didn't work out so well."

"We'll need something better," Eli says. "Towers are pretty traditional, right?" She spins a glance around the room, only half-kidding. "I could put together something impossible to scale. With an Eli-only door."

Zara's finger finds Eli's belt loop. "The problem with towers," she says, "is that girls don't like staying locked up."

Zara walks Eli backward until they're pressed against an old armoire. Their lips meet: easy. The new challenge is keeping them apart. Eli slides her mouth to Zara's throat, and a groan spills out. Someone might hear them. But the whole thing is so unspeakably hot, Eli has a hard time caring. Zara steps up the kissing from sweet to intense, running her hands up and down and everywhere.

Under the stage, in her living room, Eli had tried to put a dimmer on her hopes: a chorus of *what if she changes her mind?* In Eli's bedroom, Zara changed Eli's mind. Or melted it. Now, in the overheated dark center of a kiss, the only thing Eli is afraid of is someone trying to stop them.

Her back slams into a loose drawer, and the whole armoire rattles. Zara and Eli hold tight. No one jumps out from the shadows or bursts into the room, but Eli can't shake the feeling that something bad is coming. "Hey," she says. "Did Kestrel recover from the snap-fest she had last night?"

Zara's face does a nervous flicker, like a fluorescent that can't decide if it's broken or not. "She looked sick at rehearsal today, but I couldn't tell if it was guilt or just a hangover."

"Jesus," Eli mutters.

Zara picks at a handle on the armoire. "I was just scared last night. Of everything. I don't think she's really going to hurt me."

Eli feels like she's getting brighter and brighter and that soon she might be burning to the touch. "She *attacked* Carl."

"That was really, really bad. But . . ." Zara shakes her

head, as if there's something in there she can't get out. "I've been around her every day for two months. She's weirdly . . . innocent."

Eli stops in front of Zara to rub her shoulders again. "You forget that I grew up in suburban Connecticut. Kestrels *everywhere*. Kids who thought they could get away with anything. Mostly because they did."

Zara sighs. "She's definitely in her own world. She took a Xanax right before the gala, and I thought it would help her stay calm, but it was like the medicine didn't even touch her." Zara speaks to her shoes, which are covered in dark spots from all the dripping. "I think I have to go back to the apartment tonight."

Eli lets her hands drop from Zara's shoulders to that curve in her back, the one that she touched the night before. Over her dress, and then under it, and then without anything on at all. "You can come home with me. You can always come home with me."

Zara tugs at a piece of her hair, which has gone clumpy and lank from the cold water. "What if Leopold notices?"

Eli wouldn't really be surprised if Leopold started to stalk Zara's movements. She thinks about going to the police again, but what would she say? Leopold Henneman raped one of his actresses twenty years ago and they have no proof? He told lies, tricked people? Got Zara drunk and forced her to kiss the same guy she willingly kisses onstage every night?

Tension builds along Eli's inner wiring. She kicks at the nearest prop with the toe of her boot, until she realizes it's a creepy doll — one in a row of creepy dolls — and promptly stops.

"You could leave, you know," Eli says, hating the words. Asking Zara to give up her dreams should be unthinkable. The idea of one of them at the Aurelia without the other is physically painful. But the idea of Zara getting hurt is worse.

White-hot. Untouchable.

"I'm not going anywhere," Zara says, crossing her arms over her wet, glorious chest. "Enna told me not to."

"Really?" Eli asks.

Zara goes into that middle distance, where the memories of the dead seem to live. Like they're always just beyond where the eyes settle, and all a person has to do is look a little farther to find them. "She said don't leave, no matter what. That's letting them win."

"Yeah, and look at how that turned out for her," Eli says, forgetting to be gentle because she's so afraid.

Zara gathers herself, as if she's making a stand. Her nose is only a few inches away from Eli's, but kissing seems miles away. "If Roscoe told you to do something, would you trust him?"

Eli nods. Grudgingly.

"You really think I would give up the only two things I've ever wanted this much?" Zara asks.

"*Two* things?" Eli teases out the words.

Zara smiles, and that warm, bright look on her face closes the distance between them. "Right. Two things. Echo and . . . Ariston."

"Ariston!" Eli says. "Now with *way* more estrogen." She wants to stay in the land of bad jokes for a while, but she can feel her nerves creeping back up, like the inching of a waterline. "Promise me you won't let Leopold near you."

Zara pulls her closer, douses her in chlorine. She kisses Eli like she can't imagine a better fate. They are so busy turning themselves from girls into steam that Eli almost misses it.

Zara doesn't promise.

xxiii

Zara has been called early for a costume refitting. Cosima isn't in the shop, but one of her assistants cracks the door. The heat has been turned down so low that the cavernous room might as well be carved out of ice.

Zara clenches everything.

"Wait here," the assistant says, waving at one of the butcher-block tables. Zara sits there dutifully for a few seconds. Then, out of the corner of her eye, she sees Leopold, and panic brushes over her.

What is the director doing here?

Did he know she would be here, alone?

Leopold raped Enna. Zara is still taking that in, a little bit at a time, because it's not something she can understand all at once. There was the look on Carl's face when he said it. The way it confirmed Zara's worst fears. The light it shed on the talk she had with Enna, right before she died. This story isn't told in a single straight line — it's more like ripples. Some bleed into Zara's thoughts slowly. Others hit her in shock waves.

Zara hops down from the table, gathers her coat in one arm, and heads for the door. But the figure in the corner doesn't move. If Leopold really is back there, she should hear breathing, or the rustle of movement. She should feel the charge in the air that seems to follow Leopold around — the same buzzy feeling that Zara gets on her skin before a storm.

When she turns back, the costume shop is perfectly still. Zara thinks she might have imagined the whole thing.

"Hello?" she calls.

No answer.

She pushes her way through racks of fabric, into a forest of wool and linen and silk. A smell rises from the costumes — baked moisture from the steam cleaner, with an undertone of bodies. Heady, spicy, sweat, the aftermath of a thousand performances.

As she gets closer to the place where she thought she saw him, Zara comes to the slow understanding that it isn't the director — just a jacket and pants and a wig that, when put together, look like him.

A perfect imitation of Leopold Henneman.

The door to the shop bangs open with authority. Zara runs and is back in place at the cutting tables just as Cosima looks up from her garment bag.

"I make this costume," she says, taking out the death-scene dress, holding it aloft. "Now I make it go underwater." She digs into the stitches with a seam ripper, small and metal and toothy. "He says everything is perfect, see you next season. Two days later I am in here making a wetsuit."

There is a fray at Cosima's edges. One more rehearsal before they put the show on its feet, and Leopold won't stop changing things. Won't stop talking about how *perfect* his show needs to be.

It makes Zara want to throw up. He acts like he's the only one who's going to be judged.

Cosima picks up a needle and starts to sew with a fury.

Zara keeps very still and tries not to think about the upcoming previews. Five minutes later, Cosima tugs the new version of the dress over Zara's head. It flows around her, heavier than the old one, like it's trying to drown her without help from the water.

"How did you do that so fast?" Zara asks, marveling at the panels that spill from her waist like waterfalls.

Cosima scowls at the dress, dismissing it with a turn of the wrist. "This is nothing."

"It's beautiful," Zara says. And it really is. Like armor is beautiful.

Cosima helps Zara slide back out of the dress. The fitting

is over and Zara knows that it's time for her to leave. But she stays, after her jeans and T-shirt have been tugged back on.

She hears Carl's voice, reasonable and cold.

People die in the theater. Ask Cosima, if you don't believe me.

Cosima has picked up a pair of long-armed scissors and gone back to work. She's putting the finishing touches on something white and delicate — Echo's act 1 dress, the one from Leopold's vision. Three months ago, all she wanted was to stand onstage in that white dress. She didn't want to think about how strange it was that her director called late at night and kept her up, sliding feverish words in her ear. Two months ago, she showed up at the Aurelia and found Roscoe, and it didn't make her change course, or even dream of running back home. In the story she told herself, saying Echo's lines in that dress in front of hundreds of people each night was the only thing that mattered.

"You knew Enna, right?" Zara asks.

"Horrible woman," Cosima says without looking away from her fabric.

Who says that about someone who just died? But then Zara remembers — most people think Enna got what she deserved. These were the stories that people told themselves, to make it easier to sleep at night. Leopold was a genius who could do no wrong. Roscoe was a crazy old man, destined to fall. Enna wrote her own tragedy without anyone else's help.

But that's not the whole story. People carve words on each other's hearts, scribble their sadness on anyone who stays put for long enough. For the first time, Zara almost understands her parents. Avoiding love, the all-consuming kind, means they'll never have to deal with losing it.

"Carl told me someone else died in the Aurelia."

Cosima drops the fabric she was tacking. It flutters to the ground, but she doesn't stoop to pick it up.

"It was someone you knew?" Zara asks.

"Vivi," she mutters, carving the sign of the cross, forehead to chest, then across her shoulders.

"Vivi?" Zara repeats.

When the costume designer speaks again, she is on the edge of something tears or fury. "Idiot girl."

The tide has turned against Zara, but she keeps pushing. She's come this far. "Please. I need to know—"

"Out," Cosima says, scissors pointed at her, the blades wide and the stabbing points leveled at her throat. "Stop asking questions and get out."

xxiv

Adrian has one dress rehearsal to make things right.

He thought the kiss at the gala was a good idea, and then Zara ran away. She hasn't really talked to him since. Obviously, they've still been kissing, because Echo and Ariston are always kissing. Adrian has to put his hands on Zara's hips, his lips on her earlobe. Earlobes make things awkward.

They have about five minutes before they go on for second dress — maybe the first one they'll actually get through — and

Zara is sitting at the very back of the wings, just in front of the cyclorama. She looks upset, and Adrian wonders if maybe it's his fault. (Was he supposed to try harder? Kiss better? Run after her?)

Adrian approaches slowly, waiting for Zara to notice. But she's folded over her phone, the little screen lighting up her face. They're not supposed to have phones back here, and until now Zara has been all about the rules.

Adrian wonders what changed.

"Hey," he says, tapping on Zara's shoulder. "Z." She gives him a quick glance, and it's sad how even that much can make him feel less alone. He's been completely on his own since he got to New York. (His publicist and his personal assistant and his dialogue coach and his driver don't count. Paparazzi definitely don't count.)

Zara turns to Adrian, and her eyes tell him that she needs to talk. He thinks she is going to bring up the kiss (he's waiting for it, he's *prepared*), and instead she blurts out, "Have you ever heard of Vivi Laurent?"

"Uh," Adrian says. "Yeah, I guess so." One of the good things about his brain is that once it has a grip on something, it holds on tight. "I never met her. I mean, I think she died before I was —"

Famous. Adrian doesn't like to think about his life before that.

"It happened ten years ago," Zara fills in. "She died here. At the Aurelia."

Adrian shivers. There's a lot of death hanging around this

theater. Roscoe died right before Adrian got there, so he missed the worst of it. But then Enna went, too. And now this Vivi person? Even if it's an old death, it still feels like they're piling up. "Yeah, I remember. She was doing really well, getting all these great parts, and then she killed herself."

Zara nods, more focused on her screen than she is on him. Extreme distraction can be a sign that a girl likes him. But why would she fixate on dead actresses? There are more important things to fixate on. Like when the two of them are going to kiss again. He pulled away when Zara kissed him in the studio, but the gala gave Adrian a taste for it and now he doesn't want to stop. And there's no reason to — right?

His fans love her.

Adrian is supposed to make them happy. They make *him* happy. He was miserable before he had fans.

"Vivi starred in a play here," Zara says, her hair hanging down in a curtain, cutting Adrian off from her. "*Winterset.* Something pretty and tragic. She landed a few movie roles. She lost — forty-seven pounds. Can that be right?" She looks up at him for confirmation.

Adrian shrugs. That's a lot of pounds. But it's been known to happen.

"And then she came back here for another show," Zara says, in a trance. "And she killed herself."

"You don't need to think about that," Adrian says, sweeping Zara's hair to the side. She jolts like his fingers are electrified.

(That's a good sign, right?)

Zara hides her phone behind the chair. "It doesn't worry you?"

Adrian shrugs. "Why would it?"

Zara shakes her head, like there are *so many* things she wishes she could tell him.

They go out onstage and the play starts. Scene by scene it builds a reckless energy that it's never had before. Adrian doesn't think he can take much credit for it. The difference is mostly coming from Zara. She sets the love scenes on fire. She strokes his arm with this soft confidence.

Is she trying to tell him something? Or is this still the play? Adrian is going breathless. Muscles tight. Kisses flowing.

And then they're torn apart, and Adrian *feels* it for the first time. There's a harsh empty space inside him. Zara is marched to the top of the platform, a metal skeleton with the image of a cliff projected onto it.

She looks down at the pool, and it's obvious that she's afraid to do the jump. The messenger says his lines. Zara's cue comes. And she just — stands there.

"Echo," Leopold yells. "That's you, dear."

Zara wavers at the very edge of the platform. She looks like a stone about to drop. But she doesn't.

Leopold calls her to the front of the stage. Whispers in her ear. Adrian drifts forward with the vague hope that he can do something to help Zara. Leopold dismisses her, turning away, and Adrian takes advantage of those few seconds to stop Zara on her way back to the platform. He can see the worry rattling around in her eyes, wanting out.

"You okay?" he whispers, rubbing her upper arm. (Girls love when he does that. They actually go a little crazy.)

"He wants to meet with me in his office after rehearsal," Zara says numbly. "In private."

"And you don't want to go." He thinks of their last meeting in Leopold's office. (Meg and Leopold, getting too close for comfort.) "Yeah, I can't blame you."

She looks at him, and her eyes spark. "Can you do me a favor?"

"Sure," he says. "Anything."

She tells him what she needs, and Adrian says yes right as the AD sends them back to places. Adrian strides upstage right, so high on this rehearsal that he doesn't even see the stagehand, dressed in black, moving with quick steps.

They slam into each other. And he's so starved for contact that even *that* feels good.

"Sorry," the girl says. "Oh my God, I'm so, so, so sorry." "It's okay," Adrian says with a humble sort of head duck. "You're great tonight," she says, biting into her bottom lip. (He loves when girls do that.) "Like, *really* great."

"Thanks," he says, seriously hoping she's right. The girl stands there, waiting for him to say more. This level of attention feels normal to Adrian now. People want to do things for him. They want to give him time, and answers, and gifts, and pictures of themselves naked. They want to give him flowers and good reviews and parts of their bodies to sign.

There was a time when he was too scrawny, too energetic.

Always disappointing his mom, who said he was a natural. Adrian's dad left when he was two, for someone younger and prettier but also with more plastic surgery than a body should be able to stand. His mom had crappy boyfriends. She told him if he was good enough, if he made enough money, they wouldn't need the boyfriends.

At ten years old, Adrian was still that weird kid, the one in the corner who couldn't get cast in the cereal commercial or the Gap Kids ad. The one with multiple learning disabilities and zero muscle definition. He worked hard and he went to every audition. At some point he discovered working out, and his body magically turned into what everyone wanted. The rough edges of his energy vanished, or maybe he just learned how to shove them down.

And then he started getting romantic leads. He acted the way he thought people *should* when they were in love. The way that nobody ever acted in his real life.

And audiences loved it.

The scene starts up again, and the cute stagehand pulls back to the wings, but lingers there. Watching him. Waiting.

Adrian thinks about asking her to meet up with him later. After his favor to Zara. He can find a supply closet, press this girl against the locked door. It's been too long since he's kissed someone. (He's starting to think that kissing Zara at the gala didn't count. Kissing her at that one rehearsal *definitely* didn't count. He forces himself not to think about Kerry, and it's like trying not to get hit by a runaway truck.)

But this new girl would only go to the tabloids or get on the Internet. Kissing her will make him more alone, not less. Kerry was right. Being as famous as he is changes everything. Adrian can't be with just anyone. He needs another actor. Someone who understands.

(Someone like Kerry.) Someone like Zara Evans.

XXV

Leopold schedules Zara's private meeting for the dead of the night, when almost all the company has gone home. As the elevator slides toward the third floor, Zara sends a text, telling Eli that she's headed back to Kestrel's.

She's used to acting, to making people believe her. Even so, she's still stunned by how easy it is to lie. Even to Eli.

But what was she supposed to do? Say no to Leopold and walk out of the Aurelia? Give up Echo and all the work she's done with so little time left before the show opens? Tell Eli that she's going to see Leopold for a private meeting, and watch her perfect, beautiful girlfriend melt down?

She makes the long walk to his office, her shoes sounding lonely notes on the linoleum.

She knocks on the door to Leopold's office.

"Come in, come in."

Zara hopes that Meg is going to be there, but it's just Leopold, standing with his back to her. He doesn't turn when she walks into the room. The desk between them feels like a magical barrier — like the line of the stage that separates the audience and the actors. She tells herself that as long as they're on different sides of that desk, she's safe.

Leopold's back moves slowly as he breathes. Up and down. Up and down.

Zara knows what happened to Enna, and she won't let anything like that happen to her. But in some buried part of her brain, Zara knows that this is just another little story she's telling herself.

"What did you want to work on?" she asks in a small voice, the one that she first arrived at the theater with. Breathy and untrained. She hears herself like a stranger would — she sounds so young. Like adulthood was just a costume she tried on. Now it's been stripped off and she's standing in front of him, exposed.

"It's Echo's death, I'm afraid," Leopold says, finally turning to face her.

For a second, she's relieved that he doesn't want to talk

about love. He doesn't want to touch her. Then the moment twists and Zara remembers she shouldn't have to be relieved that the director doesn't want to touch her. She should be able to take that for granted.

"I need you to close your eyes for me," Leopold says, trailing his fingers along the surface of the desk. "And scream."

This is a fairly simple direction. Zara should be able to follow it.

She closes her eyes.

That's where her feelings are waiting. Down there, in the dark. It isn't really true blackness behind her eyes. It's the bloody color of the curtains. The color she saw on the day that Roscoe died.

Here in this closed-in place, she knows how afraid she is.

She screams and screams and screams, bright sound pouring out of her like blood. She screams until her throat is throbbing inside, a secret pain. She thinks of Roscoe on the floor, Enna in the dressing room. Vivi — a girl who sounds too much like her — dead somewhere in the Aurelia.

She opens her eyes and sees how much Leopold loves it, how he's savoring every bit of her hurt. He doesn't even try to hide it. He levels his gray eyes and stares at her and she's still screaming, screaming, and now the sound is a bright ribbon that he is tearing out of her. His tongue comes out of his mouth, and he licks his lips. They are glistening pink, slightly open.

"Very good," he says.

The sound falters. Dies. Zara puts a hand to her throat. It feels hot to the touch.

Leopold smiles, like she's made him happy and proud. The look that she used to crave now makes her swallow back disgust. "Much better," he says. "I believed your fear this time. And there was something new in there." He searches her for the answer. His eyes have the urgency of fingers, working their way over her. Pushing their way in. "Loss. There is something you are afraid to lose now." *Eli. Eli. Eli.* "Can you tell me what it is?"

No. "It's love. I love this place so much. The Aurelia. I love this show. I love being on the stage. Being an actress."

He walks toward her, crosses the barrier she picked, the line between his desk and the rest of the room. He sets his fingertips to her warm throat. Will he be able to tell that she's holding something back?

Will he demand more?

Zara's body jolts, and it takes her a moment to match her reaction up with the door flying open. Adrian Ward comes in, completely out of breath, his hands slightly curled. "I thought I heard . . ."

He looks from Leopold to Zara.

Zara gave him an entrance to make. Adrian is late — but at least he's here. The golden boy of the Aurelia. Nothing bad can happen while he's in the room. He's too important.

"Miss Evans and I were just working on her death scene," Leopold says.

"Oh," Adrian says. "Yeah. That makes sense. You good, Z?"

She's not good. That feeling is on the other side of a locked door and she has no idea how she'll open it again.

"I'm afraid that will have to be all for tonight," Leopold says, holding a hand to his face — a fluttering, delicate hand.

Zara doesn't wait to watch him collapse into a heap of visions. She doesn't care about his genius.

She rushes out of the office and down the hallway. Adrian sticks close until she stops on the landing to the stairs. That's far enough, some vague but necessary distance that makes her feel like she can stop and breathe for a second, nursing the sting in her throat. Trying to forget the way Leopold's hand felt on her skin.

She slides down to sit on the concrete landing. Adrian sits down next to her, cross-legged. "Hey." He puts a strong arm around her shoulders and it shouldn't make her feel better, but it does. "You all right?"

"Yeah. Thanks for agreeing to do this. I know it must have sounded strange when I asked you but . . ."

"It's no problem, Z," Adrian assures her. He leans in and stage whispers, "In case you haven't noticed, this whole place is strange."

Zara almost manages a laugh. Adrian keeps getting these half-chuckles out of her at the least likely times. Of course, her muddle of panic and relief probably has something to do with it. "You really did save the day," she says. "Good job with the whole hero thing."

He leans in toward her, softly, his mouth so close that she can feel its warmth. Zara pulls back. "What are you doing?" she asks with an edge of hysteria that turns her words ugly.

Adrian's shrug is hard, defensive. "That rehearsal when you kissed me? The kiss at the gala? Then . . . tonight?"

"That was acting," Zara says. "I'm an actress." Her voice sounds weak, even though she's insisting.

"We have chemistry," Adrian says. "You can't fake that."

Zara didn't see anything like this coming. She remembers Toby: *Adrian Ward, with whom you have about as much chemistry as a cat and a cold bath.* Besides which, Adrian is a movie star. This can't be real. But that's not even remotely fair to him. Adrian is sitting right here, smelling like sandalwood and boy-sweat, confused hurt brewing in his face as he waits for her to say something. Adrian is a real person — he wants love as much as anyone else. And Leopold has been pushing him, too. Pushing him toward her. Zara owes him something. Not a kiss. The truth. And the truth is, they're not always a cat and a cold bath. Not when they're onstage and Zara is channeling the strongest feelings she's ever had. "I'm not faking it. I'm feeling it for somebody else."

Adrian's gray-green eyes cloud with instant misery. "There's another guy?"

Zara wishes she could tell Adrian the truth — *Eli, Eli, Eli* — but what if he lets it slip? What if he's jealous enough to tell Leopold on purpose? "I'm not going to answer that," Zara mumbles.

"Which means yes," Adrian says.

294

"I'm —"

"Don't say sorry," Adrian mutters.

He gets up and pounds down the stairs, filling the landing with hard, hollow sound. Zara should go after him. Find some way to explain. If she doesn't, the play is in trouble. Adrian and Zara have to stand in front of hundreds of people every night and convince the world that they're in love.

Zara gets up and starts to run. She has to find the one person who can make her feel better. She checks the lighting booth, which is locked. She tries the greenroom — empty. She walks into the wings, and there's Eli, standing on the stage, looking up.

She walks slowly, neck craned, one arm lifted as she squints. It looks like she's trying to keep the sky from falling. She's muttering to herself in Spanish, or maybe she's talking to the lights.

Zara grabs Eli's hand. "Hey."

"I thought you went back to Kestrel's," Eli says, stroking Zara's palm with her long fingers. Even that little brush sings through Zara's entire body. The locked door inside her eases open.

"Are you okay?" Eli asks.

No.

But if Zara lets out that truth, she'll have to tell the rest of it. She doesn't want to admit she was stupid enough to go see Leopold alone. That she lied to Eli. That she let him stand there while she screamed and screamed.

"Hey," Eli says. "Let's get out of here. Get some food. Or

just go home." Eli looks beautifully nervous. "Let me take you home."

Zara is flooded with a new impulse. She pushes Eli toward the wings, but not all the way. Zara wants the stage under her feet. The height of the flies, taking the lid off her sense of possibility. She wants the Aurelia. Not Leopold's Aurelia. The one that she walked into that first day of auditions, the one that felt like hers. Zara wraps the thick red curtains around them so they're alone in the middle of the theater.

"Privacy," she whispers.

Eli is smiling, shaking her head. "The first time I saw you, these curtains . . . It's hard to explain."

"Later?" Zara asks, because she wants to know about the first time Eli saw her. She wants to know everything.

But first: this.

She tips forward. Their lips touch. Fingertips kiss, then palms slide. Their breasts come together, pressing. Soft sounds twine with Eli's breath, which comes faster and faster. Zara wishes she could do this every night, center stage. This is the story she wants to tell. It's *Echo and Ariston,* but better.

Eli stops kissing her just long enough to ask, "You sure you're okay?"

Zara nods. She brushes a thumb over Eli's lips, turning her worry into a wide smile.

But now, when they start kissing again, Zara has to work to hold herself in the moment. The curtains turn into a musty prison of trapped air and old velvet. Zara presses harder, anchors her hands in tangles of black hair.

296

A creak comes from the theater — a creak that has nothing to do with their kissing. Zara's eyes snap open.

"Shit," Eli mumbles, forming the word against Zara's lips. One of the doors in the house just opened.

Eli's body hardens into a plank against Zara's.

If you have anything to hide, keep it hidden.

The sound of footsteps on the stage holds Zara in place. She can feel Eli's heartbeat fighting hers, out of time with each other.

That's when the singing starts.

A soprano is onstage, her voice so high-flung and glittering that it sounds like stars in a cold night. It takes Zara a few words to place the song — "Tonight." *West Side Story.* Another tragic play about love. The woman sings about how it is all beginning and the world is falling away.

Zara is afraid to look, and at the same time, she can't stop herself. There are too many mysteries in this theater, and one is standing right next to her, begging to be known. She uncurls the curtains just an inch. A figure stands downstage center, her blond hair shining in the dim light.

Zara turns to Eli and mouths, *Meg.*

Eli mouths a string of curse words, one after the other, firecrackers going off without a sound.

Meg is tiny, but she seems to take up the entire theater. Whatever it is that makes people's eyes stick to certain actors, she has it. Presence, beauty, a balance of human frailty and otherworldly strength.

Zara can't believe what she's watching.

Meg moves into the second verse, her voice growing stronger, and it's like she dropped a stone into the most secret parts of Zara. The impact creates rings, and the rings move outward until they touch her lungs and she is holding her breath; they touch her eyes and she wants to cry.

Then, from somewhere out in the house, Zara hears a sigh rise like steam. "That was beautiful," Leopold says.

Zara gasps.

Meg turns and looks straight at her.

xxvi

Is something wrong, my dear?" Leopold asks, inspecting Meg's face as she stares toward the wings.

"No," she says. "I thought I saw something, but it's gone."

She turns back to face him, looking much more like a personal assistant than a starlet. She wears the same clothes she did at rehearsal: offensively boring khakis and a button-down shirt. Leopold pictures her in the white lace dress that she wore as Maria. And then he pictures her in nothing at all.

There are so many versions of Meg, and they only have one thing in common.

They are all his.

She came from nowhere, like Zara Evans. No pedigree, little training. She was ready to be molded. People adored her Maria. And with each drop of their love, the dark sea of his jealousy grew.

He decided to keep one actress for himself.

Meg made it easy. She was in love. When Leopold was younger, women threw their bodies at him like birds against a windowpane. He had never been particularly interested — in women, in men, in anything but theater.

But he heard them call Meg a goddess, and soon she would know they were right. She would leave the Aurelia. She would leave him behind, even though he made her what she so desperately wanted to be. So Leopold whispered three small words in her ear and — like magic — she stayed.

West Side Story closed after seven hundred and twelve performances. It was easy enough to make a few discreet calls, to sow a few rumors. People were all too willing to believe that Meg was impossible, unstable, selfish. She was an actress, after all. He told them a story with a tired old script, which is exactly what people love best.

When Meg came back to his apartment after auditions, Leopold would take her small hands in his and say, "Don't worry, my dear. Parts will be flooding in soon." After two dry seasons, when the money ran out, he said, "Work with me at the Aurelia." He whispered into her ear, "You will never have to stop acting."

At some point he bought her an apartment. At some point he stopped touching her. He tried to explain that this is love in its purest form.

He watches her. He worships her.

The song ends on an impossible high note that sounds too pure to be formed by a human voice.

Sometimes when Meg sings for Leopold, it quiets his mind. The visions let him be. He felt one coming on in his office, with Zara Evans standing there. He knew what was coming, so he called Meg.

There is only one vision left that hasn't come true. It keeps him up late, scratches at his mind until it is ragged. It tells him he must do a dark thing. He doesn't want to think of that tonight.

Meg stands on the stage, turned back into a woman creeping toward middle age.

He knows how to make her beautiful again.

"Sing another," Leopold says. Sometimes he is soft with her. Sometimes rough and demanding. Meg always says yes.

Zara presses her phone against her ear so hard that it generates heat. As if that will bring Eli closer.

"What. Was. That," Eli says.

Zara is speeding through the lobby of Kestrel's apartment building, past the fake Christmas trees. "I don't know," Zara says. "I don't know."

They've been going over the same things in a loop since they left the theater.

"Did she see us?" Eli asks.

"She saw me," Zara says.

"But . . . *us*? Plural?"

"I don't know, I don't know."

The elevator dings and Zara gets in. Alone, thankfully. The doors slide closed.

"Why was Meg singing?" Eli asks.

It's a good question. But Zara feels like they're missing a more important one buried just beneath it. How was she that good?

"Wait a second," Zara says, shifting the phone away from her ear. She does a quick search for *West Side Story*, adding *New York City*—which dredges up too many results—and then *Aurelia*. Here are rave reviews of a production that happened when Zara was only a little girl. She thumbs down to a list of the cast and crew. Leopold directed it, of course. Right at the top of the cast is a name that Zara would never have noticed until tonight.

She puts the phone back to her ear. "Meg played Maria at the Aurelia fifteen years ago."

"Meg?" Eli asks. "White-toast-with-nothing-on-it *Meg*?"

"She was Margaret Jones back then."

"Ugh," Eli says. "Of course Leopold would cast her in that role. Why not? There are *so many* leads for Latinas on Broadway."

Zara flares with anger. When she first came to New York, she expected a cast that mirrored the city—prettier, maybe, but just as diverse. Now she knows better, that most casts are mostly white, but Leopold's *Echo and Ariston* is *entirely* white, as if anything else wouldn't match his idea of perfection.

The elevator rises up too far and Zara's insides float. They lurch back into place as the elevator settles at Kestrel's floor.

Eli's apartment is the only place Zara can imagine wanting to be right now, but there's a possibility Kestrel will start caring where she's been spending her time. Zara made up a lie about her parents being in the city last night, which only makes her feel a thousand miles farther away from them than she already did.

"I don't think Meg saw you," Zara says again.

"Good." Zara pictures Eli sitting on her flowered couch, then jumping back up to pace. Eli flipping through the blades on her Leatherman, one by one. "I think we can trust Toby not to say anything. He's gay. There's an honor code."

Zara walks the long, quiet hall toward Kestrel's door. "There's also Adrian."

Eli's voice bursts at the seams with disbelief. "You told Mr. Front Page that you're having girl sex and you expect him to keep it to himself?"

Zara comes alive with a full-body blush. "Well, we're not exactly . . ." She tries again. "I mean we haven't had . . ."

"It's a figure of speech," Eli says, but underneath the bluntness, there's a smile in her voice.

Zara's not blushing anymore. She's officially on fire.

She lingers outside Kestrel's door, whispering in case her roommate is right inside. "I didn't tell Adrian about *you,*" she says with a little muscle. "Just a general someone who isn't him."

"I can't tell if that makes me feel better or worse," Eli says. "How can I want to tell everyone and also want to keep it a secret? It's like being in the closet. Times a thousand. It's like being in a thousand closets."

Zara feels it differently, like she's standing onstage in the dark. She can play all the same scenes as she would with the lights on — flirting, kissing, falling in love — but no one else can see them.

"Good night," Eli says.

"Good night," Zara says.

"Good night," Eli says again.

"We could do this forever."

"Yeah, I'd like that," Eli says. "Call me if Kestrel does anything remotely strange. Including singing show tunes."

They say a few more rounds of good night, and then Zara hangs up.

When she enters the apartment, it has an untouched quality, the quiet of a new snowfall. There's a potted evergreen on the coffee table with tiny twinkle lights and a paper star on top that looks homemade. She wonders if it's the one ornament that survived Kestrel's childhood.

Zara drops her purse in the corner of the little entryway and crosses the living room. Opens her door.

The room has been warped past recognition. No more pristine white and modern glass — it looks like a murder scene without a body. Shredded sheets, broken windows, furniture marred by deep scratches. Worst are the pieces that don't fit the scene, like artifacts ripped from a nightmare. A hacked-apart mannequin. A row of dolls staring up at her with those round, blinkable eyes. Words drawn and scratched on every surface, bleeding at her in shades of red paint. The same words, everywhere.

STOP ASKING QUESTIONS.

xxviii

Eli finds herself skimming across the city in a late night cab. Her feet carry her into a hotel, through a lobby filled with hideous armchairs and Christmas music played on a grand piano. Crystal lamp shades and chandeliers cast yellow light, making the whole place look stained. Eli double-checks the room number on her phone as she rides the elevator up. When she knocks, Zara answers.

And then it rushes Eli all at once.

Zara could have been in danger. Zara *is* in danger. And Eli can't do a damn thing about it.

Zara lets her in, crosses the room on timid feet, and curls up on a leather couch. Eli walks slowly through the suite. There's a monstrous TV, a minibar, a king bed looming in the background. Zara must have spent a fortune.

Eli told her to take a cab to her apartment, but Zara didn't want to be anywhere that people from the Aurelia could find them.

Zara is giving off porcupine vibes, so Eli sits down one cushion away. "It had to be Kestrel."

"Kestrel," Zara echoes.

"There's no other explanation. Right?"

Zara looks over, but not really *at* her. "Someone could have broken in."

"Was the lock forced?" Eli asks. "Was the door kicked in? Was the window over the fire escape broken?" God, she wants to help. She wants to be right. She wants this to be *over* so they can get to the real business of being in love with each other.

Zara shakes her head. "Nothing like that."

"Look, we know Kestrel isn't trustworthy." She ticks the evidence off on her fingers. "Screaming at nobody? Throwing glass at people's faces? Making up fake boyfriends?"

"She never said it was a boyfriend," Zara says with a bristle that Eli cherishes. "Just that she had a secret date."

"While I appreciate the open-mindedness, that still means she *invented a significant other.*"

Zara nods, but it's a hollow motion, all the meaning scooped out. "Kestrel's like this little girl who never grew up."

"Wrecking that room doesn't sound like a tantrum to you?"

"The words on the walls, I can't think of a single reason she would write them," Zara says. She looks at Eli and actually connects with her for a second. "Cosima told me something like that when I went in the other day. *Stop asking questions and get out.*"

Eli knows this is not the time, that she shouldn't push, but what Zara is saying makes no sense. "You think an eighty-year-old woman stole a key and went uptown to re-create a scene from a horror movie."

Zara shrugs.

She hands Eli her phone without even looking at it first. Eli has spent enough time watching Zara to know what she looks like when she's being herself and when she's being Echo. Right now — she's nobody.

"What's this?" Eli asks, nodding at the phone.

"I took pictures of the room," Zara says. Eli opens the photo roll and the first thing that comes up is the bedroom at Kestrel's. The warnings on the walls and the furniture and the floor — it's way past creepy.

"Those dolls," Eli says.

"Yeah."

Eli turns toward Zara fast: she can't hold this in. She has something to say. Something *real.* Her pants give a soft flannel swish as she hikes a leg up on the couch. That's when Eli realizes she's wearing pajamas. She didn't even notice when she left the apartment — she just ran in the direction of Zara. No wonder she was getting those spiky looks in the lobby.

"I've seen them," Eli says. "*Those* dolls. In prop storage."

"So you think Kestrel stole them?" Zara asks. "Or . . . what if she's dating Barrett?" Her words speed up to match Eli's racing pulse. "If he's Kestrel's secret boyfriend, he would have keys to the apartment." Zara grabs her phone back from Eli, and their fingers brush. Just like old times.

Zara scrolls through her pictures, all the way to the little dressing room right after Enna died. "Here," Zara says, thrusting the phone into the space between them, which is getting smaller by the second. They push together, hip to hip, inspecting the handwriting on the walls of the dressing room. "It's the same," Zara says. "The handwriting is the same."

"No," Eli says. "The *Hamlet* quote here looks different. That was the real clue. Barrett was trying to bury it."

"Shit," Zara says.

"Hey." Eli nudges Zara's shoulder with her own. "You stole my line."

Zara hasn't let up her death grip on the phone. Her hands are about to explode the thing into tiny pieces. "But . . . why would Barrett kill Enna? Or Roscoe? It doesn't make sense. There's no motivation."

"That's a very actorly thing to be worried about right now."

Eli pictures that props bastard passing through the secret walkway. Pushing Roscoe. It's not hard to believe, not at all. "We don't need to figure out *why* he did it. The police can be in charge of that. We just need enough proof to get them to pay attention." She thinks darkly of her first trip to the police station. "Believe me, that's the difficult part."

"We can show them the pictures of the handwriting," Zara says.

"We need more. If we go storming into the precinct without enough evidence, they can't arrest Barrett."

Roscoe's death has always been the wrong color, but it's one thing to know that and another to be two breaths away from catching the person who killed him. Eli doesn't know if she should be happy or terrified or just very, very tired.

"I have an idea," Zara says, her voice pre-stubborn, like she knows Eli will fight whatever she's about to say next. "Kestrel knows more of the story than we do. She can tell us what happened."

Zara was right. Eli hates this idea. For one thing, she's still not entirely convinced that Kestrel isn't dangerous. She might have noodles for arms, but she's not afraid to use them. "I'll talk to her."

"No," Zara says. "She barely knows you. She'll talk to me." Zara looks over at Eli like it just fully registered that they're in the same room. "Previews tomorrow. We should get some sleep."

Eli nods down at her pajamas. "I came prepared."

Zara smiles. If she wasn't looking at Eli before, she's making up for it now with some very direct staring.

Sleep would be good, Eli thinks. For both of them. But looking around the hotel room — two hotel rooms, really — Eli gets the feeling that they're not going to take Zara's very good advice.

Zara has never kissed anyone like this — it's a study in heat and impatience. She pushes against Eli with such force that she can't feel skin, only pressure. The leather of the couch crackles as Eli slides against her.

They were being careful with each other before, like they were holding something breakable between them. But now, with Eli's hair spilling through Zara's hands and her own body moving with a kind of spellbinding confidence, Zara's not afraid. Or maybe she's afraid of the right things. Barrett. Leopold.

Not having this.

Eli takes Zara's hand in hers, and Zara lets herself be led, kiss by kiss, across the suite, although she has a very good guess where they're headed. Eli stops just shy of the door to the bedroom, untangles herself long enough to ask, "Should we —"

"Yes," Zara says quickly. She doesn't need to hear the rest of the question. If Eli is asking, the answer is yes.

The bedroom is almost entirely filled with a huge white bed — a blank canvas. Zara gives herself one simple objective: get closer to Eli. There's a winter coat between them, and two shirts, which are just getting in the way. There are Zara's stiff jeans and Eli's flimsy pajama pants. All superfluous.

All gone.

Eli's fingers skim Zara's stomach and sink into the low curve between her legs, fitting there. Snug. And then one finger gets adventurous and starts to draw circles, and soon Zara can't breathe.

Zara doesn't know exactly when they cross that line — the one they left uncrossed in Eli's apartment — but whether it's one specific touch or all of them added together, they're definitely having sex. Zara's entire body is wired with brightness. It's like Eli has taken what she can do with light and slid it inside Zara; she wouldn't be surprised if her blood was running starry white. The good feeling between her legs reaches a breaking point, and when Zara's back lifts off the mattress, Eli is there, cradling her hips.

"Now Echo and I have something else in common," Zara says when she can breathe again.

"What's that?" Eli asks.

"A love scene."

Eli laughs, which is a good thing, and then there are more very good things, and a well-earned collapse. They are a pile of sheets and skin, a collection of warmly lit curves and dips of shadow.

Zara turns on her side to look at Eli. She tries to picture them like this after *Echo and Ariston* closes. When this forever-long winter ends. She touches Eli's bare shoulder and gets a flash of that same curve lit up by the sun. Of Eli's eyes half-closed against springtime brightness, her smile flung wider than a screen door. The two of them sitting cross-legged on a scratchy blanket in some park Zara doesn't even know the name of yet. She can see it — how she'll fall in love with every tree. Zara can imagine them together, a season from now, and a year, and longer than that, stretching out into the unknowable.

That's the scariest thing yet. How good it could be.

Preview night is on a Friday, which means that Midtown is even more crowded than usual. There are thousands of people on the sidewalks. There are countless snowflakes spinning above Zara's head.

She's supposed to duck into the alley next to the Aurelia. Actors enter the theater through the stage door. That's part of the magic. Zara should slip in unseen, as if she doesn't exist until the moment she appears onstage.

Tonight, she breaks the rules. She needs to see the Aurelia, to feel like the theater is on her side. Zara lingers on the sidewalk in front of the wide set of glass doors. The lamps are pricked with points of light, the lobby as red and alive as a beating heart.

She passes through the plush and gilt into the grit and sweat and chaos of backstage. The rush of chorus members and stagehands makes her feel like she's trapped in a fast-moving stream.

She wades into the dressing room. There are chorus members everywhere, so focused on their reflections that it wouldn't surprise Zara if they missed a murder happening right behind them. At the far end of the makeup table, Kestrel puts the final touches on her lipstick, a purple shade that makes her look like she belongs in a very glamorous morgue.

Zara stares at Kestrel. She's lived in close proximity to this girl for nearly two months. Zara wants to believe that if Kestrel was really dangerous, she would know it. But Kestrel is a good actress. Good enough to be Echo.

"Could you come help me with something?" Zara asks.

Kestrel's head snaps in her direction. "Your hair?" she asks, staring at the hanging mess that should be pinned up by now.

Zara doesn't answer. She waits for Kestrel to join her in the little dressing room. As soon as the door clicks shut, she thrusts her phone into Kestrel's hands. Zara takes off her coat as Kestrel studies the picture, squinting her cat-eye makeup

317

into two long, dark lines. "Is that my apartment?" Her voice tilts upward, toward panic. "What's going on, Zara?"

"That's what I wanted to ask. I found that when I came home last night." She takes the phone back and waits to see what Kestrel will say next.

"Do you think I did this?" Kestrel sounds bewildered. "Why would I mess up *my* apartment? Why would I even go into that room when you're not there?"

A stray punch of guilt hits Zara. She definitely went in Kestrel's room without her permission. "Nobody broke into the apartment, so either you did this or it was someone you let in."

Kestrel crosses her wire-thin arms. Zara takes stock of all the throwable things in the room. "Was it Barrett?"

Kestrel is shaking her bright-red hair. The bones in her chest rise and rise as she inhales. "Zara, I swear on my life. I had nothing to do with this." She doesn't deny that Barrett was in the apartment, though.

Kestrel's breathing goes from bad to worse. Soon she is gasping for air. "Xanax," she says. "My bag."

Zara flashes through the outer dressing room and grabs the leather purse from under Kestrel's makeup station. When she makes it back to the little room, she takes out the prescription vial and spills tiny blue ovals all over the makeup table. She plucks one up between her thumb and forefinger and holds it out to Kestrel, who swallows it with a cough.

They wait for what feels like an endless minute.

That's when Zara starts to wonder.

She turns back to the pills. They're all roughly the same color, the same shape. Zara holds up one pill and matches it to another. The word *Xanax* is on both, but only one is carved with machine-like precision. It's like looking at a shadow that doesn't match the person casting it.

"The night of the gala," Zara says as if she's watching a scene being lit one set piece at a time. Soon she'll be able to see all of it — nothing left in the shadows. "That pill didn't work, did it?"

Kestrel shrugs.

"Someone put fakes in here. Good fakes." She tries to hand Kestrel a *real* pill, but Kestrel shakes her head.

And then the shaking spreads — to her shoulders, her hands, her entire body. "Who would do that?"

"Who would be able to?" Zara asks. The answer is right there between them, unspoken.

Someone who makes props.

Zara is worried that Kestrel will start screaming. But she does the opposite. She goes perfectly still and takes one long, careful breath. She closes her eyes and lightly places her thumb and one finger on the lids. It's the kind of adult gesture that backfires and makes Kestrel look even younger than she is. "Barrett loves me."

But she can't say it with her eyes open.

"He comes on to every girl in a mile radius," Zara says. "You must be able to see that."

"He flirts. We both do," she says, but she does it with the kind of delivery that Leopold hates. Flat. Lifeless. *Memorized.* "Barrett just wants people to like him."

"He's a dangerous person, Kestrel," Zara says. The little dressing room has long been scrubbed clean, but Zara can still feel the words around her — the words that Barrett wrote on the walls.

Zara sat in here with Enna once upon a time, talking with her, listening to how she felt. Enna might have thought terrible things about herself. Maybe everyone does. But she wasn't a ruined victim. She was imperfect and screwed up and brave. She was still fighting. She told Zara to keep fighting.

"Barrett hurt people," Zara says.

Kestrel opens her eyes calmly, sucking in her cheeks as if she's biting them on the inside. "You're wrong, and he can explain this."

And then Kestrel is moving, out of the little dressing room, flashing through the larger one and into the hallway. Zara follows. She can't stop herself — she can't let Kestrel accuse him alone.

She might get hurt.

They both might.

"Come back!" Zara yells, but Kestrel is quick, and she knows how to dart around the racks of costumes and the stage-hands. And maybe it's stupid or innocent, but as Zara runs, she gets a wild flash of hope. The future plays out in Zara's head, scene by scene: Kestrel confronts Barrett, he confesses, and the curtain rises, only a few minutes late, on a triumphant *Echo and Ariston.*

With so much going on backstage, no one notices Zara and Kestrel moving against the tide, slipping into Storage Room Two. The huge door clicks into place behind Zara. Kestrel is only a few steps ahead of her, wading into the catastrophe of props. The space that used to feel like a sort of cathedral now just seems dusty and gray and overstuffed. There are rustling noises toward the back of the room. At first Zara thinks there must be mice.

Then the groaning starts.

"Are you all right back there?" Zara asks, thinking someone must be hurt. *These things come in threes.* She hears one low groan, a man's voice, over and over. Then another joins it — higher and louder, like breathy punctuation.

Zara can feel Kestrel's full-body flinch.

"I know you're here," Kestrel says, projecting so that her voice fills the space. "I know what you're doing." Her tone is sharp enough to draw blood. "You brought me here, too. Remember?"

Barrett rises up, naked, surrounded by antique umbrella stands. A crew girl with dark hair stands up next to him, tugging down her shirt, quickly urging her pants up over her hips.

"Hello, girls," Barrett says, not trying to hide what he's done. Not even bothering to act like he feels guilty.

Kestrel starts hurling things — pillows, old records, insults. She pitches an ashtray. It falls short, smashing on the floor. Zara pins Kestrel's arms behind her back, as gently as she can.

"Are you kidding me?" asks the dark-haired girl, taking in Kestrel with sad eyes. "She's a child."

Kestrel shrieks.

With his clothes halfway on, Barrett runs through the maze of old gramophones and decorative screens. Even if she wasn't holding Kestrel, Zara wouldn't be able to stop him. Barrett knows every path through this room. There is the sound of a door yawning open — it bangs shut.

The dark-haired girl passes them with one hand up, shielding her face.

Kestrel melts down to her knees. Her face is lacquered, a layer of tears over the dark eyeliner and purple lipstick.

Zara kneels in front of Kestrel. They have something as good as evidence now. If Kestrel tells the truth, maybe all of this will wash clean. "Tell me everything," Zara says. "Whatever Barrett told you. Even if it's small."

"How about this?" Kestrel asks with a harsh little smile that does nothing to hold back her tears. "Barrett is Leopold's son."

xxxi

Meg sees the two girls coming out of Storage Room Two, Zara's arm around Kestrel's heaving shoulders. Meg sees everything in the theater.

She follows them to the dressing room, where the acrid bite of hair singed by curling irons fills the air. Meg waits as the girls dither; unlike the hair and makeup artists, who hover impatiently, Meg knows how to make herself unseen in a room. She waits patiently for Kestrel to go back to her chair, for the hair and makeup artists to do what they can with the mess that is Zara. When they emerge from Zara's little dressing room, Meg moves quickly toward the closing door. She knocks.

"Come in!" Zara yells at top volume. It's an amateur mistake. Shouting only showcases the tremble at the center of her voice.

Meg opens the door, putting on her best director's personal assistant face. She is concerned, capable, here to help. Zara looks up. "Oh," she says with relief. "I thought it would be Leopold."

And just like that, Meg is not the director's personal assistant. She's an actress, a young one with an improbable starring role, waiting for Leopold to make his rounds before a performance. Meg used to live for those moments. The butterfly of her pulse, Leopold's beautiful words. He gave her so few that when they came, it felt like the return of the sun after a long, cold season.

"The director is indisposed," Meg says.

She left him lying in a heap on the floor of his office. There were animal sounds rising from his throat. Meg shook out a dose of Oxycontin, pressed a cool cloth to the back of his neck, and told him to count to one thousand. Sometimes, when his visions are already raging, there's nothing else she can do.

Meg closes the door behind her, sealing them in.

Zara turns back to her little compacts of paint and powder, pretending to be focused. "Is everything all right?" Meg asks, her voice as cool as a compress. "I saw you and Kestrel coming out of the storage room. You looked upset."

"Oh, it was nothing," Zara says, smudging a spot of

pancake at her neckline that hasn't quite blended. "I mean, not nothing. Barrett and Kestrel were dating, and . . . she caught him cheating. I went because she wanted to confront him."

If this is all about Kestrel, Zara shouldn't look so pale under her makeup. So cold inside her skin. As though she's caught at the center of a snow globe that has been violently shaken and won't stop swirling.

"Is that all?" Meg asks. Zara cuts a look toward Meg, sharp with distrust. Meg takes a deep, supported breath, the kind that actors draw on for their performances. "I know you saw me onstage last night. It must have given you all sorts of ideas. Give me a chance to explain." Meg doesn't want to say these words out loud, but there's no real way around it. Barrett has caused trouble, she can sense it, and she needs to regain Zara's confidence. So she takes this one sentence at a time, treating her life like a story that happened to someone else. "When I was a girl, not much older than you, I left the place where I grew up, a small town in Louisiana. I came to New York and auditioned for shows. I met a charming director."

Zara's eyes, darkly outlined, meet Meg's in the mirror.

"He made me believe that I was the most talented, perfect creature," she says. The bitterness has been inside her for so long; it has grown so intense that it feels like poison. "He told me I was the most worthless girl he'd ever seen. While Leopold was building me up, he was also tearing me down. Slowly. Methodically. I didn't see that until it was too late."

Zara holds her arms tight across her middle. Fear is making its way through her, finding a proper home.

Good. Meg was never afraid enough.

"Whatever is happening, whatever is troubling you, I can help. That's what I'm here for. To help the actors. That's why I keep coming back. Not for him. We're about to start previews, Zara, and I don't want you to go on like this. Leopold will notice, for one thing."

"All I wanted was to be Echo," Zara says, wooden and scraped.

"I know," Meg says. A bit more poison leaks out. "Echo is your dream. Our dreams have another side to them, though. We wake up. Sometimes more roughly than others."

Zara turns around to face Meg fully. "Barrett is Leopold's son. Did you know that? Maybe that explains why he is . . . like he is." She holds out her phone, and Meg takes in the picture on the screen. "He did this. Last night."

Meg is going to kill Barrett. It's that simple. The stage manager's hard knock sounds. "Places!" Meg opens the door just a crack; the actresses are lining up. "I need a minute," Meg tells the stage manager. "Hold the curtain if you have to."

The stage manager looks like she wants to dismember Meg, but that sort of anger doesn't touch her. People who need to hurt you don't always make a show of it. They find quiet ways.

This time when Meg closes the door, she locks it. "You know about Leopold's visions."

"They show him how to stage his plays," Zara says. But the shiver in her voice makes it clear she's not sure about anything, including the ground she's standing on.

A strand of Zara's light-brown hair has broken away from the rest. Meg captures it and gently tucks it back in, adding a pin from the lineup on the table. "He's been having visions of the deaths before they happen."

Zara blinks. "Roscoe and Enna? He saw them?"

"Leopold told me that the Aurelia's curse made a home for itself in his mind," Meg says dryly. "It took over his visions. They're not just about the show anymore." It feels good to let out a small measure of truth. Meg has been holding back so much for so long. That's how she ends up throwing glasses at the wall.

Zara stares at their shared reflection in the mirror. "Who else did Leopold see?"

"He won't tell me."

When Zara speaks again, her pretty voice is in pieces. "Eli told me that people saw someone who looks like Leopold coming out of the Aurelia on the day Roscoe died. But she also said he wasn't in the city that day. He was with Toby."

Meg sighs. "After talking to you at the Dragon and Bottle, Toby confided in me. Leopold didn't go on that trip to his cabin upstate. He asked Toby to lie for him. You know how . . . persuasive Leopold can be."

Zara falls silent in a permanent sort of way.

Meg sticks a final pin in the girl's hair and sends her to take her place.

xxxii

It has to be Leopold.

Zara can't believe she ever thought it was Barrett. The motivation that was missing is suddenly clear. Leopold trusts his visions. He believes in what they show him. *It has to be Leopold.* This version of the story finally connects Roscoe and Enna. And it doesn't rule out Barrett's role. Leopold could have asked him to steal the pills for Enna's murder, replace them with fakes so Kestrel wouldn't notice the missing ones, threaten Zara when she refused to stop asking questions.

It has to be Leopold. Zara's whole body pulses with the knowledge. Which is a problem, because she's onstage.

There are people out there in the dark, watching her, waiting for her to show them something glorious, but this doesn't feel like a performance. It feels like a dream gone wrong.

She floats into the scene with Echo's father and mother. When Carl scolds her, it feels like he's scolding *her*, not Echo. She remembers Leopold giving him permission to trap her with his body, a moment that keeps coming back to trouble her. Enna's understudy blinks at her with soft blue eyes, naive. She has no idea what's going on in this theater.

Zara stands upstage while Echo's parents argue. She spreads her fingers wide to keep them from shaking. When her first monologue comes, her voice starts out small, a series of nervous steps.

"I would touch without feeling,
Kiss without taste."

When Zara leaves the stage, Leopold is there, waiting. He grabs her away from the spot by the curtains where she is supposed to wait for her next entrance. "What was that?" he asks, his accent flattened.

In that moment, trapped between the curtains and his body, she finds another key.

Leopold never would have picked her if he thought she couldn't handle this role. He cares too much about his own reputation. About *perfection.* He knew from the start that she was good enough. But he also knew she was young and hungry and unsure. He chose her out of nowhere, spun her life in a circle and clothed it in the prettiest dreams. He wanted an Echo who would be desperate to please him. An Echo he could control.

Zara rushes into act 2, already midflight. Running away from Leopold gives her plenty of motivation.

She pulls up the hood of the rich cloak that Cosima made. It's just Echo and the woods now. This part of the play has always spoken to Zara in an urgent whisper — there is something here, a feeling that lies underneath the rest of the story, sliding against the happiest moments, rubbing off on them in ways that foreshadow the ending.

Trees made of darkness crowd her path. Roscoe's stencil created these patterns, but it's Eli's touches that have turned the woods truly menacing. The lighting is perfect. One more thing Leopold was wrong about.

"I must find a way
To a place that does not know
The girl I once was.
A place that does not know
The name I left
Like a leaf, shed and dying."

As Zara spins through the woods — talking to herself, to the trees, to the strangers she meets along the way — she notices that people are collecting in the wings. Everyone presses to the farthest edges of the curtains — Kestrel, Toby, even Carl. Everyone is watching her. No one knows what to expect from this Echo.

She is burning. Bright. Alive.

Her certainty has lit her up in a new way, and it leads her back to Eli. The thought of Eli, warm in her mind. The memory of Eli, hot on her skin.

When she enters the market scene, she's ready to fall in love. Ariston marches in from the other side of the stage. He says his lines beautifully — they slide out of him like he's not even trying. But no amount of acting can cover up the anger trapped in his arm muscles, the hurt flinch in his eyes that only Zara is standing close enough to notice. Zara hoped that a day apart would calm him down. But everything that went wrong on the landing is still there.

"*I dreamed of a beautiful girl,*" he says. "*To see you is to watch that dream wander on new shores.*" The words are the same as always — Adrian has learned them well — but tonight he uses them to sting her.

Eli's light is there, like a firm hand at Zara's back. It reminds her of how she felt when she was at her brightest and most beautiful. The Aurelia is full of Zara's voice and Eli's light, and Zara soars through the rest of the scene on a feeling that no hate or fear can force back to earth.

And then — Adrian stops trying to fight her. All the sweetness that she's seen in him, the need for love, it's there in the way that he puts his hand on her waist. In the way that his eyes warm up before he smiles. Soon they are in some rarefied atmosphere, breathing the dizzy-thin air.

The lines burn up fast. Here is the love scene, begging to be played like it never has before. The bed that Ariston made for Echo is the only thing onstage. As Zara climbs onto it, she wills herself to forget that Leopold chose this bed. She does a furious rewrite in her head, turning it into a bed from another story.

She thinks Eli. She wants Eli. And when she closes her eyes and kisses Adrian, she is kissing Eli.

xxxiii

In all of her time sitting in theaters, watching stories play out scene by scene, Eli has never had to make it through a performance like the one Zara's giving. It feels like watching the girl she loves set herself on fire.

Like any good fire, the result is beautiful. Like any fire in the history of fires, standing close to it is scary. Up here in the booth, Eli usually feels safe: there's distance between her and the stage.

Not tonight.

Eli listens to the stage manager over the headset. She calls the cues to her board op. They'll reach the end of the play soon, and then Eli can find Zara and help her do a reverse phoenix. Unburn herself. Everything will be fine two scenes from now. Eli just has to keep hitting the cues.

And she has to stop thinking about Zara's trashed room. About what might have happened if Zara had been *in* that room instead of rolled up inside a curtain with her.

One scene left before the end. The soldiers come for Echo and Ariston. The love bubble gets burst, every time. They drag Echo away by the roots of her hair while she screams a bright-red scream. The two strongest soldiers pin Ariston's arms behind his back. Adrian Ward isn't a movie star tonight. He's Ariston, in messy doomed love with Echo, and Eli can feel what he's feeling.

She takes them to black, but there's no relief in it. The audience can sense the ending coming now. They know where Echo's story is headed, faster than a falling body.

This is why Eli hates the play, the real reason, the secret that she hasn't told anyone. Eli is a romantic. And the ending of this play *hurts*. To wrap herself in those words of love, to watch the flare between Echo and Ariston, and then every night, to see her gutter out — Eli needs to believe that love doesn't have to end this way night after night.

Echo after echo.

When the lights come back up, the platform is set. The cliffs rise above the stage, fleshed out from a metal skeleton into a harsh outline of rock. The water waits below, dark, blue, patient.

In the corner of the stage, Ariston puts up a fight, but not a winning one. Shouldn't he be trying harder? If he really loves Echo, shouldn't he be finding some way to stop the soldiers? But he can't.

He can't.

Zara trembles at the top of the platform, her breath a shallow mess. Is she acting? Or terrified? Eli can't tell. The lines between this play and life have gone past blurry. They've vanished.

Eli takes out her Leatherman and pushes the blades around, setting them against her skin without letting them cut. The touch of the metal is a comfort, because it reminds Eli what's real.

Zara trembles at the edge of the platform. She's supposed to jump, and then Eli will call the blackout.

But Zara isn't moving.

The messenger's voice sounds the final notes of the play, even though Zara hasn't jumped yet. *"She was pulled down, where love could not reach. Her old name died with her, before it could be revealed that she was Echo, the same Echo that Ariston should have wed. He returned to his kingdom and wept every day for a year, and when he had cried enough tears to drown himself, he woke and ruled his people."*

Zara is still standing there, unmoved. She spreads her arms, a bird stretching sleek wings. She takes a tiny step backward. And when she leaps —

"Go," Eli says.

The board op hits the blackout, and Eli reels in the fresh darkness, an image of Zara burned into her eyes. Zara still on the platform. She didn't jump. Her toes left the ground, but she never took flight. There's the sound of a body smacking. Eli drops the Leatherman, which she forgot she was holding. "Houselights," Eli says to the board op, skipping the last several cues. The play is over, anyway. "Go. Go!" Hard white hits the theater.

She tears off her headset and runs.

Eli's boots are thunder by the time she arrives backstage. None of the stagehands pay her any attention. They're all watching the stage, which they've just finished resetting, waiting for the cue from the stage manager to start the curtain call.

Leopold made a huge deal about his choice to keep Echo out of the curtain call. It made Eli so angry the first time she heard it. Zara did all that work and Leopold insisted that she stay backstage while everyone else took their bows because it *breaks the illusion of her death.*

Now Eli is just glad that everyone else is busy and she can get to Zara faster.

Eli rushes for the handle in the floor backstage, the one that opens to the traps below. When she tears it open, Zara is climbing up the ladder, right toward her. She's favoring one hand, but otherwise she seems okay. Eli breathes for the first time since she left the booth. When Zara sees her, her eyes do that flashburn thing, the one that makes it very, very clear that Zara wants to kiss her.

Eli pulls her up the last step, the water from the pool spreading into Eli's clothes.

"Are you okay?" Eli asks in low tones, surprised by how husky her voice is. It sounds like she's been crying.

"Yeah," Zara says, holding out her left wrist. "I hit the edge of the pool, but it's just a bruise, I think."

There are waves of energy coming off Zara. "I have to tell you something," Zara says. "Not here." Eli nods, her face a bare inch away from Zara's. Their bodies barely touch. Their hands linger for a second, then part.

That's all they can have for now.

It isn't enough.

It's too much.

Because when Eli pulls away from Zara, Leopold is rushing toward them through the wings. And if she wasn't sure whether he saw them, the way he looks back and forth between them, so knowing, so smug, so *playful*, proves it. Eli swears under her breath in Spanish, the most bristling and barbed words she knows, and hopes that Leopold doesn't understand.

Actually, she hopes he does.

Eli changes the blocking at the last second. She stands as close to Zara as she wants, presses their arms side by side, knots their hands. If he already saw them together, there's nothing else to lose.

"Miss Vasquez," Leopold says. "I've been informed by the stage manager that you called your cue early."

This isn't what Eli was expecting.

"I should have known you were too young, too

inexperienced to take this seriously. I never should have kept you on after Roscoe's terrible accident." Eli used to flinch at that word. *Accident.* Now it batters her like a massive wave. It takes her down. "I'm afraid I'll have to ask that you leave the Aurelia."

Last night, Eli thought she couldn't hate anyone as much as Barrett. But now he has company.

"What?" she asks numbly.

"Leave," Leopold repeats coldly.

Eli's been living in fear of those words since the first day she got here, and when they finally come, it's like a cut: so deep and clean and fast she doesn't even notice until she starts to bleed.

"You can't do that," Eli says.

The stagehands are watching, gathered in a little fringe, a tiny audience. They can't look away from her misery.

"I can, and I'm afraid I must," Leopold says. "For the safety of my actors."

"So that's it," Eli says, challenging his truth. "One bad cue?" She knows that she's being sent away because of what Leopold just saw. She wants him to say it. She wants the real truth, out in the open.

Everyone else should have a chance to see how ugly it is.

"It wasn't just any cue, my dear," Leopold says, acting like he's *so* concerned for everyone's well-being. Leopold shakes his head heavily, but there is a glint in his eyes, just for her. A dead giveaway. "Roscoe would be so disappointed."

338

"You don't know shit about Roscoe," Eli says.

She's saying whatever she wants now, whatever is true. But Zara's silence is starting to worry her. At the mention of Roscoe, she goes brittle against Eli's side. Glass to Eli's live wire.

"You knew him for a few short months. I knew him for half his life, Eliza," Leopold says, and it rings so damn false. Nobody calls her that. She is Eli. She is Luzecita. She is Zara's girlfriend. She is Roscoe's assistant. His friend. These are her truths. Leopold's are all the wrong color. Dark as bruises. Dark as storms. "Roscoe would be very distressed to see what has happened here. A lighting designer who jumps the most important cue in the show? Who puts the entire production in danger?"

"I'm not hurt," Zara says, her voice this weak little thing.

"Please," Leopold says, his eyes still on Eli. "For the good of the Aurelia, gather your things and leave."

Eli doesn't have power here. She never has. But there's one thing she can do: she turns to Zara and holds the wet tips of her hair in both hands. Zara is as cold and pale as a whiteout sky.

"Come with me," Eli says.

Zara's lips part, but the words come from Leopold, as if he's changed the wiring and he can speak through her now. "Miss Evans is currently under a contract that binds her for the duration of the play. If she were to step away from it now, the consequences would be quite unpleasant." Leopold digs back into Eli, harder this time. He's done with the fun and games and now he wants her to know that he means what he's saying. "This little career you're trying to build is already in trouble. Fired from a major New York theater at such a young age? That's not going to sit well with directors. Of course, if I call and give you a reference . . ."

Eli looks him directly in the eyes and says, "Fuck your reference."

Leopold laughs, as if all the fight in Eli is just a little light amusement before the real show begins. "If that's the way you feel. I can turn things in a different direction if you'd rather."

It's true that Leopold has influence. But there's no way he controls the entire theater world, like he seems to think he does. This is Eli's dream and she doesn't want to lose her grip on it, but right now, it isn't Leopold that makes her scared.

It's Zara's silence.

"Come on," Eli says, tugging and tugging at Zara's unhurt arm. "This isn't real. He can't hurt us."

Zara looks at her like she has no idea how wrong she is. "I think you should go," she mumbles.

"Zara . . ." Eli says.

Zara shakes her head, this tiny brush back and forth, and Eli's heart does the most predictable thing in the world.

It breaks.

She turns her back on the scene, rushes past the red, red curtains, and bangs through the door that leads out of the backstage area. Just a few more steps and she is away from the Aurelia.

340

One more door between her and the nettles of snow on her skin. Eli needs the bottomless cold and the fractured pavement. She needs the lights that never turn off, their harsh, predictable glow.

She needs to get away from this story.

This is how it goes: siempre, siempre.

ACT III

Leopold is alone in the theater on Christmas Eve when he feels it coming on. The prickle of a headache, like the air waking up, electric, before a storm. There is a weighted feeling in his limbs. When he closes his eyes, the curtain rises on his third vision.

It's opening night at the Aurelia. Leopold isn't in his body, not yet. He's floating, detached. A sort of spirit. Or perhaps he *is* the theater — he can feel a hollow sense of expectation as the doors open.

Warm lights line the lobby. The coat check is accepting a flock of black and gray wool. Tickets are inspected and programs with shining white covers handed out. Patrons murmur in low voices, cut by a sparkling cry of excitement.

Leopold enters the lobby from the top of the balcony staircase, looking as delighted as he ever has. *Echo and Ariston,* his *Echo and Ariston,* has come together beautifully. All eyes turn to him.

A chime sounds with a muffled underwater quality. The sound goes on and on, which means that it's time. There is no turning away. The patrons laugh and talk as they bleed into the theater.

Leopold waits, a comfortable smile on his face. He is vaguely aware that his body is in pain outside the vision, that it is imploring him to stop. But the Leopold within the vision doesn't care about that.

He has to let this scene play out.

Three visions, and each one ends with a death. Leopold still doesn't know if the Aurelia's curse is living through him, or if he has simply known the story for so long that it left a lasting shadow on his imagination.

In the end, does it matter?

All the patrons are in the theater now. Leopold has a seat reserved in the center of the orchestra section, as always, but he doesn't want to be there now. He stays in the lobby, watching through a slitted door as the audience settles.

Soon, *Echo and Ariston* will unfold with elaborate precision,

346

like a clock that he has made and wound himself. This is how the human heart keeps time. Stories like this one.

The houselights go down.

Darkness spreads and contracts, blurring out the details. Leopold hears himself telling Meg that he needs a few moments. He sees himself pulling away from the great doors, walking down the hallway. The vision contracts, narrowing on him like a relentless spotlight.

Leopold, no matter how he fights, is forced into his body. Into the pain. It feels like a thousand bright screams passing through him, a candle that flares dangerously bright, and then — nothing.

Leopold can feel himself dying.

ii

Zara spends Christmas Eve wandering around. She takes the subway, packed with last-minute shoppers and holiday travelers with bulky bags, but when Eli's stop comes, she can't get herself to move toward the door.

Zara made her choice when Eli walked out of the Aurelia. There's nothing she can do to change that now.

She pockets Eli's Christmas present: two tickets to *Hamilton*.

Zara spent a ridiculous amount of her Aurelia money on them, but she's never really had money to spend before and this is the best thing she could imagine. Sitting in the dark with Eli. Whispering together before the curtain goes up. Remembering why they do this—why they love this. Now it seems so stupid and hopeful. The date on the tickets is April 16.

She drifts back to Kestrel's apartment. The little potted tree twinkles on the coffee table. There's a black-and-white movie on in the background—*Miracle on 34th Street*—but Kestrel isn't watching. She's looking out the window. The moon is a lidless eye, and Kestrel has gotten into a staring competition.

"You're back late," she says without turning around. "Did you make up with your girlfriend?"

The question hits Zara like a dropped counterweight. No one has ever called Eli that—not outside Zara's own head. And now it's gone: the girl, the word, the possibilities that went with it.

Zara never should have believed that they could make it through this show together. Eli was right, to stay away from her for so long. To keep her distance. Her silence.

"Who called her that?" Zara asks.

"You mean besides everyone? The entire crew saw you two holding hands. Not. Very. Discreet."

"Well, she's gone," Zara says, stubbing the toes of one boot against the heel of the other so she can kick it off. Her toes slip, and even that tiny failure floods her with anger. "I don't think she'll ever talk to me again. Eli's like that. All or nothing."

"That's a bit dramatic, don't you think?" The irony of Kestrel being the one to say it makes Zara laugh so hard that she has to pretend she was coughing.

Kestrel twists to reveal that she's curled up around a dusty bottle of Scotch. She offers it to Zara with a flourish. "My gift to you."

Zara considers the bottle. She considers the last few days of her life. She takes a tentative sip. "Tastes like hellfire." It's a very Eli way to think of it, which is comforting and painful all at once. She doesn't want to stop thinking Eli thoughts. She doesn't want to go back to the Aurelia without her.

Zara could have walked away and hoped that Leopold would spare their careers. That he wouldn't hurt them in even worse ways. But she couldn't take that chance.

She takes another — longer — swig. It chokes her. She remembers how hot her throat was, screaming in Leopold's office.

"Good, right?" Kestrel says. "Mama left it in the liquor cabinet. And she did *not* sufficiently hide the key." Zara pulls herself into a tight shape on the couch. At least Kestrel knows that Zara's heart is broken — she doesn't have to pretend. To hide. She's done so much of that, and now the sobs come out of her in jagged slices. She wonders if anything could make the burn in her chest go away. The Scotch just makes it burn harder.

Kestrel waits until she's done. She stares at the moon, patiently.

"If it makes you feel better, you can ask me whatever you

want about Barrett. I'd like for him to be strung up, preferably by his nether regions. I'll tell you *anything*." She stretches her fingers wide, a plea for Zara to give back the Scotch. "I took a Xanax, a real one this time. I am so very relaxed and ready to talk."

"You're not supposed to mix those," Zara says, stuffing the bottle between the couch cushions. She's suddenly furious with Kestrel, the full force of her emotions swinging around to land on her roommate. "That's how Enna died. You know that, right?"

Kestrel waves a hand back and forth, like Zara's words are annoying smoke that got in her eyes. "Ask me stuff."

Zara knows that she should start with Barrett's connection to Leopold, how much he knew about Roscoe and Enna, but a different question slips to the head of the line.

Zara can understand wading through this much pain for someone like Eli. But . . . *Barrett*? "Why him?"

For a minute Zara thinks that Kestrel won't answer. When the words come, they're messy and true, the opposite of the precise, grand way Kestrel talks onstage. "He knew I wanted Echo. I was trying to act so indifferent about it, so *fine*, but he could tell. He said that he and I were more alike than I could ever guess. Ambitious. Overlooked." Kestrel runs one long, thin finger down a streak of moonlight on her leg. "Barrett came to the city thinking Leopold would give him a job. That was all he wanted. A chance to prove himself. When Leopold said no, Barrett threatened to tell everyone the truth."

"About Barrett being his son?" Zara asks. The only thing keeping her upright now is the idea of Leopold being punished. Paying for everything he's done.

Kestrel shrugs. "Lots of people have illegitimate children. No one would be so very shocked by Leopold Henneman's bastard." The word sounds like an antique — something that should be kept in prop storage and dusted off for period pieces.

"All right," Zara says. "So what's the secret?"

Kestrel leans forward, as if whatever she knows is weighty and wants to tip itself out. "There *is* no Leopold Henneman. He invented himself out of thin air and fake European ancestors. His mother was a nurse. His father was a drunk." Kestrel's eyes glitter with a kind of hard glee. "Here's the best part: *he's from Indiana.*"

Zara should feel the same bitter delight as Kestrel, but all she's left with is a frantic desire to tell Eli.

What would Eli say next? "You know that's blackmail, right? Barrett was blackmailing Leopold."

Kestrel's response is half whine, half slur. "The way Barrett said it, it sounded so reeeeeasonable."

Zara decides to move on. "So what happened?"

"Leopold stuck him in props and kept him there," Kestrel says. "Barrett has loathed his father ever since."

Zara's thoughts come full circle, back to the deaths. "Maybe Barrett trashed my room, stole your pills, did everything Leopold told him, because he thought Leopold would finally give him a better job. That's what he wanted, right?

What the blackmail was all about? Did Barrett say anything about a promotion?"

Kestrel nods, biting her lip until it glistens in the moonlight. "He said things were about to get better for him. He made it sound like I would be there with him as long as . . ." She sighs, like she can finally hear how silly the words sound. "As long as we kept it secret for a while."

Zara winces. She wishes she'd never asked Eli to keep their relationship a secret — but what choice did they have? Maybe they should have waited until *Echo and Ariston* was over. It seems so obvious now, but when she was staring into Eli's eyes in the shine of a lantern under the stage, the thought never even occurred to her.

She wants to crawl into bed, nurse her heartache and her brand-new Scotch headache, and forget. She wants all this to disappear, the way the snow does at the end of the winter. Dirty and gritty and built-up and then — gone. But her life isn't going to work that way.

Zara needs to wash it clean. Otherwise what happened to Zara and Eli, what happened to Toby and Michael, what happened to Carl and Enna, what happened to Meg, will just keep happening.

Leopold killed two people. He might kill another one on opening night. Zara can't let this go. Not yet.

"I need to ask you something," Zara says.

Kestrel speaks with her eyes closed. "I fell asleep."

"It involves getting back at Barrett."

The corners of Kestrel's lips hook upward slightly. "I'm listening."

Zara has an idea — a way to connect Enna's scribbled words to Leopold. She should have thought of this sooner. Not just what the words meant, but who they pointed to. "The production of *Hamlet* that Enna was in," Zara says. "The one where she played Gertrude. I need to know who at the Aurelia was involved with that play."

Kestrel is quiet for so long that Zara thinks she might have actually fallen asleep. And then, as softly as the snow that has just decided to start falling, Kestrel whispers, "Leopold. He directed it."

iii

Zara stands in the lighting booth, alone.

It's early. Too early. But Zara's sleep was shredded into long, ragged strips—awake and restless or asleep and mid-nightmare. The sad part is that she would have loved the nightmares if even one of them had Eli in it.

Today is Christmas. The Aurelia is dark. This is one day when the city feels like it's gone dark, too.

What is Eli doing? Did she go back to Connecticut to spend the day with her family? Did she stay in the city and start looking for a new job? Did she go out and try to meet another girl as quickly as possible? One who was prettier than Zara? Easier to love? One she wouldn't have to stay in the dark for?

The lighting booth is nothing without the assistant designer. No stacks of loose paper with her deeply slanted handwriting. Zara inhales, hoping to catch Eli's smell — spicy pencil shavings and electrical sparks and mint lotion.

Nothing.

That's not why Zara's here. She needs evidence of what Leopold did. If she can find evidence, then she can stop Leopold from hurting anyone else. If she can stop Leopold, then she stayed for a reason and not just because he told her to.

The booth is supposed to tell her more about Roscoe, to give up some clue that she and Eli missed the first time around.

Zara falls to her knees, bones meeting the floor abruptly. Trying to prove Leopold's guilt was supposed to distract her, but it's not enough.

She plays a new game.

You're allowed to crumple on your side, but not cry.

You're allowed to sob like someone reached down your throat and is trying to tear out your lungs, but you're not allowed to cry.

The tears leave with hot fury, like they're angry at Zara for not letting them out sooner. How could Eli ask her to leave? How could Zara say no?

You're allowed to stay here for a while and think about her. As long as you don't cry.

Zara wipes away the blurry salt. She sees something on the floor. It's shiny and metal and familiar. Zara clutches it in her left hand, forgetting the bruise until it's too late. She's holding Eli's Leatherman, with its mismatched teeth and sharp fingers that fold out from the handle.

Eli left without her things. The stage manager had the lighting booth emptied, stripped of Eli. The crew must have missed this. Zara should return it. But as she turns it over and over, she knows that she has no intention of giving up the one piece of Eli that she still has.

That's not right. She touches the keys that hang around her neck.

She has two things now.

A sound startles Zara into dropping the Leatherman. It takes a few rings to realize that it's her phone, trying to leap out of her pocket. Zara has thought about calling Eli so many times. But what would she say?

Zara takes out her phone.

The little screen is lit up with a single word. *Home.*

She hasn't talked to her parents in over a week. She can't imagine doing it now. Her finger finds the button that will send them to voice mail — but they shouldn't be calling her so late. They never do. Zara's heart twists, finds a new way to be terrified.

"Mom?" she asks. "Dad?"

"Hi, honey." Her mom's voice is half sigh.

"What's wrong?" Zara asks. She finds herself back on her feet. Moving. "Is something —"

"Everything's fine. Except that we can't get in touch with you." Zara wants to apologize, but she can't find a single *I'm sorry* to wring out of her body. "I know your rehearsals run late, but . . ."

"Yeah. I've been hard to get a hold of. I know." The distance in Zara's voice makes her wince. The air in the lighting booth is a mess of unsaid things. Leopold and his visions. Love and death.

Eli. Eli. Eli.

"We're coming to see you in a few days and we need to make sure we're all set," her mom says.

"No." Zara can't have them here, not until Leopold is gone. Besides, there's still one more problem to deal with. *The curse ends on opening night.* "You should come later in the run," Zara insists. "The show isn't ready yet."

She tells them about her wrist — one little dark truth she can admit without dragging the rest of it into the light. Besides, it backs up her story about the play needing more time to get on its feet. She definitely doesn't tell them how it happened. *My girlfriend hit the blackout too early, probably because she thought I was in danger.*

She rewrites that in her head.

Ex-girlfriend.

"Zara, honey, should we be worried?" her mom asks. The tone of her voice sends Zara back to a time when she was a little girl watching her mom's hands reach into the darkness of their medicine cabinet, searching for cotton balls, cough medicine, Band-Aids. Whatever would make it better.

"Honey," her mom says. "Are you still there?"

"Yeah," Zara says. "Still here." Her view of the stage becomes a watercolor. She blinks, trying to give the world solid edges.

"Here's your dad," her mom says, handing off the phone.

You can tell them you love them, but only if you don't cry.

"Merry Christmas," her dad says, which is sort of a family joke.

"Merry Christmas," she says back, her voice halfway gone.

"Are you excited about opening night?" he asks, probably just to be saying something.

"I'm scared," Zara says.

At least she doesn't have to lie.

iv

Wandering around the empty Aurelia makes Toby feel like Hamlet's ghost. He passes through the hall where audience members wait to be admitted through arched doors. Narrow vines of stairs lead up to the balconies. This place was built a hundred years before his time, but Toby can't help feeling like he's a fixture here. A sconce, or a gargoyle — permanent, decorative, easy to overlook.

The hidden door that leads up to the lighting booth flies open and Zara flies out, a storm of tears and snot.

"Taking a turn around the grounds?" Toby asks.

Zara whirls around with pink, feral eyes and a switchblade held out blindly. He throws his hands up in mock terror. "So you've joined one of those ingenue gangs. It was only a matter of time."

Zara breathes herself back to normal. She folds the knife back into its little knife home. "Toby. I'm sorry, I . . ."

He brushes the air lightly with his fingertips. "No need."

Toby wants to tell Zara that he understands. Oh, he understands all too well. Eli, the girl of the midnight texts, is gone. Zara is putting on a brave face about it, but it makes Toby feel better to know that she's capable of falling apart.

He stopped crying a long time ago.

He takes one of her arms and links it through his. "Did you know that company is the best way to stave off heartbreak?" Zara shakes her head as they begin to stroll. "It's not a cure, of course. There's only one cure."

Zara looks up with wide, needful eyes, and Toby wishes he had something better to offer than "Tequila."

"Oh." Zara drops her eyes to the ground. "Right."

He doesn't ask what she's doing here on Christmas, of all days. When a heart is broken, it doesn't follow a schedule. He takes her up the balcony staircase, the scenic route to the linoleum parts of the building. Toby is needed elsewhere, but at least they can walk together for a bit.

"Can I ask you something?" Zara says.

Toby feels a strange responsibility toward this girl. Or maybe it isn't strange at all. Maybe, given his history and his involvement, it makes absolute sense. "Anything in the world, my love."

"Why didn't anyone speak up about Leopold?" Zara asks. "About what he does to people?"

"He was very good at hiding it for a long time," Toby says, disgusted at how easy it became not to see the truth. "I, for instance, didn't know why Michael left me. Not for years. I thought he had simply moved on."

"How did you find out?" she asks.

"A friend." Meg. "She discovered something unsavory about Leopold, and as soon as she started digging, well . . . let's say there was plenty to unearth." He takes a set of keys from his pocket and unlocks a door on the balcony that leads to one of the building's inner staircases.

A door swings open, several landings up. Carl appears in the gloom, showered by red light from an exit sign. Meg is behind him. And Cosima. Barrett is there, too, at the very back. When Zara catches sight of him, she stiffens.

Toby can't say that he blames her.

Carl calls down to Toby. "It's late. We're heading for the Dragon and Bottle."

"We were just chatting," Toby says.

He turns back to Zara. "Do you want to come to the bar with us? Christmas tradition. Anyone who doesn't have plans is welcome. The bartenders make perfect, horrible eggnog. With *eggs* in it."

Zara shakes her head. It doesn't surprise him, but he felt he had to try. He can't promise that the pain she's in will lessen anytime soon. There is something he can say to make her feel better, though. He sets one hand on Zara's shoulder and dusts off his very best I'm-a-wise-adult voice one more time. "Don't let Leopold worry you, chickadee. He'll be done hurting people soon enough."

There is only one rehearsal to fix what went wrong in the previews, so Zara's not surprised when Leopold chooses to devote it to running Echo's death. She's not surprised, but she is terrified. The end of the curse is coming on fast — a third death — and she has no reason to think that it won't be her.

"Again," Leopold says, walking through the shadowy house, his voice coming from a new place every time he speaks.

Zara climbs the platform.

"Jump," Leopold says.

Zara lets herself fall.

When the lights have been cut and the tank has been lowered, a stagehand helps Zara over the side of the tank and she walks, shivering and shedding water, up to the stage to start again.

Adrian catches her arm just as she clears the wings. "You okay?"

"How do I look?" she asks through teeth gone mad with chattering.

Adrian subjects her to one of his most soulful stares. "Hey, I'm sorry about Eli. You know that, right?"

Zara shakes her head. "It doesn't matter now." She barely recognizes her own voice. She barely feels herself in her own body.

She goes out onto the stage and finds that Leopold has climbed up the rehearsal stairs. He's waiting for her — his suit pressed and lovely, his face feverish and blistered with sweat. Leopold smiles at Zara and she feels like she's dying. He puts a hand on her arm and she wants him to die. She has never wished for something so horrible. It's a swallowing pit that opens up inside her.

"Only a few more times," Leopold says, ever so gently. "We both need this to be right."

Zara is playing the statue game with all her might. Stillness is her only defense. Otherwise she will do something reckless. Spit onto Leopold's clammy skin. Claw out his eyes.

Tell the truth.

365

All of it.

Leopold doesn't move — are they waiting to see who will break first? But then his weight sags into hers, and it becomes clear that he needs her to hold him up. The muscles in his cheeks drag, his lips parting with the slow melt of honey.

He's having a vision.

Zara doesn't turn away. She pays attention to what Leopold looks like when he's in pain. There's a savage happiness involved — whatever Leopold is seeing right now hurts him, and Zara wants him to hurt.

He's watching someone die.

Zara wants to scream at him.

Who do you see?

But she can't give away how much she knows. Her innocence put her in danger for so long. Right now, it's her only defense.

Meg rushes to the stage with a little orange vial in her hand. She gets to her knees and feeds Leopold a pill, opening his mouth and pushing the pill to the back of his throat. Zara can see the old-fashioned silver fillings in his molars. Her gaze flicks away, only to get stuck on the vial in Meg's hand.

Oxycontin.

vi

Adrian doesn't expect Zara to show up at the door to his private dressing room, looking determined. "I'm coming in," she says, sliding past him on an angle and then closing the door with a bang.

Good thing Adrian's already changed. Getting stuck in a small space with his costar and none of his clothes would not be his idea of fun. He's done with the whole naked-in-front-of-Zara thing.

"What's up?" he asks, throwing on his coat. The last week of December has gone furiously cold.

"What I said to you onstage isn't true. It still matters. All of it." It looks like she's about to add something, but she veers in a new direction. "I need you to do me a favor." Zara pulls an envelope out of her pocket. "Can you hold on to this? Give it to Eli. If anything happens."

"What kind of anything?" Adrian asks.

Zara's got the wide, unblinking look that she wears during the last scenes of the play, when the soldiers are on their way and nothing can change what's coming. "You'll know."

Adrian lets the envelope hang in the air between them, dangling from Zara's fingers. Before he takes any sort of job, he wants to make sure he can get it right. "I'm supposed to hold on to this note, and maybe give it to your lesbian lover?"

"Don't use that word," she says.

"Lesbian?" Now Adrian's really confused. He didn't see the whole two-girl scenario coming, but now that it's here, he's trying to roll with the punches.

Zara winces so hard that she actually closes her eyes. "She's not my *lover.* Anymore."

"Yeah, I kinda got that."

Zara looks up at Adrian, and it feels like they've cleared away layers of smoke and they're seeing each other for the first time. No Leopold to push them together, no earlobe kissing to get in the way. "I'm sorry about the other night," he says.

"I'm sorry I didn't tell you the truth," Zara says.

368

Adrian wishes they could just skip this part. Thinking about how he tried to kiss her on the landing has become a hot poker of embarrassment. "I mean, it would have made things easier, you know?"

"If you thought I could only fall for a girl?" Zara asks.

"Yes," Adrian admits.

Zara sighs, like she's weighing something — deciding between an easy lie and a hard truth. "I don't think that's how it works for me. I've dated guys before. I've thought girls were pretty."

"Girls *are* pretty," Adrian confirms.

"This is the wrong time to talk about it," Zara says.

"Is there a better time?" Adrian asks. "Because this whole play has been a hot mess."

Zara sits down, tucking her hands between her knees. "I don't know how to say this."

"Don't worry," he says with his very best smile. (The real one.) "I can help you with your lines."

She doesn't really say it to Adrian — she says it to the ceiling. "I'm bisexual."

Adrian feels like something just went right between the two of them. Finally. "Did that feel good?"

"It made me so *nervous,*" Zara says. She mutters, "There are bigger things to be nervous about right now."

"You mean the play."

"Yeah." There's a weird and sudden hollowness to her voice. "The play."

Adrian feels like he's missing something. He slides to sit on the counter, making the brushes rattle and a few of the little makeup pots fall to the floor. "Well, the media will be shitty about it, especially since we just kissed. And my fans can get . . . intense. But I'll do a press release about how that kiss at the gala was just for fun, you know, since we're such good friends. I'll say that I'm still looking for my perfect girl. They love that sort of thing."

Zara gets out half a smile. "Thank you."

"Bisexual," Adrian says, fiddling with a makeup brush. He knows he should stop talking, but he wants to help. "That's good news, right? You have more people who can help you get over Eli."

Zara looks at him like it's the stupidest thing he ever said. Adrian wants to find some crawl space in the theater and hide for a while. "First of all, no. That's not what it means." Her voice softens, and she goes to some other place, somewhere that isn't the Aurelia at all. Some place in her head where all the best memories are locked up tight. "And second of all, I'm in love with her. Even if she's gone. I love her."

Those words hit Adrian squarely in the chest. His mind goes back to the night when he packed a single suitcase and left his entire life in LA. There was the hug in the driveway. The stupid, stilted good-bye. The days and weeks he spent dismissing every thought of Kerry.

He already found his perfect girl. And he lost her.

"Hey, Zara Evans," he says, giving her a pained smile. "I think we have something in common."

370

Zara looks at him in pure confusion. He'll have to give her more than that.

"Her name is Kerry," Adrian says. "She's back in LA."

Zara nods like she understands that perfectly.

Maybe that's the real reason Adrian came to New York. Why he signed on for this play, picked it out from all the projects in the world. Ariston's heartbreak is the same one he went through, the same that Zara is living right now. Adrian gets that, in a sudden and not very pleasant way. Tragedy is the glue. It connects every smashed-up person on the planet.

"So why aren't you trying to get her back, if you love her so much?" Adrian asks.

"Just . . . take this," Zara says, holding the envelope out, arm shaking. "Please. You said you were sorry, and this is how you can help." She puts the letter in Adrian's hand, and their fingers do that sliding thing. But it doesn't make Adrian want to kiss Zara. For the first time in months he lets himself think about Kerry, her long fingers. Kissing them. Her skin always smelled amazing, like ginger and grass and some third thing that he could never quite name.

Zara walks out of his dressing room, and Adrian immediately opens the envelope. She must have known that would happen — right?

First of all, there are two tickets to *Hamilton* in there. That's a really good idea. Maybe he should send some to Kerry. And then he sees the other paper, the one folded on itself so many times it can't fold anymore. He picks it open, carefully.

371

On one side is *Echo and Ariston.*
The gods have not given me leave to speak
And yet I will
For to leave this unsaid would be a violence
Against all things.

It's one of the best monologues in the play. (It's also when Zara and Adrian do the sexy lantern dance. But he's not going to think about that right now.) He turns the page to the side where Zara's plain block handwriting stands out against the white, the words of the play showing through where the light hits.

Eli,

   There are so many things I want to tell you.
(Everything). But first . . . I was trying to tell you
on preview night, and I never got the chance.
   It was Leopold. It was always Leopold.

Adrian doesn't know what that means. Maybe Leopold was the one who kept them apart? Adrian can't imagine letting someone else come between him and the person he wants to be with.

Only that's what he already did. He chose his fans over Kerry.

The letter goes on, cramped with memories, so many that the margins are almost black. Adrian stops reading, because some of this is *way* personal. What would happen if he wrote a letter like this and sent it to Kerry? Would she read it on her little balcony with the Spanish tiles, the sunshine hot on her shoulders? Would she take him back? The right words matter, but they're not a guarantee.

Maybe he and Zara are both dead in the water.

vii

Zara can't help noticing that New York is different a few days after Christmas. The lights stay up, but everything else goes back to normal. The city was putting on a show. Now it's over.

Now it's opening night. Zara finds a spot onstage and warms up, sliding her muscles to the very edge of their abilities, coaxing her voice to new heights. She is merciless with herself, thinking pain might crowd out fear.

The curse ends on opening night.

When the stage manager tells the actors to clear out, Zara rushes to her dressing room. Loads her face with makeup. Stabs her hair full of pins. Slides on her act 1 costume, the white dress.

The curse ends on opening night.

The stage manager comes knocking, calls fifteen minutes to curtain, and Zara echoes, "Thank you, fifteen."

Zara tucks Eli's Leatherman down the front of her dress, snug in the fabric of her bra — the only place she can keep it close without having it show through the outline of her dress. It sits like a cold fist an inch away from her heart.

If Eli isn't here tonight, she can't get hurt.

That's what Zara has been telling herself. That's why Zara asked Adrian to wait. She wants to believe that if Eli knew the truth right now, she would come to the Aurelia. But then she would be in danger. Zara has already failed her enough.

And if something goes wrong, at least Eli will know the truth.

She would hate what Zara is about to do, but Zara's out of time, and she can't see any other way. No matter how many stories she collects, no matter how firmly they all point to Leopold, it's not the same thing as hard evidence.

So there's one thing left.

Zara can try to stop him.

The director isn't backstage. He isn't in the men's dressing room, at least as far as Zara can tell by hovering outside. She storms around in the same restless pattern — greenroom, backstage, dressing rooms, greenroom, backstage, dressing rooms. She runs the length of the hall and checks the loading dock, but all she gets is a slap of cold air to the face.

Zara feels blank, emptied of possibilities. Would Leopold go up to the studios? She thinks of the mirror scrawled out along the whole room. She wonders what it would be like to die there, caught staring at her own panicked reflection. But no — too many people have access to those studios. She needs to think of a private place. Away from the crowds.

And then she remembers his office.

The fear in Zara's system is taking over, a panic that pushes on her nerves and plays tricks with her pulse. It feels indistinguishable from stage fright. Some of it *is* stage fright. She has to get onstage soon and give the best performance of her life.

Zara runs up the stairwell, and when she opens the door to the hallway, she sees blond hair shining from a pool of overhead light.

It's Meg.

"Have you seen Leopold?" Zara asks.

Meg's eyes cut to the far end of the hall. The emergency exit. "No," she says slowly. "I came up here to find him. But he's missing at the moment. Probably not feeling well." Meg puts on a soothing tone, a textbook sort of calm. "Can I give you a bit of advice, from one actress to another? This is what you've wanted so long, what you've worked hard for, and now it's here. If there's one thing I know, the chance won't come twice." Meg's blue eyes bear down on her. "Stay focused."

The words travel backward in Zara's brain, searching for

something. An echo. Or — what comes first and creates the echo? An origin? A source? She's heard these words before.

You need to stay focused on the play.

Carl said that at the gala.

"Let's go down," Meg says. "Have they called ten yet?"

Zara should leave now, forget about Leopold. She cared only about being Echo for so long — she wishes she could have that back now. But she feels as drunk and dangerous as she did on gala night. She swings an accusation at Meg. "You know he hurt Enna and Carl and Toby. You probably know more people he hurt, and you're not doing anything."

"Of course I do, and of course I am," Meg says. "You just can't see it. It's one thing to know what he's done, and another to try to get people to believe. So many would find a way to ignore it. To put it in a little compartment in their minds and say, yes, he was a monster, *but* he made such beautiful things. I've seen how people treat him. I've lived with him. *I know.*" Meg catches Zara's hands between her two small ones. They smell comforting and predictable. Lavender soap. "Go downstairs and put everything you think and feel into this play. Forget about Leopold."

Zara feels the world swinging around her — or maybe that's the nausea part of stage fright setting in. "Why would you tell me all that, about his visions, if you wanted me to forget?"

Meg closes her eyes and sighs. "I wanted you to be *careful.*" She opens her eyes again, tightens her cheeks, adds some impossible cheer to her demeanor. "Let's go down. All right?"

And Zara does, trailing right behind her. The audience will be taking their seats now, sliding into place.

Zara has one last chance to disappear into the fantasy of her childhood — the love story. She used to pick and choose, remembering Echo and Ariston's epic love and forgetting the unspeakable ending. That doesn't work anymore. She can't believe in love without knowing it could end in pain. She can't care about Echo's life and keep her death at arm's length.

Everything in her training tells her that if someone's eyes flick to the emergency exit, there's a reason. Zara isn't going to let that go, to pretend it never happened and hurry to places.

As soon as Meg disappears down the hall, Zara heads back up the stairs, taking them at a blinding run. Her toes bruise immediately. The shoes that Cosima gave her aren't much more than slippers. They were made for a girl who was kept inside, kept safe.

Zara pelts down the hallway, putting a shoulder to the metal exit door. She shoves with all her weight. The door opens, blowing cold air in at her. The metal fire-escape stairs are waiting. They eventually lead up to the roof — to the open wound of the winter sky.

There is a sound far above, like the shadow of steps. She thinks of Eli, of how she wouldn't want Zara to do this, especially not alone. But Zara can be braver than she ever showed Eli.

Zara can be *more*.

And she hopes that, if this all goes wrong, she can some-day be forgiven.

She takes another frozen breath and tells herself that she can do this. Maybe it's just a story, but it's enough to make her believe.

Zara starts up the stairs.

Leopold's toes are set against the marble edge of the Aurelia's roof.

Buildings crowd and jostle on their way to the sky. When Leopold looks up, he sees the endless stretch of clouds, milky gray on black. New York City, no matter how hard it tries, is only a handful of glitter cast into the darkness.

When Leopold looks down, he feels like he is already falling.

The gun was an option, but in the end, he couldn't take it seriously. It was more suited to a man stealing cigarettes from the corner store than someone who had staged Shakespeare's histories for the RSC. Leopold went through all the knives and ropes and less obvious tortures. For days and weeks, his mind glistened with weapons.

And then there were the days and weeks Leopold spent *not* thinking about it — shoving the notion of his death down, watching it float back up. Now it has broken the surface and become real. This moment. His feet pushing forward. The scrape of marble against his shoes.

And still he hesitates. He tells himself that what holds him back, like a hand to the chest, isn't fear. It's a simple question.

Is this the best way for Leopold Henneman to die?

Such a long plummet — twenty stories — will leave no body. At first, this thought gave him trouble. People have been known to plan their own funerals, but what he really craves is the wake. Everyone shuffling by in a long, respectful line, shedding memories instead of tears. Would they do that for an empty casket?

But in the end, Leopold isn't his body. He is the story that he leaves behind.

He raises his arms, spreads them wide. He thinks that maybe if he catches the perfect updraft, it might lift him away, and he will be gone.

He won't die. He'll disappear.

Leopold was glad that his visions gave him a say in the matter. In other cases, they were painfully specific. Roscoe's death was a flash of falling, and then his body on the ground, marooned in a small ocean of blood. Enna was a paper flower, long past its prime. A crumple of drink and death.

Leopold closes his eyes, but he's not inside the vision, which is a mercy. That would send him over the edge too quickly — no swan-dive rush of cold air, no heady sense of the afterlife. What he feels now is a simple darkness closing in, the claustrophobic final shutting of a door. Like death is a closet to be stuffed into, left to suffocate forever. Nothing grand about it.

Leopold will have to furnish the beauty himself. It's a fine challenge, really. He closes his eyes and gets ready to leave the world one last picture.

ix

Zara takes a step onto the roof and finds that it has started to snow. Not the soft, wayward snow of the gala night. These are driving, reckless flakes that race to see how fast they can land.

They fall on Zara's arms, burden her like a secret. She brushes them off, not wanting to ruin the white dress. It has nothing to do with being the perfect Echo or making people love her. She doesn't want to hurt the costume that Cosima worked so hard on — even now, she's a little afraid of the costume designer.

The snow is so thick it's almost like a curtain has been drawn. Zara fights her way forward, into the wind. Leopold is on the far side of the roof, standing gently on the stone margin, his palms upturned.

For a moment all Zara can do is appreciate the artistry — the scrawl of the city reduced to a backdrop for an epic scene. Noise and life below them, darkness and eternity above, and Leopold caught between the two.

Even now, he is directing.

Even now, he is maddeningly good at it.

But there's an emptiness at the heart of his work. He has no idea how to tell a true story. He's just following the pattern. That's why he needs his actors to be hollow, to be *his*. He's made a little set of puppets to play with, and he uses them to tell the same tired stories over and over again.

Leopold dangles one foot off the edge, into the darkness. The wind up here has muscle and teeth, and it is searching for something to destroy. One moment of grappling with it could send him over the edge.

Zara walks toward him — it's a wide roof, littered with protruding vents and strange slanted bits. Even taking a few steps feels treacherous. Snow seeps through the fabric of her shoes.

"What are you doing?" Zara shouts into the wind.

Where is the third victim?

Leopold looks over his shoulder like she's come up here to consult him about an acting note. "Echo," he says, a tremor in his voice contradicting his body's calm state. "You should be downstairs. The play is about to begin."

She takes another step toward him — but what if he is waiting there so he can pull her over the side? What if he set this scene for her, like setting a trap? What if Zara is the third victim? "I'm not coming any closer."

"Good," Leopold says. "I wouldn't suggest it." He runs his hands through the cold plumes of air, toying with them like ribbons. He dances a few steps forward, then places one foot back to find his balance. "This is it," he says. "The final act."

Zara is cold down to her bones, and even farther. There is a pit of cold in the center of her brain. She needs to keep Leopold talking until she figures out what to do. "I know about the first two visions," she says. "The ones that told you to kill Roscoe and Enna."

Leopold blinks at her like she's a mirage. "My visions come true."

Heat rises in Zara. Her voice should be able to scald the snow into melting. "You *make* them come true."

Leopold lifts his arms, as if to summon a different explanation from the night, from the darkness. "You think I wanted them in my head, screaming? You believe I've relished the notion of my own death?"

"*Your* death?" Zara asks.

"What — did you think I was taking a little stroll on the

edge of the roof for no reason?" Leopold rattles on, as if all he wants is to be listened to. "The curse took Roscoe and Enna. It's here for me now."

"You didn't kill them?" Zara asks. She feels dizzy, then burning, then numb. She wonders how long it takes frostbite to set in.

"Of course I didn't." His eyes are on fire — a terrifying, truthful blaze. "What have I been telling you this whole time? What have you ignored so often? I need this play to be —"

"Perfect," Zara says, stepping on his line. She can see Leopold's motivation clearly now. If he knew he was going to die, he would need his final production to be flawless. But —"You hurt people. That's what you do. Over and over again. Roscoe and Enna are dead. And you want me to think —"

"I don't care what you think," Leopold says, his voice blunted by the cold. "Why are you up here again?"

"Meg," Zara says blankly.

"She told you about my visions, did she?" Leopold asks with a bitter wisp of a smile.

Meg didn't tell her that Leopold was on the roof, but she obviously knew. She did tell Zara about the visions, about Roscoe and Enna. She never *said* that Leopold killed them, though. She just led Zara to the cusp of the idea and let Zara push herself over the edge.

"Wait," she says, her mind suddenly kindled, working against every cold thing about the night. "Meg knew you were going to do this? Come up here and . . . jump?"

Leopold curls a wrist, such a natural movement. Zara wonders how long it took to cultivate. How fully he had to train himself to become the person in front of her, to erase the nobody from Indiana and become a set of careful lies. She thinks back to the costume shop and the hollow set of clothes that looked like Leopold Henneman. That's all he's ever been.

"Meg knows everything," Leopold says.

And the fire inside Zara's mind starts to rage.

"She told me about the first two visions," Zara says. "Meg *wanted* me to think that you killed Roscoe and Enna. But she said you wouldn't tell her who died in the third vision. She let me think you were going to kill someone else tonight. Probably so I would be afraid and stay away from you." Every step, every action, every death could have been carefully staged. "I think — I think *she* made this happen. I think she's trying to kill you."

"Impossible," Leopold says with a smile that calls on all of his old charms. "Meg is in love with me."

"No," Zara says. "She isn't." The Meg she saw in the little dressing room — that version spoke with honesty and telling flares of emotion. That version is closest to the truth. "Meg despises you."

Leopold doesn't seem to hear her, or if he does, it doesn't dent his belief. In Leopold's mind, Meg still loves him.

He looks down at his watch, adjusting the dial, squinting at the face in the dark, and the action is so grounded in the ordinary that it almost convinces Zara everything will be back to normal soon. No murders. No impossible choices.

No pulse beating so fast that it feels like wings about to take flight.

"It's time," Leopold says. "Go downstairs. Take your place."

Zara's whole body strains toward the theater. Her dreams are downstairs, waiting for her to play a starring role in them. She could slip into that so easily, like a warm robe, like a full bath, like a kiss.

Zara could let Leopold go over the edge. She has as much a reason as anybody else to want that.

He sent Eli away.

Zara's skin remembers Eli's skin. Her lips remember Eli's lips, spread into a smiling kiss. Her hands remember the first and last times they tangled up with Eli's, and all the times between.

Her heart remembers *everything*.

Zara could let him fall.

Standing on the roof of the Aurelia, Zara decides — this is not how opening night is going to begin.

"If you don't come down from there, the play doesn't happen," Zara says, taking a step back, the snow lashing her. "You can be known as the director who killed himself because he *failed*. The man who couldn't keep one little nobody actress in line. I won't go onstage." He peers over the edge, like he might have misjudged how far it is to the ground. "Is that the legacy you want?"

"You wouldn't do that," Leopold says, laughing. The sound is as cold as everything else on the roof, but also fragile, like if Zara reached out and touched it, his icy voice would shatter. "You wouldn't do anything to stop *Echo and Ariston.* You love this show. You want it too much."

He still thinks that Zara let Eli go because she cared too much about Echo to walk away. Which means he really *didn't* kill Roscoe and Enna. If he'd done it, he would have been able to guess that Zara stayed because she was afraid of the threats he made at previews — about what he'd do to her if she tried to leave the Aurelia.

Leopold isn't a murderer. But that doesn't make him right.

Echo is the role Zara has always wanted, but not like this. She's already let Leopold write too much of her story, scribble too much of himself into her margins. He isn't going to decide how this plays out.

Not tonight.

Zara crouches on the roof, keeping herself out of the wind as much as she can. She looks up at Leopold.

She watches. She waits.

Downstairs, they must be holding the curtain.

Up here, she is rubbing her hands together so fast it feels like she should be able to start a fire.

When Leopold steps down from the marble beam, he looks angry enough to kill her. She believes that he won't, but she makes him walk first across the roof, just in case, and keeps a hand on Eli's knife.

xi

The lights dimmed long ago. Evening gowns rustle around Meg like restless leaves before a storm.

The curtain should have risen on *Echo and Ariston* nine minutes ago. Meg has a good view of the waiting audience from her seat, third row center. At her side is an empty chair, even though every other seat in the house is taken.

This one is reserved for Leopold.

Meg savors that empty chair.

Leopold told her about the third vision before the production started. At first, she thought it was a joke. Another little cruelty. But then she heard the worry in his voice. Worry became fear, which deepened into panic. He truly thought that seeing himself die meant it was going to happen. He believed in his visions with the white-hot fervor of a saint. Leopold questioned everything in the world except his own genius.

But his one mistake was trusting Meg, not thinking that she was smart enough to eventually figure out how her career had withered, and hate him for it. Of course, she buried her loathing under admiration and helpfulness.

She is a very good actress.

The woman next to Meg digs into her purse and comes up with a chocolate bar. She makes a crinkling mess of the wrapper. Meg wants to turn to her, take it from her hands, eat it very calmly in long, even bites, and then stuff the wrapper down the woman's throat.

The lights blink — a magical, firefly blink — and the audience resettles. This can only mean one thing.

The show is about to begin.

xii

When the curtains sweep apart, Zara is standing in the wings. Her hands loose at her sides, her breath a tightened knot. The audience is out there — so many people. They bring a weight to the room, a heat, a sheer force of wanting.

Zara takes a step onstage.

She thought it would be impossible to let go of what happened with Leopold on the roof, but everything drops away. Everything but *this*. Her skin drinks the light. There is a potent silence. She can feel her heartbeat pounding in each fingertip.

Zara has been trying to get to this moment for so long. Since before Leopold and Meg, before Enna and Roscoe.

Even before Eli.

This is what she wanted. But it doesn't feel like Zara has arrived. It's more like she's just getting started. She stretches and slides into this new reality, finding Echo. Her chin tilts. Her feet arch differently. Her shoulders pin back.

For once she isn't afraid of taking up space. She wants an Echo who can fill this world, the world that everyone at the Aurelia created — bounded by the wings on both sides, the cyclorama behind her, the steep drop-off of darkness that waits past the stage lights.

The chorus joins her now, weaving in from every direction. Kestrel gives Zara a slight, almost invisible nod as she passes.

And then Kestrel's voice takes over the room. She is different tonight. Less polished, more truthful.

"Echo refused a love
To find a path,
Not knowing that it would lead
Past love, to death."

All Zara has to do is take one step backward, to find the beginning. The innocent girl who doesn't see where this is all headed. She's lived through her own *Echo and Ariston*. She doesn't have to imagine. She *knows*. Her hands curl and tighten around the truth. She will give those people out there

394

in the dark something better than Leopold's *perfect*. She will give them trying, failing, seeking. She will give them living, breathing, dying.

Being an actor is all about finding keys from the real world that open imaginary locks. Zara will toss every key she's found into the air and watch where they land.

Meg is watching Zara.

She can't stop.

This Echo is stronger than ever, a diamond-bright surface over a deep sea of urges and needs. Meg tries to escape what Zara is doing, but it's there when she closes her eyes — Zara's sweet, breathy voice pulling Meg under.

Zara shouldn't be able to do this, to make Meg almost believe in love again; it's been a wrecked ship on the shores of her life. This girl, who just lost the person she loves, shouldn't still be able to blaze like this, to *believe*.

At intermission, Meg stands up, careful not to look too eager. She waits as her row shuffles out, holds her head up as she walks through the lobby, avoiding the rest of the audience as much as possible. They are suspended in a dream. She is firmly rooted in the real world.

As soon as Meg has the double glass door in sight, she knows that something is wrong. Or rather, *not* wrong. There should be lights, sirens.

Leopold should be dead by now.

Meg leaves the lobby and goes back to the place where she left Leopold pretending to be brave. Snow roars down, blotting out the sky. Meg's black dress leaves her shoulders bare; she can feel everything. There is lightning embedded in the clouds, thunder to match the enraged wind.

She finds Leopold huddled under the lip of the roof, helps him to his feet. She runs her hands up and down his arms to stop his shaking.

"She made me go downstairs," Leopold babbles into Meg's shoulder as she holds him a bit closer. "She told me to leave. But she can't do that. The Aurelia is my theater. So she told me to stand in the wings, where she could watch me. But she's not supposed to be watching me."

Meg pats his back in circles, soothing him like a child. Every second of being this close to him is pain and revulsion. "Who told you all that?"

"Our little Echo." He looks up at Meg, his hair a matted

397

mess, his eyes the color of a soiled winter. "She said you're try-ing to kill me."

"That's absurd," Meg says.

Meg is a very good actress.

"The visions come true," Leopold says, holding tight to that idea but losing his grip on it just as quickly. "If I haven't jumped yet . . . maybe this one *won't* come true. I might live," he says, his voice circling from confusion to hope and back again. "The visions come true, they always do," Leopold repeats, a broken mutter.

"Yes," Meg says.

She's been making sure of that.

She knows what she has to do. The failsafe was always in place, in case Leopold lost his nerve. She can't push him over the edge; he would take Meg down, down, down with him, she has no doubt.

She slowly unzips the little purse at her side and lowers her hand in, fishing around as if she's looking for tissues. But her fingertips are brushing the cold metal of a knife. It was a gift from Barrett in prop storage. He was a terrible person to involve in her plans; she can see that now. Impulsive, selfish, disgusting to a fault. She still can't believe the idiot threatened Zara in her own bedroom. Like that would really keep the girl from asking questions.

Still, Barrett gave Meg a very good knife. It's not the kind that actors use for stage fighting. It's an ornamental dagger that would be used for set decoration, perfectly heavy and just sharp enough.

This won't look like a suicide anymore. Zara ruined that for everyone. In one minute, she destroyed all of Meg's careful work. A perfectly woven story, one thread tugged out of place.

Leopold only has long enough to be surprised before the knife slides into his chest. There is no pain in his eyes. No betrayal. To feel those things, you have to care first.

He doesn't even scream.

Zara is losing her grip on Echo.

After everything she did to get here, and everything she did to stay, Zara is losing her.

She made it away from Echo's parents and through the woods. She found Ariston and fell in love. All of that felt right, but now the end is coming. The stark blue water. The fall.

She keeps thinking about Leopold and Meg. The story that she stumbled into, the one that's bigger than *Echo and Ariston* but made out of the same fabric — love and death. There's still so much that Zara doesn't understand.

She doesn't have to. Not right now. She just needs to let Echo's next line bloom from her throat. The words are ready, waiting, wanting to be said. But Zara can only think about Meg and Leopold and love and death.

And Eli — always edging in at the corners of her mind.

Always Eli.

Adrian is keeping a hand on her arm tonight, even when it's not part of the blocking. He must be able to tell something's wrong. Zara can feel that he wants her to come back and finish the play. She's barely onstage with him, even if her feet are planted on the boards.

Adrian lays her down gently, and her mind is there, tangled up in the heat of kissing him and the memory of kissing Eli. And then her mind slips, and it shows her other people kissing. Meg and Leopold, Kestrel and Barrett, Carl and Enna, Toby and Michael — all of them twined up together.

All of them in love, and doomed.

Meg, touching her hands and telling her not to worry. Roscoe falling from the ceiling, Roscoe lying at her feet. Enna, cold on the dressing room floor.

Eli, Eli, Eli.

She was the answer to the question that Leopold asked at auditions: *Who do you love most?*

Zara just didn't know it yet. But time has doubled over on itself, and she can see the whole story, laid out beginning to end. Eli was in this room when Zara first stepped onstage.

Eli saw Zara with the curtains and thought — something. She never did tell Zara what.

When she makes her next cross, she notices a new terrible thing. Leopold is missing from the spot where she planted him backstage so she could keep an eye on him during the show.

She takes a breath at the wrong time, arrives at the end of a line with nothing left to give. And there are hundreds of people in the audience wanting *more*. The lights continue to pound and words that Zara used to worship are pouring out of her like sand.

I hate this ending, she wants to tell Eli.

I hate it. Let's write a new one.

That will never happen. Zara is alone with the part that she wanted so much. She has to get to the end of the play. And then Meg will be arrested and everything will be fine.

But fine is not beautiful, fine is not *Eli*.

Echo and Ariston's home by the sea becomes a place for the lovers to huddle together as the story tightens around them like a noose.

With a sick flush, Zara realizes Meg was behind more than just Leopold and the roof. If she could frame him for two murders before he committed suicide, it would change Leopold's entire story. He wouldn't be the darling of the theater world anymore. People would see him for what he was. An *art monster*. Leopold didn't kill Roscoe or Enna, but using the deaths to expose him as a monster was a twisted, brilliant piece of theater.

A lie that tells the truth.

The blackout comes on fast, and quick as a held breath, a beacon stamps itself onto the dark. A lantern. It's not coming from the stage, from Ariston. It's out there in the audience, a lighthouse blink in the ocean of darkness. Zara's heart flares a single word.

Eli.

Zara runs back to the wings. Cosima is there. Waiting. A stagehand is supposed to help Zara into the binds, but tonight it's the tiny costume designer, with a new length of rope.

"Last-minute change," she whispers in a voice that has the same basic properties as a dull pair of scissors. "I tie these on, you go in the water, your hands won't fly apart. No smashing the wrist again. Good? Good."

Zara doesn't have time to agree or disagree. Was that even a real lantern, or did Zara just invent one bright moment out of madness and hope?

"You wait for the blackout, you twist, the ropes come undone," Cosima says, demonstrating with her own wrists. She turns them halfway around, a swift unlocking motion. "This knot is special," she says. "It will come apart, no problem."

Zara nods, hoping her brain has absorbed all of that.

In the final moments of the blackout, Cosima leans forward and whispers, "Leopold killed her. My Vivi. He said she would never be good enough, pretty enough. No one would love her. But *I* loved her. That girl was as good as my daughter. And he killed her."

And then, with a shove, Zara is back onstage.

She feels sorry for Cosima and sick for Vivi. Another girl he plucked from nowhere and pushed until she broke.

Zara's mind splits in two, like forked lightning. One branch is racing through the play, fully present, electrified. The other is reaching for Eli; she is the ground. She is there, past the storm, waiting. She is what Zara needs to touch.

It's not hard tonight to put on her bravest face while the messenger unspools the story of Echo's final moment. It's nothing to climb the stairs and stand at the top, balanced on her toes.

It's easy, sublime, to leap, because every movement brings her closer to Eli.

In the cold water, she does what she's supposed to do. She pretends to struggle. The ropes around her wrists seem to shrink with the touch of the water, to bind tighter. And even though she took the deepest breath her actor's lungs would allow, when the ropes catch, she wants more.

Air. Air. Air.

Now Zara is not so much fake struggling as she is real struggling, and she wonders if anyone in the audience can tell.

She wonders if Eli can tell.

The blackout comes on time, and Zara tries not to let out the rest of her air in a blind panic. She pedals through dark water, feeling her muscles start to prick with fatigue. She turns her wrists, the way that Cosima showed her.

Nothing happens.

Her hands budge less than an inch, and the rope is a tight,

wet heaviness, despair turned into something she can touch. The lights are out, which means Zara is allowed to surface and breathe, but with her hands bound like this, she can't.

The tank lowers into the stage, and now she is away from the audience, and she can't help feeling like she is slipping into some underworld. But that's the Greek tragedy talking. As soon as the tank locks into place, there will be a stagehand, and the stagehand will help her up the ladder, and Cosima will show her how those binds were *supposed* to work, and Eli will be there waiting and —

There is no stagehand to help her out of the tank. There is only Meg, pale eyes locked on Zara as she struggles.

Meg, who is watching her drown.

Eli can't sit here and watch Echo die. Again.

She hated this part when she was up in the booth and she hates it more now. At least when she was working it kept her mind busy enough to interrupt the constant spin cycle of *the girl I think is cute is dying, the girl I want to kiss is dying, the girl I love is dying.*

The woman on her left and the man on her right — both in full evening dress, the lady drizzled with beads — are sitting with their mouths open. It's like they're wearing their heart-beats outside their clothes.

Eli stands up, ruffling her entire row. She passes them one at a time, bumping into knees, not even caring. "Excuse me," Eli whispers. "Coming through."

She shouldn't be drawing more attention to herself. She isn't, technically, a ticket holder. Eli used the oldest trick in the broke-theater-girl book: dress up, wait until intermission, and then flood into the lobby with everyone else. Claim a stall in the bathroom, wait until the last second, check the theater for an open seat. The woman on Eli's left gave her a quick, prod ding glance and then left her the hell alone.

Eli could have kissed her.

She breaks through the double doors and heads straight past the ushers. It's a miracle they didn't throw her out after the lantern trick.

When Eli left the Aurelia, she was fully prepared to be angry at Zara for days or weeks, but she just ended up angry at herself, Leopold, and the entire world, in that order.

Why did you make her choose? Eli asked herself as she boxed up her books and her ripped jeans and her chipped bowls. She spent all Christmas day packing. Her parents called a dozen times: *M'ija, come home. ¿Dónde estás? It's Christmas. We're all here waiting for you.* But she couldn't do it: couldn't face them with a broken heart and a life in glass splinters. She'll be back with them soon enough — no way she can afford Manhattan without the Aurelia money. Eli wanted to be mad at Zara for that. She wouldn't have been fired from her dream job if she hadn't fallen in love with the wrong girl.

But what made her wrong in the first place? The world, Leopold, and Eli, in that order.

Cue guilt. Cue emotional meltdown. Cue kicking at packed boxes until her toes went numb.

Eli imagined a thousand different phone calls — but what was she going to say? *I'm sorry I asked you to give up your dreams for me, when I built my whole life around mine. I'm sorry that Leopold is a controlling asshole of the highest order. I'm sorry I don't want you to die.*

That's why Eli is here. Zara might not want her back, but there was no way Eli could sit across town while Zara fought her way through opening night alone. *The curse ends on opening night.*

It makes Eli sick sometimes, thinking she could have changed things if she'd been there the day that Roscoe died. She's not going to let that happen twice.

But Zara made it to the last scene of the play perfectly alive, so it's time to go. Still, Eli hesitates in the lobby.

Twelve hours ago, right around dawn, there had been a knock at Eli's door, and hope had blinded her. It was the most painful thing Eli ever felt, but also beautiful — like staring straight into a cloudless sun.

When Eli opened the door, it wasn't Zara. It was an even less likely person. Adrian Ward.

"Don't kill the messenger," he said, looking very Hollywood in a leather jacket and dark glasses. He ran a hand through his thick, dark hair, shocking it straight up. Eli couldn't help thinking: he would make a pretty cute lesbian.

"Look," he said, taking an envelope out of his pocket. "I'm not supposed to give you this until later, so I'm going to give it to you now. If Greek tragedies have taught me one thing, it's that what you don't know always comes back to bite you in the ass."

Eli just stared at him.

"I'm going to leave this right here," Adrian said, crouching down to deposit the envelope on her apartment doormat. "Now, if you and Zara don't need me anymore, I'm going to call my girlfriend."

"You have a girlfriend?" Eli asked, latching on to the least confusing of the very confusing things he'd said.

"It's a long story." And with one last hair scrub, he was gone.

Eli has the letter now, folded into a thousand squares and stuffed in her bra. One corner spikes into her skin. Leopold killed Roscoe, but Zara made it through opening night, safe. Eli should leave, but the letter is proof: Zara loved her. *Loves* her.

Eli kept thinking that she wasn't enough for Zara, but sometimes it was too much for Eli. The secret keeping, the constant fear. All she ever wanted, besides her light board, was to fall in love with someone and have it be this good, simple thing. Maybe *she* was being painfully innocent.

The lobby is empty, no patrons yet. Eli waits until the ushers are turned away, and then she slips through the door that she knows, from plenty of experience, will lead her backstage. She strides right down that hallway like she belongs. It's a good thing everybody else is in the wings.

Eli can slip into Zara's dressing room before the actors and crew flood out of the theater. She can be waiting for Zara when she gets back, and finally help Zara out of that wet dress. But in front of the men's dressing room, a few steps from her final destination, Eli hears voices.

She tucks into the doorway, ready to rush away if the door flies open.

"Stop it," Carl says. "We have to go out there and bow."

Someone else is in there. Someone is crying.

Toby.

Eli's fear is a freshly struck match.

"Pull yourself together," Carl says. "No one can see you acting like this."

"I defended you. I told Zara you would never hurt Enna. . . . I *believed* it."

"Is that really what you're worried about right now?"

"All I had to do was tell one little lie," Toby says, panic welling in his voice. "That's what you said."

"And that's all *you* had to do," Carl says. "All Cosima had to do was make costumes and follow Meg's orders. Some of us had to do more." His tone is bitter, bleak. "It all went wrong."

Eli blinks. *What* went wrong?

"Meg will think of something," Carl says. "She always does."

Toby cries harder. Carl must be bringing him toward

the door because footsteps are growing close and loud. Eli quick-strides into the women's dressing room. It's empty. The door to the little dressing room stands open.

Zara should be back from the pool under the stage. She should be here by now.

xvi

With her hands bound and her breath almost gone, Zara has to do the hardest thing imaginable.

She has to stop fighting.

It's the struggle that's killing her. The thrashing, the kicking. It's twisting her up in the godawful heavy layers of Cosima's costume. This costume wants her to die. Meg wants her to die.

Zara lets her body go slack, melting into the weight of the water. She has to sink down — down is the right direction. She hits the bottom of the tank and uses every bit of strength in her legs to propel herself *up*—

She hits the air, heaving and gasping. Meg is still watching, standing calmly at the side of the tank, hate roaring through her pale-blue eyes. "Why did you stop him from jumping?" she asks. "I was doing this for you. For all of us. You only had to stand back and let it happen."

Zara tilts her face up toward the stage tiles that have been put back together, creating a ceiling like a low, black night. Footsteps echo across the boards above her. Actors are coming out from the wings in ones and twos to take their bows. The company is smiling and joining hands.

No one will miss Zara. Not for a while, at least.

"I finished it," Meg says. "Leopold is dead."

Zara gasps, and this time water comes in, mixed with the air.

"I'm going to try this one last time," Meg says. "I'll help you out of the pool, and you can be Echo, if you forget what you saw. There will always be a place for you here at the Aurelia. Just. Forget."

Zara tries to nod, but it dips her head under, sends burning cold water sluicing into her nose.

She fights her way back up. "Yes," she chokes. "Okay." If she can't convince Meg that she believes her, she'll be dead before she can come up with a plan.

Meg's voice curves with satisfaction. "Come to the edge."

Zara goes under and tries to work her way over to the side of the tank, her feet like useless flippers, her hands still bound.

413

Cosima did this.

Bound Zara's hands.

And there was that costume, in the corner of the shop. Cosima made it so someone else could dress to look like Leopold. It would have to be convincing enough that strangers on the street would be able to confirm that they saw Leopold coming out the front door of the theater that day.

And who better for the role than Leopold's son?

Barrett never wanted to help Leopold — he hated his father. That's what Kestrel told Zara. Meg must have been the one who promised Barrett a better job when Leopold was gone.

But Barrett couldn't have used the costume to give Enna the pills. To poison her. Enna wasn't a stranger on the street — she would have seen right through the disguise.

That had to be someone else.

Zara doesn't have the time to figure it out. She only has half of the truth, and she is going to take it with her into nothingness. It's stunning, how certain Zara is that she's going to die. The water tells her so. Her brain starts to sponge with black at the edges.

Zara chooses Eli for her last thoughts. Eli, somewhere in the Aurelia. Eli, waiting to tell her it's okay and to take both of Zara's hands in hers. Her smile. Bright, hot, white. Her blue-green tattoos, a whole world scrawled on her arms. Her black curls, everywhere.

Her Leatherman.

It's still tucked into Zara's bra. She can feel it there, hard against the workings of her heart.

Zara lets out her breath all at once, sinks to the bottom of the tank like a dropped stone. She has one chance to get this right. No rehearsal. No running it again if she messes up.

Zara tugs at the neckline of her dress until she has the Leatherman in a clumsy double grip. She pries at it, freeing several of the knives at once, slicing into her own fingers, pointing the Leatherman toward her wrists. The water pinks with blood as one long blade struggles through the rope.

Then she pushes against the bottom of the tank, and when she makes it to the surface, she ignores the screaming pulse in her cut fingers and lashes at Meg. The director's assistant steps back — not quickly enough. The blade catches her in the arm, and sticks.

Applause rages above them.

Zara can feel it in the bones of the building. She can hear it over the sound of her scraped breath.

It covers Meg's screams.

Zara pulls herself over the side of the tank, her arms doing things they shouldn't be able to after so long tied together, going numb. Blood runs onto the floor — her blood, Meg's blood. She's afraid of how much she hurt Meg. She's afraid that she didn't hurt her enough.

Zara runs, floor slippery, hands sticky. Her feet are a nervous drumbeat on the ladder, pounding until she makes it to the top. She uses the last of her strength to lift the door above her head and crawl into the wings. The actors are onstage, looking out at the audience. There are no crew members on this side of the wings. The assistant stage manager stands on the far side of the stage, but she's not paying attention as Zara waves one bleeding hand. Meg will be after her soon. Zara needs help. She needs —

Zara thinks she must be wrong, she must be hallucinating. She might be dead.

Because Eli is there, in her dark-blue dress, running through the wings. She doesn't have the shining look of a prince coming to save someone. She looks tired and desperate and painfully in love.

Zara collapses.

Her breath is gone. Her muscles are failing one by one. She's bleeding. A lot.

Eli kneels down next to her, looking so beautiful that it's just another ache. "Tell me what happened," she says.

Zara speaks, pouring words as fast as she pours blood and water. She tells Eli about the roof. About Meg. "She's down there," Zara says, nodding at the ladder. "I stabbed her with your Leatherman."

There is a glint of pride on Eli's face, underneath the shock. She puts her arms around Zara and takes most of her weight, leading her to the back of the wings. The white sheet of the cyclorama cuts off the stage from the back of the theater, creating the thin passage the actors and crew use to pass from one side of the stage to the other. They turn, taking careful sidesteps.

The audience is on the third round of applause for the full company. Zara realizes, with a hazy feeling like waking up after a string of dreams, that some of this applause is for her.

Eli keeps her eyes on the far side of the wings. They're moving so slowly.

"How did you find me?" Zara whispers, each word a ferocious burn. Too much water got in her throat.

"I heard Toby and Carl talking," Eli whispers. She tells Zara what she heard, and another piece of the story becomes obvious, as if it were waiting in the dark for someone to shine a light on it.

I pray you, pardon me.

The scribbled quote didn't have anything to do with the Aurelia production. Those were Gertrude's last words — the words of a woman who had been poisoned by her husband. Carl must have given her a drink, a pill, several pills, and told her that he only wanted to help her relax.

Enna still trusted him.

"It was Carl," Zara says. "He killed Enna. To fulfill the visions. He wanted revenge for what Leopold did to Enna."

"He got revenge for Enna by killing her?" Eli says, like she's just trying to get things cleared up.

"The revenge was for himself, too. Who he and Enna used to be. What Leopold did to them when they were in love. Carl thought she was miserable, ruined by what happened. He believed Enna was as good as dead already." There is a horrible heat in Zara's chest, and she doesn't know if it's rage or sadness or just the water, burning.

"You're saying it was all five of them?" Eli asks as they come out on the other side of the cyclorama.

"Yes," Zara rasps.

The whole thing was like a little play.

Cosima made the costumes. Barrett did the props, the set dressing. Meg was the director. Carl was the lead actor, playing a role only Enna would ever see. Toby was a supporting actor, providing Leopold with an alibi and then conveniently taking it away. Toby didn't know about the murders until the curtain came down. Neither did Cosima — but she was still willing to bind Zara's hands. Meg must have told her to do it. Cosima must have been in too deep to question why.

The part that makes Zara close her eyes — the part she doesn't want to look at — is how they tried to warn her, to protect her from what they were doing. They ignored Zara at first, keeping her at arm's length from the day she arrived. They avoided talking about Roscoe's and Enna's deaths. The more Zara and Eli insisted on the truth, the more all five repeated the same words, in different variations.

Focus on the play. Don't ask questions.

It wasn't until Barrett painted it on the walls of Zara's bedroom and gave himself away that Meg told her a little story, a slightly altered version of the truth. She couldn't risk Zara figuring out what actually happened, so she made Zara believe that Leopold was responsible for the deaths. The story to frame him was already in place.

All Meg had to do was tip Zara's mind in the right direction.

418

As Zara's thoughts whirl, Eli pulls her out from behind the stage, to where the assistant stage manager and a few stagehands are waiting. They stare at the two girls, but they don't seem to understand what they're looking at.

Zara kneels, trying to catch her breath. It feels impossible. Eli crouches next to her, a hand on her back. "Call 911!"

The stagehands hold up empty palms. No one has phones backstage.

And then Zara catches sight of Meg's blond hair shining across the stage, on the other side of the wings.

The audience launches into one more round of applause. They're unstoppable. They love *Echo and Ariston*.

They always do.

Meg heads for the cyclorama. Zara's mind does a fevered turn through the Aurelia. If she and Eli head backstage with Zara moving this slowly, Meg will catch up to them before they can reach the lobby or the loading dock. "Come on," Zara says, setting her eyes on the one place they might be safe. She stands up, grabbing the rich red velvet of the curtains.

Zara pulls Eli onstage.

After being buried in water and bricked under the stage, this is where Zara belongs. The stage is bright, like being flooded with early spring sunshine.

At first, the audience thinks Echo has finally arrived to take a bow. The applause grows wild at the edges. It's already a standing ovation. With the houselights up, Zara can pick out individual faces. People are delighted.

And then people are confused.

Because Echo is bleeding. Echo is breathing hard. Echo is dragging someone behind her like a life preserver.

Silence overtakes the theater.

Adrian rushes up. Zara can feel him wanting to help. Kestrel, too, runs toward them. Chorus members break the ranks of the curtain call, starting to ask questions. Carl watches Zara with hard eyes. Toby starts to cry.

Zara is where she belongs, but she can't tell the story that needs to be told, not with her throat damaged from nearly drowning. "I need you to do the talking," she whispers to Eli.

Eli nods. And then her voice springs out, louder than Zara's ever heard it, filling every corner of the Aurelia. "Someone call 911!" she says. "There's been an attempted murder."

Zara whispers in Eli's ear.

"And an actual murder," she adds.

The silence in the theater shatters into a thousand voices — people calling for help, crying out, yelling into phones.

"Was that okay?" Eli whispers, leaning her head in to touch Zara's.

"Brilliant."

Zara doesn't know what to do next, or what to say, or how to stop bleeding. But Eli is there. She kneels down, tears off a piece of Zara's dress, and wraps it around her fingers. "You were right," Zara murmurs. "This play has a terrible ending."

Eli looks out at the lights, the faces, the beautiful body of the theater. "This isn't how it usually goes."

"I like this ending better," Zara whispers, pulling Eli a little closer until they're at that distance where every word sounds like an invitation and the meeting of their bodies feels fated.

Zara touches her lips to Eli's. Every time they do this, they're inventing so much — themselves, each other, what it means to be in love. This is the best truth that Zara has. She and Eli stand together at the heart of the Aurelia, kissing and kissing as the lights burn into them. Now everyone can see.

This is their story.

This has always been their story.

ACKNOWLEDGMENTS

This is the book's curtain call, where the audience gets to see — and applaud — everyone who helped create the magic.

I love this part.

First, thank you to every artist I have ever shared a stage, backstage, or greenroom with. Many years as an actor (and a few stabs at playwriting) have taught me that theater people are some of the best in the world. I would not be an author today without those bighearted companies and chances to connect with other people. Like Zara, I found my voice in the theater.

A special thanks to my sister, Allyson Capetta, an inspiring theater artist in NYC, who was very sweet about answering my frantic e-mails with subject lines like "QUESTION ABOUT SUBWAYS." Thanks to Kitt Lavoie for sharing his knowledge of running a New York theater, Brian Brookhart for letting me run around — I mean research — in the fly space, and Sara Watson, who provided information and inspiration for Eli's career as a young lighting designer.

When I became a YA writer, I discovered a second artistic community that is just as supportive, wildly creative, and tireless in its search for beauty and truth. Big love to the VCFA family and those who heard the first public reading of this story in January 2015. A spotlight for my agent, Sara Crowe, who championed this book from the first draft. Tossing roses at the feet of my incredible early readers: Katie Bayerl (mystery choreographer),

Yamile Saied Méndez (brilliant director of all things Eli), Ann Hagman Cardinal (who found Eli in real life and stage-managed an entire draft), Mary Winn Heider (old theater hand and wondrous giver of feedback), Tirzah Price (who was there from the first rehearsal), Julia Blau (who waited patiently for opening night), and Cori McCarthy (my live-in story designer, who read every word—multiple times—and helped me make them *more*).

The Candlewick team is the best crew I could imagine for this book, making things run smoothly behind the scenes and finding every possible way for the story to shine. Clapping so hard that my hands sting for Emily Wagner and her early enthusiasm; interns Courtney Burke and Sofia Elbadawi; copyeditors Susan VanHecke and Maggie Deslaurier; catalog writer and live-texter of story excitement Christine Engels; proofreader Martha Dwyer; Jamie Tan, Wonder Publicist; Matt Roeser, who gave this book its epic cover; and Sherry Fatla, who designed its gorgeous insides. Cheers for the readers whose targeted feedback made the book stronger: Sarah Ketchersid, Andrea Corbin, and Melanie Cordova. A standing ovation for Hilary Van Dusen, who believed this was a Candlewick book and gave it the perfect home.

The final bow goes to Miriam Newman, my editor. Finding her was a moment of pure distilled luck. Working with her has been a mind-sparking act of collaboration—the kind of story-making I love best. Miriam: Zara and Eli wouldn't have their love story without you. I'm sad to leave the Aurelia, but I like to think it's always there waiting for us.